THE KERRIGANS
A TEXAS DYNASTY
HATE THY NEIGHBOR

THE KERRIGANS
A TEXAS DYNASTY
HATE THY NEIGHBOR

WILLIAM W. JOHNSTONE
with J. A. Johnstone

PINNACLE BOOKS
Kensington Publishing Corp.
www.kensingtonbooks.com

PINNACLE BOOKS are published by

Kensington Publishing Corp.
119 West 40th Street
New York, NY 10018

All Kensington titles, imprints, and distributed lines are available at special quantity discounts for bulk purchases for sales promotions, premiums, fund-raising, educational, or institutional use. Special book excerpts or customized printings can also be created to fit specific needs. For details, write or phone the office of the Kensington sales manager: Kensington Publishing Corp., 119 West 40th Street, New York, NY 10018, attn: Sales Department; phone 1-800-221-2647.

ISBN-13: 978-0-7860-4046-9
ISBN-10: 0-7860-4046-7

First printing: June 2017

10 9 8 7 6 5 4 3 2 1

Printed in the United States of America

First electronic edition: June 2017

ISBN-13: 978-0-7860-4047-6
ISBN-10: 0-7860-4047-5

BOOK ONE

An Ill Wind

CHAPTER ONE

Behind the stately façade of Kate Kerrigan's four-pillared mansion lay a household in turmoil.

The cook and the scullery maid, a rather unintelligent girl, the parlor maids, the butler, and two punchers who happened to be passing the house when the tumult began were all summoned to Kate's bedroom, where her personal maid was trying to calm her distraught mistress.

The maid stepped to the window and her hands parted, pinched forefinger and thumbs two feet apart, and studied something against the light that would have been invisible to the casual observer.

"Well?" Kate said. "Is it as we feared?"

The maid shook her head. "I'm sure I don't know, ma'am."

"You don't know! Why I have a good mind to box your ears, you silly girl. It's as obvious as . . . well, as the picture on the wall over there." Kate nodded in the direction of a framed portrait of an elderly gent with a walrus mustache. Hiram Clay was the president of the local cattlemen's association and a man powerful enough to be courted. He'd given Kate the portrait as a gift and had begged her to keep it in her bedroom so that he could be close to her "ere fair face touches pillow and you drift into the sweetest dreams of your ever devoted Hiram."

Kate thought the picture hideous in the extreme and had vowed to get rid of it just as soon as a new association president was elected. But now, apart from using Hiram as a test of the maid's vision, the portrait was far from her mind.

Anxious people crowded into the bedroom where Kate's breakfast lay untouched, her coffee untasted. As each one examined the long hair in the window's morning light, Kate asked the same question. "Well?"—"Well?"—"Well?"

And each time, fearful of losing their positions, the answer from cook, maids, and butler was always the same. "Ma'am, I can't really tell."—"I can't see without my glasses."—"It could be, but I'm not at all sure."

Finally, Willie Haynes the puncher, a tough little cuss who'd ridden for Charlie Goodnight back in the early days and was anything but the soul of discretion, stared at the hair, screwed up his face, and then said, "Yup, seen it right off. It's as gray as a badger's ass, boss."

Kate was taken aback by Haynes's bluntness and after a few moments of stunned silence her icy voice matched her chilly demeanor. "Thank you, Willie, you can go now. You can all go. I want to be alone."

Haynes nodded and said, "Any time you need my opinion on a thing, Miz Kerrigan, you only have to ask." As his fellow punchers tried unsuccessfully to steer Willie toward the door, the little cowboy added,

"An' I'm right sorry about the gray hair, boss, and how you're all undone by it an' all, but cheer up, you got plenty of red ones left."

Kate's smile could have turned a Louisiana swamp water pond to ice. "Thank you. And thank you all," she said. "Now I'm sure you have work that needs attending to."

The bedroom cleared rapidly as people beat a hasty retreat and Kate sat on the edge of the bed and studied the shoulders of her yellow silk robe for other treacherously ashen turncoats. There were none. She glanced at her breakfast tray, but was much too upset to eat. Well . . . perhaps she'd feel better after a piece of toast.

Kate nibbled on a corner of the triangle of toast and her gaze fell on the chafing dish in the middle of the silver tray. No, she was too distressed to eat a bite, not even a crumb. But then, there was no harm in lifting the cover to take a look. She owed it to Jazmin, her wonderful cook, to at least see what she had prepared. Hmm . . . a nice plump pork sausage, slightly scorched the way she liked it, crispy bacon, and a sunny-faced egg.

Well, perhaps just a bite or two. After all, she mustn't disappoint Jazmin.

The chafing dish was empty but for a morsel of bacon when Kate's butler, old Moses Rice, tapped on the door and stepped into the bedroom.

"Gennel'man to see you, Miz Kate," he said.

Kate felt slightly full, as if she'd eaten too much.

"Who is he, Moses? If he's a drummer, tell him he must talk with Mr. Cobb."

"Ma'am, the gent says he'll only talk with you," Moses said. His wrinkled face took on a look of wonder. "He says he's a prince."

"Prince indeed?" Kate said. "Prince of what?"

"Of the plains, ma'am." Moses scratched the gray wool on the side of his head, remembering. "He said for me to tell you his name is William Frederick Cody, Prince of the Plains, and showman ex . . . extra . . ."

"Extraordinaire," Kate said.

Moses's face lit up and his smile flashed. "That was it, Miz Kate. Do you know the gennel'man?"

"I've heard of him. Show him into the parlor and offer him coffee. Tell Mr. Cody I'll join him directly."

As her lady's maid helped her change into a rococo, a pleated day dress of white cotton with a built-in corset that laced up the front, Kate tried to recall what she knew of William F. Cody, Buffalo Bill as she'd heard him called. He'd been an army scout and Indian fighter and now had his own Wild West show that contained picaresque elements of frontier life. Bill's show had crossed the ocean to perform for old Queen Victoria, or was he about to do that? No, she couldn't remember which. One thing was certain, Mr. Cody had become a very famous man, and it was said that he cut a dash with the ladies.

So why his visit to the Kerrigan ranch? Perhaps he was passing and decided to stop and pay his respects.

Kate checked herself in the full-length mirror and was pleased to see that her hair fell over her shoulders in thick ringlets of burnished red, not a traitorous gray in sight.

"How do I look, Flossie?" she said.

"Like a princess from a fairy tale," the maid said.

"Then I'm fit to meet the prince," Kate said. "Very well, I'll see Mr. Cody now."

Flossie, remembering the affair of the hair, nodded and said, "You look very young and lovely, ma'am."

"Then let us hope that Mr. Cody appreciates the efforts we've made on his behalf," Kate said.

"Oh, any fine gentleman would, ma'am," Flossie said. And then worried for a moment that she'd spoken out of turn, she whispered, "If you don't mind me saying so."

But Kate, moving with all the grace of a Celtic queen, was already opening the bedroom door and didn't hear.

CHAPTER TWO

When Kate Kerrigan stepped into the parlor, a tall, broad-shouldered man wearing gloriously beaded white buckskins rose to his feet. A large red bandana draped loosely around his neck, and in his hands he held a plumed, high-crowned hat with a prodigiously wide brim. He wore polished, thigh-high black boots and around his hips, as Kate noticed at once, hung a silver-studded gun belt and in the holsters a pair of ivory-handled Colts.

"Mr. Cody, I presume," Kate said, offering her hand.

Buffalo Bill made a leg and bowed with a sweeping gesture of his feathered hat that was worthy of Athos, Porthos, or Aramis and for sheer elegance and grace probably out-courtiered all three.

Bill kissed Kate's hand, and when he straightened, he said, "Your obedient servant, madam." Then, in an overly dramatic display, he raised his hat as though shielding his eyes from the sun. "By all that's holy, Mrs. Kerrigan, I'm blinded by the dazzling beauty of your person." Bill adopted a heroic pose, threw back his head, and declaimed, "Thus did King Menelaus of

Sparta stand in astonished awe when he first beheld fair Helen on the massy ramparts of Troy."

Kate, well used to compliments from men, was nonetheless impressed by the frontiersman's rhetoric and knowledge of the classics. "You are very *gallante*, sir," she said. "Please resume your seat."

She was uncomfortably aware that Buffalo Bill Cody was a fine-looking man with a rampant masculinity that even Frank Cobb, her rugged segundo, would have trouble matching.

Kate sat and said, "Have you . . ." She had trouble finding her voice, coughed, and tried again, "Have you had coffee, Mr. Cody?"

"My dear lady . . . may I call you *Gloriana*?" Bill said.

"No. Kate will do just fine."

"Then Kate it is."

Bill placed his hand on his heart as though he was about to impart a secret of the most private kind, as indeed he was. "Kate, it has been my lot since boyhood to enjoy but one daily cup of the sable brew that sharpens the wits and invigorates the body. But after the cup that cheers, I feel drawn to partake in . . . what shall we call it? Ah yes, stronger stuff."

"How remiss of me, Mr. Cody," Kate said, rising. "Would bonded bourbon be more to your liking?"

"Not a drop, dear lady." Bill made one of his heroic gestures, his right hand extended, warding off temptation. "Not so much as a taste."

Kate moved to sit again, and Bill exclaimed in some haste, "But . . ."

"Yes?" Kate said.

"I could not but notice the exquisite slenderness of your hands, dear lady," Bill said. "I think three fingers of bourbon from you would be a small enough portion of the viper that resides in the bottle."

Kate smiled, moved to the drinks tray, and poured Bill a generous glass of Old Crow. After she'd settled in her chair again and Bill had begged her indulgence to smoke a cigar, they made small talk until he'd finished his second bourbon and the cigar had burned down almost two-thirds of the way. Then Kate said, "As much as I enjoy your company and your dashing tales of derring-do on the plains, Mr. Cody, I suspect that your visit to my ranch is not entirely a social call."

"And indeed it is not, dear lady," Bill said. "You have gone right to the heart of the matter. Indeed, your arrow has sped unerringly to the bulls-eye. In short, I am here to humbly beg a boon."

Now Kate was slightly wary. "What is the nature of this favor, Mr. Cody?"

Bill leaned forward in his chair and his long, silvery hair tumbled over his shoulders. "Let me precede my request by stating that that our fair land is in winter's frosty grip, torn by tempests, blasted by blizzards, snowbound, icebound, and, worst of all, homebound. In short, the weather up north is rotten and folks are staying home."

"So I've been told, Mr. Cody," Kate said. "A traveling lightning rod salesman assured me that the extent and severity of the snowstorms are most singular and the government had declared them potentially a disaster of the greatest moment."

"The drummer spoke the unvarnished truth, dear lady," Bill said. "Everywhere is as cold as a banker's heart and I am reliably informed that in Kansas boiling water freezes so fast the ice is still warm."

Kate smiled and said, "Mr. Cody, say no more. I understand your predicament, and I'd be honored to have you spend the winter on my ranch. I have twelve guest rooms and I'm sure we can find one that suits you."

"Kate, your generosity is boundless, but, alas, if it were only that simple," Bill said. "No, dear lady, there is indeed a major complication."

"Ah, you have someone else with you, a lady perhaps?"

"I have six hundred someone elses," Bill said. "And almost twice that number of horses, buffalo, and other animals."

"Six hundred people, Mr. Cody?" Kate looked shocked. "And animals? Buffalo?"

"Yes, ma'am. And cowboys, Indians, and sharp-shooters. And my private train."

"Private train, Mr. Cody?"

"Yes. That is why I'm asking you if I can use your railroad spur," Bill said.

"My railroad spur, Mr. Cody?"

"Yes, dear lady, to offload my people, animals, supplies, wagons, and tents. With your gracious permission we would set up camp, and spend the winter far away from the northern tempests."

It took a while for Kate to find the words, and then she said, "How . . . I mean, how much land would you need?"

"Not much, dear lady, just ten to fifteen acres, a small corner, the merest morsel of your range."

"But, Mr. Cody, the Kerrigan ranch can't feed that

many people, to say nothing of the animals. Our winter graze is thin and our supply of hay limited. I do not wish to sound uncharitable, but . . ."

"Fear not, dear Kate. Buffalo Bill's Wild West is self-sufficient. We have to be since we travel all over the country and around the world. We bring our own food, fodder for the stock, and even our own cooking stoves and firewood. All we need is said railroad spur and a small patch of ground amid your boundless acres."

Bill sat back in his chair, flashed his most winning smile, and said, "Now, being a businesswoman as well as a rancher, I'm sure the thought uppermost in your mind is remuneration. In short, how much will Mr. Cody pay me?"

In fact, payment was the last thing on Kate's mind, filled as it was with visions of stampeding buffalo, wild Indians, and even wilder cowboys.

"Ah," said Bill, "I see that good breeding makes you hesitate to name a figure that would be agreeable to both parties. Well, I will not beat about the bush, dear lady. Three things cannot be hidden, the sun, the moon, and the truth, and the truth is that you see before you a man in the most impecunious circumstances. The bank won't let me draw breath and as a result I'm down to my last tail feather. In a nutshell, Bill is broke."

"Mr. Cody, I'm so sorry to hear that," Kate said.

"Do not despair, dear lady, I beseech you," Bill said. "Come spring we leave on our European tour and I will soon recoup my finances. A letter from the British ambassador in Washington informs that Queen Victoria is eagerly awaiting our arrival. The lady is, Lord

Barclay told me, all in a dither. As for the Kaiser, he is looking into providing buffalo sausage for his army, vittles that will be named after my humble self. The British say they'll be called Bill's Bangers, but I don't set any store by that. The British and Germans are never on very good speaking terms."

Kate glanced at the watch that hung around her neck from a silver chain and Buffalo Bill took the hint. "What I offer in remuneration, my dear Kate, is to provide a show on the day before our departure just for the Kerrigan ranch. There! What do you think of that? Is that not a handsome offer indeed?"

"A show, Mr. Cody?" Kate said.

"Indeed, madam. You will be the first to see, before even Queen Victoria or the Kaiser, such new spectacles as *The First Scalp for Custer* and *Buffalo Bill Saves the Mexican Maiden.* And you will meet our shining new star, the amazing lady sharpshooter Annie Oakley, The Texas Bluebonnet."

To Bill, the fact that Annie was born in Ohio was neither here nor there. On tour she changed birthplaces as often as she changed her dress. His face now anxious, he said, "Well, dear lady, do we have an agreement? As my old friend Wild Bill Hickok, God rest him, was wont to say, shall we make this a happy day?"

Feeling more than a little overwhelmed, it took Kate a few moments before she replied. Hesitantly, she said, "Well, I suppose so, Mr. Cody, so long as your being here doesn't interfere with the work of my ranch."

Bill beamed. "Be assured, dear lady, that our presence here will hardly be noticed, even by your cows.

My people will keep to themselves, and I assure you that even the savages, those panthers of the plains who led the gallant Custer to his destruction, will remain in their teepees. In short, we'll be as quiet as church mice."

Kate rose to her feet. "Then it is settled. When do you wish to move onto a campground?"

"Today, dear lady. Instanter!" Bill said. "I have already taken the liberty of pulling my train onto the spur, but I told the engineer to keep up steam in the doleful event that you saw fit to turn me down."

It seemed to Kate that Bill Cody's powerful personality lacked neither charm nor confidence.

"I'll have Frank Cobb, my segundo, help you choose a campsite, Mr. Cody," Kate said. "He's out on the range at the moment with my sons, but I expect him to return shortly and I'll have him meet you at the spur terminal." Then, in a deliberate attempt to regain the initiative, "This winter I plan to expand my range west as far as the Rio Grande and south to the big bend of the Nueces. In the coming weeks you will see my riders coming and going, but please tell your people not to be alarmed. My men mean them no harm."

"Ha! An expanding cattle empire indeed, Mrs. Kerrigan," Bill said.

"And hard won, Mr. Cody, with many battles against man and nature still to be fought. Now, let me show you to the door. It has been indeed a pleasure talking to you. You must come again and I will bake a sponge cake to mark the occasion. My cake, with a cream and strawberry jam filling, is old Queen Vic's favorite, you know."

"And I will be sure to tell her that I ate a piece

under this very roof," Bill said. "I know the old lady will be very impressed."

Once outside, Buffalo Bill Cody mounted a milk-white stallion with an ornate silver saddle. And being Bill, he made the horse rear as he waved his hat above his head before galloping away, sitting tall and straight in the saddle.

Kate watched him go and then whispered to herself, "You have the trappings of a gallant knight indeed, Mr. Cody, but something tells me that I'm not going to enjoy having you for a neighbor."

As Bill Cody himself might have said, "Truer words were never spoke."

CHAPTER THREE

As Kate Kerrigan watched Buffalo Bill Cody leave and then closed the door of her mansion, an event was unfolding in the New Mexico Territory that would soon impact her life and place her in more danger than she'd ever known.

McLean was not a town—it wasn't even a settlement. It consisted of a combination general store, eating house, saloon and flophouse, a blacksmith's shop, and pole corral, all jammed into a narrow canyon among the western foothills of the Brokeoff Mountains. It was a lonely, remote place surrounded by scrub desert, the haunt of mule deer, javelina, wintering elk, and golden eagles.

Mclean made no claim to be other than what it was, a robbers' roost in the wilderness, only occasionally visited by passing cowboys, prospectors, men on the scout, and travelers. If such a traveler had the time and inclination and could keep his nerve, the proprietor, a former bare-knuckle prizefighter by the name of Gold Lawson, would regale him with hair-raising tales of the eighteen men who'd met their end by gun, knife, or billy club in his establishment since he'd opened for business just five years before.

"And that's not counting them as died from drinking too much rotgut," Lawson would say to the trembling traveler. "Aye, and let it be said, from the pox as well."

It was unfortunate then that because of prevailing winds and a furious rainstorm, an old man named Professor Lancelot Purdon and his assistant, a much younger man called Josiah Mosely, had trouble with their hot-air balloon and were forced to land just a few yards from the door of Lawson's violent establishment.

What followed was cold-blooded murder . . . for no other reason than sheer meanness and the urge to kill another human being for amusement.

The out-of-control hydrogen balloon, its burner extinguished and envelope ripped, crashed onto the open ground in front of the general store, unceremoniously spilling the professor and Josiah Mosely into the mud.

Despite his eighty years, Professor Purdon was spry. Lashed by rain, he sprang to his feet and yelled, "Josiah! Secure the balloon."

Mosely, eighteen years old that last summer, grabbed a trailing rope and battled to drag the now limp balloon into the shelter of some scrub pine.

"Don't forget our bags, Josiah," Purdon yelled above the dragon hiss of the downpour.

The professor was a small, bearded man with a mop of unruly white hair sticking out from under the black top hat he'd just rammed onto his head. He wore goggles and a threadbare broadcloth suit, and was half-mad. In 1845 he'd crossed the English Channel by balloon, there and back, and five years later had ventured a flight over the darkest jungles of darkest Africa. That adventure had not ended well. The fuel in the burner had exhausted itself while the tree canopy below him still stretched for miles in every direction, a green and leafy roof over a savage world. He was forced to land and as the professor told the story was promptly captured by natives ("The biggest damned savages I ever saw in my life"), that were inclined to cannibalism, their favorite dish a white man baked over an open flame in a crust of mud. "Rather like the meat in pastry dish we British call Beef Wellington," Purdon would thoughtfully explain.

Fortunately, the professor was saved by a group of Dutch missionaries and being a man of considerable means, he later found a berth on an Italian tramp steamer bound for Portsmouth town. Like his flight, the voyage ended in disaster when a storm struck the ship and it sank a few miles north of the equator within telescope view of St. Paul Rock. After eighteen days in an open boat, the professor and seven companions, more dead than alive, were picked up by an American ship and taken to New York. Professor Purdon decided to remain in the United States, and during the Civil War he advised the U.S. Army on the use of observation balloons, often while under heavy enemy fire. This gallantry earned him a captain's commission and a gold medal. After the war the lure of balloons remained and he became a rainmaker, firing colored rockets into the sky from the basket of his soaring airship, a hazardous occupation that drew the admiration of seventeen-year-old Josiah Mosely, then a lowly clerk in a Boston countinghouse. Impressed by the youth's enthusiasm, the professor took Josiah on as an assistant. Mosely was a quick learner and things were going well . . . until the disaster that afternoon in the stormy skies over McLean.

Dene Brett stepped out of the store, took one look at the rain and decided to forgo a trip to the outhouse. He unbuttoned and pissed over the side of the rickety porch that ran the length of the building.

Cannibals couldn't kill Professor Lancelot Purdon, nor could tempest, shipwreck, cannon fire, or the odd balloon crash, but four outlaws, cowardly border trash who'd cut any man, woman, or child in half with a shotgun for fifty dollars, did.

The day the balloon dropped out of the sky, Marty Hawley, his cousin Dene Brett, Floris Lusk and Jesse Tobin had just come off a killing, a man named Hooper, shot in the back for the fifteen dollars in his wallet and his fancy brocade vest.

When the balloon hit the ground, spilling its two occupants, Brett's eyes popped and he hurried inside. He stepped through the store into the saloon and yelled, "Hey, come see this. We got visitors."

His three companions and a couple of slatternly doxies just one step removed from the hog farm rushed outside and gathered on the porch.

"Well, lookee here," Jesse Tobin, a small, narrow man with stone eyes, said. "Seems like Methuselah fell out of heaven and landed right here in hell."

One of the women buttoned up Brett's pants and then cut loose with a piercing, mocking laugh. "Hey, pops, you got yourself a flying machine that don't fly, huh?"

Professor Purdon found his silver-topped cane in the mud, brandished it, and yelled, "You men, lend a hand there. My assistant needs help to tie down the balloon."

But Josiah was already stepping toward him. "It's secure, Professor," he said. "The damage is not as bad as I thought." The youngster was dripping wet. His thin hair plastered flat over his head and round, wire-rimmed glasses hung lopsided on his face.

Purdon waved an arm. "Then come along out of the rain, Josiah. I believe we can obtain lunch here and perhaps a place to lodge for the night."

The old man stepped onto the porch, the end of his long life now just a few minutes away.

Jesse Tobin, who'd already killed a man for his vest, took a liking to Purdon's cane, the ornate silver cap carved to look like a steer skull with rubies for eyes. "Hey pops, I'll give you fifty cents for the cane," he said.

"It's not for sale," the professor said. His eyes moved to Gold Lawson, who wore a stained white apron. "I say, my good man, can you provide me and my young assistant with a meal and a bed for the night?"

Before Lawson could answer, Tobin reached into his pocket, produced a couple of coins, and said, "Here, pops, take the fifty cents. Now give me the damned cane."

"I told you, sir," Purdon said. "It's not for sale at any price. This cane was a gift from Mr. John Chisum after

I provided his range with a downpour and I will not part with it."

"Then that makes me want it all the more," Tobin said. He reached out to grab the cane's ebony shaft. "Now give me the damned thing."

"Indeed I will not," the old man said. He raised the stick in a threatening manner and said, "Now mind your manners, young man, or by the lord Harry I'll give you the heavy end of it."

Tobin grinned, casually drew, and fired one shot into Purdon's belly. As the oldster fell backward off the porch, Tobin fired again, this time a killing shot to the chest. Professor Lancelot Purdon was as dead as a stone when his body splashed into the deep, filthy mud.

"You all saw it," Jesse Tobin said. He fought hard to keep the grin off his face. "The old man came at me with the cane. He could've bashed my brains out."

"Damn right, Jesse," the dull, brutish Floris Lusk said. "It was self-defense. The old coot was trying to kill you. Anybody could see he was crazy."

"Fair fight, Jesse," Gold Lawson said, wiping his hands on his apron. "We all saw it plain."

Tobin turned his attention to Josiah Mosely, who stood stiff as a board in the hammering rain, a carpetbag in each hand and a horrified expression on his mild young face.

"How about you, boy?" Tobin said. "How did you see it?"

Faced with four killers and a couple of women with

Medusa eyes, Mosely swallowed hard and said, "It was an accident. The gun went off by itself. Twice."

Tobin grinned and after a while said, "Yeah, boy, right enough. That's what it was, an accident." He looked around him. "Ain't that so, everybody? The gun went off by itself twice."

This last was met with shouts of approval, and one of the woman laughed. Her name was Annabelle Lowe, and Tobin turned and said to her, "Go get me the damned cane."

"Jesse, it's raining out there," the woman said.

"I know it's raining, and I told you to get it. Now do as I say or I'll give you the back of my hand."

The woman pouted but stepped into the mud that immediately covered her high-heeled ankle boot. She bent over, grabbed the cane, and said, "Jesse, he's got a watch and chain."

"Then bring it here, stupid," Tobin said.

The watch was a German silver hunter of no great value, and Tobin shoved it in his pocket and then grabbed the cane from Annabelle. He pointed the stick at Josiah Mosely and said, "What you got in your poke, boy?"

The youth hefted the carpetbags to waist level. "These?"

"Yeah, those," Tobin said.

"Clothing, a few books, and nothing else."

"Bring them bags over here and let me take a look."

Mosely timidly stepped onto the porch, and Tobin grabbed the bags out of his hands. He opened them and rummaged through their contents. "Rags," he said. "Here, what's this?" He removed a bone-handled razor, a soap brush, and a silver-backed hairbrush. He tossed them to Lusk and said, "Here, Floris, make yourself presentable for the ladies."

"That ain't ever never gonna happen," Annabelle said, a crack that earned her a smack in the face from Tobin.

"When I want to hear sass from a whore I'll ask for it," he said.

Tobin stepped to the edge of the porch and threw the carpetbags into the mud, scattering their contents. "I need a drink," he said. "We'll go inside out of this damned rain."

Tobin walked into the store and the others followed. The woman named Annabelle had a red welt on her cheek that was the same size as Jesse's Tobin's hand.

Josiah Mosely kneeled in the rain beside Lancelot Purdon's lifeless body. The two .45 balls had torn great holes in the frail old man, but his face was tranquil in death, as though he'd just met up with an old enemy he'd been avoiding for years.

Gold Lawson stepped to the edge of the porch and stood behind the shifting curtain of the rain. "You can move that later, take it somewhere," he said. "You can't bury a dead man around here."

Mosely looked up at him, rain running down his face like tears. "How come I can't?"

"We got an inch of topsoil on top of bedrock," Lawson said. "You need dynamite to blast a hole, and I ain't got none of that."

"I can't leave the professor here in the mud," Mosely said.

Lawson shrugged. "Suit yourself, but you ain't bringing a stiff into my place. I've had enough of them stinking up my spare room already."

The man turned and walked inside and Mosely watched him go, hating his guts.

A small man makes for a light body, the mud was slick, and the youngster had no trouble dragging the old man into the pines. Mosely stumbled on the foundation of an old stone cabin that probably predated Lawson's establishment by twenty years, half-hidden by bunch grass and brush. It looked like the place had been built with a base of rough-cut sandstone topped by logs. Over the decades the logs had rotted, and most of the blocks had loosened and fallen, unless Apaches had attacked the cabin and deliberately pulled them down.

Whatever had happened, Josiah Mosely had found a fitting resting place for Professor Purdon. He would bury the old hero under a mausoleum of red stone.

CHAPTER FOUR

The gray day was shading into a thundery evening when Josiah Mosely placed the last stone on the pile that covered the mortal remains of Professor Lancelot Purdon. Except in times of war, young men seldom bury the dead and Mosely never had before. He had no prayers, no words, and let ten minutes of remembering silence say what had to be said. For the past few years the old man had been his friend, his mentor, and constant companion, a man of letters, wit, and endless stories of adventure in savage and distant lands . . . but none were more savage than right there in McLean.

After one last, lingering look at the grave, Mosely picked up his sodden carpetbags and walked to the store. Above him the sky roared as it was torn apart by the violent thunderstorm.

Gold Lawson stood behind the counter, an array of canned goods spread out in front of him. He had a ledger and a yellow pencil in his hands and seemed to be taking inventory. He looked up when Mosely slopped inside and said, "What can I do fer you, young feller?"

"I need a room for the night."

Lawson nodded. "Upstairs, room to the left. It will cost you a dollar and another dollar for a pillow and blanket." He looked Mosely up and down, not liking what he saw. "You got two dollars?"

Mosely reached into his sodden pocket, found the coins and rang them onto the counter among the peach cans. "Key," he said.

"There ain't no key on account of how there ain't no lock," Lawson said. "This is the New Mexico Territory, boy, not the Ritz."

"I guess it will do," Mosely said, as thunder crashed.

Lawson grinned. "You look a tad peaked, boy. Thunder scare you?"

Mosely shook his head. "No. I bring the thunder," he said.

Upstairs, roughly above the store part of the building, was one large room partitioned into two by a couple of ragged army blankets hanging from a string. The room to the left was furnished with an iron cot and a dresser that supported a jug and a basin, both empty. There was a corn husk mattress on the bed, much stained, and a chamber pot under it that Josiah Mosely did not care to investigate. He threw the muddy contents of the carpetbags on the rough timber floor and then set the seemingly empty bags on the bed. But both had a false bottom, one of Professor Purdon's little secrets since each compartment held a British Bulldog revolver and a box of cartridges. The little guns were made by Webley & Sons of Birmingham, England, and both were engraved with the words ROYAL ULSTER CONSTABULARY. The lovely little five-shooters were in .455 caliber and sported walnut grips and a nickel finish. How the professor acquired them, Mosely did not know. The old man had never shot the revolvers but kept them meticulously cleaned and oiled. Josiah Mosely had never shot them, either; in fact he'd never fired a gun of any kind, and Purdon had never encouraged him to take an interest in revolvers—a gap in his education that Mosely now regretted.

Well, now it was time to make up for it by getting in some practice.

The Bulldogs were unloaded and the noise from the saloon area had grown in volume as the four killers and their women got drunker. A gun in each hand, Mosely triggered imaginary shot after shot at Jesse Tobin and his friends—click—click—click—click. The Bulldogs were snarling, spitting fire.

It is one of God's tender mercies that the novice shooter, having known no other, will blithely accept a heavy double-action trigger pull under the illusion that such is the norm. Only later when he understands the ways of the revolver will the joys of light, smooth triggers enter into his thinking. It should be noted here, as Mosely clicked, clicked, at his phantom targets, that women learn this faster than men. But now Mosely had to adapt to the Bulldog's notoriously heavy trigger faster than anybody.

After a while he stopped, realizing that shooting an empty gun at shadows was far removed from the harsh realities of a gunfight. All the youngster had going for him was the element of surprise and a consuming anger that made him determined to take his hits and keep on shooting.

Professor Purdon was dead, buried out there in the thunderstorm under a pile of rock. No matter the cost, there had to be a reckoning.

Josiah Mosely loaded the Bulldogs, shoved them into the pockets of his damp coat, and stepped downstairs. He had ten shots and could afford six misses. Even so, the odds were not in his favor.

The saloon was a close, rickety room with a few tables and chairs and a bar made from two beer barrels supporting a warped timber door from an old barn. Behind the bar a shelf held half-washed glasses, several jugs of rotgut, a few dusty bottles, and a small keg that may once have contained brandy. There was no beer. Above the shelf a framed, embroidered sign read HAVE YOU WRITTEN TO MOTHER? and a couple of smoking oil lamps hung from the ceiling beams, glowing dimly against the advancing darkness.

Josiah Mosely stepped to the bar and turned to face the room.

Jesse Tobin took his hand out from under the unlaced corset of the woman named Annabelle and glared at Mosely with undisguised contempt. "What the hell are you doing in here, boy?" he said. "Gold Lawson don't sell milk, so only men are allowed in here."

Annabelle laughed and said, "Maybe he's got some sarsaparilla, huh, Jess?"

Tobin grinned and said, "Get the hell out of here, boy, before I get angry and spank your butt."

Mosely said nothing, but his eyes were busy, fixing the positions of the four men, the sprawled half-naked bodies of the two women.

Floris Lusk said, "You still here, boy? Jesse just told you. You ain't drinking among the men."

"Or the women, Annabelle said.

"Or the whores," Tobin said.

"Jess, I ain't a whore," Annabelle said, pouting. "And neither is Bonnie Sue."

"Then if you ain't whores, then what the hell are you?" Tobin said.

"We're ladies."

This last occasioned a loud explosion of mirth among the men. Annabelle jumped from Tobin's lap and flounced to the door, her open corset and undone Mexican blouse revealing her breasts.

"Git back here!" Tobin said, suddenly angry.

"She'll be back, Jesse," Lusk said. "You ain't paid her yet."

More laughter followed.

Josiah Mosely was pleased. The woman's leaving gave him a clear shot at Tobin. But it wouldn't be easy.

The gunman drew his Colt, thumped it onto the table, and said to Mosely, "Go bring me my woman, boy. If she ain't here on my knee in two minutes, all undone, I'll shoot you right between the eyes."

The youngster straightened. "I'm a rainmaker," he said. "I bring only the thunder."

"What the hell are you talking about?" Floris Lusk said.

A moment later he found out.

* * *

Josiah Mosely reached into his pockets and suddenly in the cheap perfume-scented gloom his revolvers flashed fire. In its black powder loading the .455 is not a particularly powerful round but at close range it's a big, soft lead bullet that can do a hell of a lot of damage to a man. Jesse Tobin didn't even have time to reach for his revolver before he took a hit. Mosely had pointed the muzzle of the Bulldog at the middle of the man's forehead but he jerked the heavy trigger and pulled his shot low to the right. The bullet entered Tobin's right eye and blew his brains out the back of his head.

One round. One kill. Nine rounds left.

Floris Lusk, a skilled gunman with three kills to his credit, jumped to his feet, his Colt clearing leather. But at that moment the woman who'd been sitting beside him decided to make a run for it, and she and Lusk collided, tangled, and the half-drunk gunman staggered back and delayed his shot. At a range of just five feet, Mosely fired at Marty Hawley and again pulled low and left. Hawley took the bullet in the lower gut and staggered back a step, shocked by pain. His cousin Dene Brett, a back-shooter but not a fighting man, was slow getting his work in. He and Mosely swapped a couple of shots with no hits, but the youngster got lucky with his third and hit Brett at the base of his thumb where it joined the wrist. Disabled, the man screamed, dropped his Colt, and bent over, cradling his shattered wrist, out of the fight.

But Floris Lusk was back in action. Assuming the duelist's position, his right arm extended, he drew a bead on Mosely. In that split second the young man knew he was dead. But then a gun roared and kept on roaring. Lusk reeled, hit several times. Annabelle stood in the doorway, a smoking Henry rifle at her shoulder. Lusk turned his head and stared at the woman, stunned at the manner of his death. He tried to raise his revolver, but suddenly it seemed to weigh as much as an anvil. Lusk raised up on his toes and then fell flat on his face, dead when he hit the floor.

Then things happened quickly, almost too fast for the gun-shocked Josiah Mosely to follow.

Splashing a trail of blood, Dene Brett, still bent over, staggered toward Annabelle, and said, "Help me."

A country girl born and bred, long familiar with rifles, now a whore with a heart of stone, the woman pumped two shots into Brett and said, "Go to hell."

Those were her last words. A single shot rang out and through the thick tangle of gunsmoke Mosely saw Annabelle grab for the doorjamb then slide slowly to the floor.

Gold Lawson appeared in the doorway, a huge Colt Dragoon revolver in his hand. He looked down at the dead woman with a face devoid of pity and gritted between clenched teeth, "Bitch."

That was enough for Mosely. He crossed eight feet of open floor quickly, raised the Bulldog in his right hand and said, "You look a tad peaked, mister. The thunder scare you?"

Lawson looked beyond Mosely at the carnage the youngster had wrought and said, "Damn you, boy, I never took ye for a shootist."

"I'm not. I'm a rainmaker, like Professor Purdon was a rainmaker. I bring the thunder."

Unnerved by the events of the past couple of minutes, Lawson raised his Colt, but he was painfully slow. He cursed his own hesitation and thumbed back the hammer.

At a range of five feet Josiah Mosely fired. The bullet hit low to the left, slammed into Lawson's belly, and the man dropped to his knees, his face shocked. "You killed me, you son of a bitch," he said.

Mosely nodded. "Yes, I did. But then some men need killing."

He fired again.

Hit a second time, Lawson gasped and fell on his face, dead as he was ever going to be.

The woman named Bonnie Sue, still pretty but worn, a woman who'd been used and abused all her life, appeared in the doorway. She kneeled beside Annabelle's body and sobbed quietly for a while and then her tear-stained face turned to Mosely. "She didn't deserve this," she said.

"I reckon she didn't," Mosely said. "But it happened."

"You killed them all."

"Not the woman. I didn't kill the woman."

"Now where do I go? Is there anyplace in the world lower than this hell, boy?"

"Nowhere. You go nowhere. Seems like now you own a grocery store and saloon. You stay right here, make a life for yourself."

"I don't own McLean or anything in it," Bonnie Sue said.

"Then who does? Gold Lawson is dead. Did he have any heirs?"

"Not that I know of. And if he had any they've probably all been hung."

Mosely nodded. "Then you're his only heir, woman. I know that out of the goodness of his heart Gold would have wanted you to have all that was his."

The woman thought that over then said, "You're right, pilgrim. I was always Gold's favorite."

"Seeing as how he shot Annabelle without too much regret I'd say that was the case."

"He was a dear man," Bobbie Sue said. "I mean really deep inside."

"Yeah, wasn't he though," Mosely said with a straight face.

"What about you? There's only me and you. Do you plan on killing me?"

"There's been enough killing," Mosely said. His smile was boyish. "I'll go wherever the balloon takes me." Then, "But first I'll help you bury the dead."

Owning the establishment so recently vacated by the late, unlamented Gold Lawson had struck a chord with Bonnie Sue. "I want Annabelle close and the others far, far away from my place."

My place. Josiah Mosely smiled inwardly at that. Bonnie Sue was a quick study, and there was more to her than he'd realized. Watching her now, he saw a strength and determination found in many females of that era. He'd been told that examples of such women lived in Texas, one or two of them wealthy ranchers, but he considered that last just a big story.

Josiah Mosely and Bonnie Sue spent the next day burying the dead. Like Professor Purdon, Annabelle was laid to rest under a cairn of red stone, but the dead men were dragged away behind their horses and left in the wilderness where the coyotes would be attentive but not kind. Then Mosely did one last kindness for the professor. He laid the old man's precious cane on his grave, and Bonnie Sue said it would stay there forever. As far as is known the cane lay on Purdon's last resting place until the 1920s, when it mysteriously disappeared.

The following day, in fair weather, Mosely reinflated the balloon from the hydrogen cylinder but did not light the burner. The prevailing wind was to the south and Bonnie Sue, dressed in a demure brown dress with white collar and cuffs, waved to him as he soared into the air and abandoned his fate to the elements.

Mosely knew that southward lay West Texas, but he did not know that Kate Kerrigan owned most of it or that his destiny would intertwine with hers and that all too soon he would again remove the British Bulldog revolvers from the carpetbags to use them to fight for what he believed in.

CHAPTER FIVE

"A fine sight, is it not, Kate?" Buffalo Bill Cody said. "A man's entire reason for existence represented by a locomotive, boxcars, flatbeds, cage wagons, and a dozen passenger cars."

Kate Kerrigan nodded. "A fine sight indeed, Mr. Cody. Do you not think so, Frank?"

Frank Cobb stood at Kate's side by the rail terminal and his handsome face bore an expression of wonderment. He grinned and said, "I bet there hasn't been this many Indians in one place at one time since the Custer Massacre."

That last was greeted by loud laughter that interrupted the *oohs* and *ahs* of amazement by the crowd that surrounded Kate. Every house servant and puncher who could make an excuse to leave his ranch chores had done so, and Kate feared that the KK must be empty. Her tall sons Trace and Quinn had quickly attached themselves to a pair of pretty young ladies Bill called "cowgirls," and Annie Oakley had emerged from a passenger car to wave to Kate and the others and fire her rifle in the air.

"Oh, look, Kate," Frank said, as excited as a boy at his first circus. "You see that black feller there with the terrible scars on his face, that's—"

"Meldrew Washington," Bill Cody said, beaming. "Kate, he's the only man in the history of the world to survive four days of torture at the hands of Apache women, the worst of them. When he was rescued by Texas Rangers he hovered at death's door for three months before he pulled through."

"A tough man, Mr. Cody," Kate said.

"Indeed, ma'am, and a damned fine wrangler to boot," Bill said. "I mean horse wrangler, of course."

"Mr. Cody, I know what a wrangler is," Kate said. "I employ several."

"Why, indeed you do, Kate," Bill said. "My mistake. Now, do you see that huge buffalo being led down the ramp from the boxcar?"

Frank Cobb shook his head, his eyes wide. "Well, cut off my legs and call me shorty. I never thought they grew to be that size. He's bigger than any longhorn I ever saw."

"Mr. Cobb, we took five Sioux and Cheyenne arrowheads and a fifty-caliber ball out of that bull's hide," Bill said. "We call him Methuselah, and when Sitting Bull first saw him he said he must be at least a hundred years old because he remembers putting an arrow into him when he was just a boy. And see there, the Indian standing on top of the boxcar wrapped in a blanket? That's Spotted Fawn, an Arapaho that was at the Custer fight. He said he put a bullet into the gallant Custer a moment before the one that killed him, but I don't know if that's true or not." Cody smiled, revealing remarkably good teeth, "The crowd loves to boo him, I can tell you that, but they cheer when I stick a knife into him." He looked quickly at Kate. "All in pretend, dear lady, all in pretend. No one really dies."

Kate smiled and shivered. "I should hope not, Mr. Cody."

Bill swept off his hat and made a gallant bow. "And now I must see to the unloading of the cooking stoves. Napoleon said an army marches on its stomach, and so does Buffalo Bill Cody's Wild West."

After Bill swaggered away in his usual swashbuckling fashion, Kate looked at the people around her and said, "You may watch until the train is unloaded, and then I want you all back at work." She turned to her personal maid. "Except you, Flossie. You'll come with me. I'm not at all sure the gray hair was the only one and I want you to search. And Frank, we need to talk about the nesters over to Fort Stockton way. I want them out before the spring roundup."

Frank Cobb nodded but said nothing. What he had to tell Kate could only be told in private.

After Flossie had been dismissed with nary another silver hair found, Frank was summoned to meet Kate in the parlor, and the doors were closed.

"Are you ready to make a report, Frank?" Kate said. "I'd hoped that Trace and Quinn could be here, but apparently they've found better things to do."

Frank grinned. "Bill's cowgirls sure are pretty though, ain't they?"

"Frank, that will be quite enough. I have no wish to discuss cowgirls, or whatever you wish to call them. We need more range now I've gotten the army contracts. Come spring I plan to ship ten thousand head, and that's all I wish to discuss at this time."

"Yes, ma'am," Frank said. "From what I've been told, there are at least six thousand acres under the plow around Comanche Springs, all it platted land and of legal occupancy."

"How many farms are we talking about?" Kate said.

"Around forty, maybe less."

Kate thought about that, then said, "We can bypass the farms and run our cattle on the open range. Later we'll put up fences to keep the sodbusters in their place, but it's the nesters that are my main concern. What about those people camped out on my range west of Fort Stockton?"

"I meant to tell you earlier, Kate, but we no longer have worries on that score. The nesters have been cleaned out. Hiram Clay and the association brought in a young rifleman by the name of Tom Horn and made him a range detective. Within a few weeks the nesters pulled stakes and lit a shuck, left four of their number in the ground. Horn rode out too, said he was headed for the Arizona Territory."

"You took all this time to tell me?" Kate said.

"I only heard it myself a couple of days ago from a Rocking-G puncher," Frank said. "He said he rode past those nester cabins and they've all been burned to the ground." Frank watched as roustabouts manhandled a huge tent canvas off a flatbed wagon, then said, "But we have nester trouble elsewhere."

"Where are they?" Kate said.

"They're mainly clustered along the Rio Grande,

Mexicans coming up from Chihuahua," Frank said. "That's marginal land for farming, sand and sage-brush mostly, but they're trying it."

Kate looked strained. "How many?"

"Several thousand, men, women, and children, but the Rangers say there's a rumor that white men are running the show down there."

"White men? Why, for heaven's sake?"

"I don't know, Kate. But I sure don't like the sound of it."

"Why won't the Rangers do something? Do they know I'm pushing my range west to the Rio Grande?"

"Well, you haven't claimed the land yet, and nobody's broken any laws. Sure the Rangers can run them off, but as soon as them big mustaches ride away the nesters will cross the river and come back."

"White men," Kate said, frowning. "I can't believe that."

"Yeah. It troubles the hell out of me, Kate."

"Me too. Why are they there?"

"I don't know."

"Do you think they mean harm to the Kerrigan Ranch?"

Frank smiled. "Kate, you've got thirty full-time hands, all of them good with a gun and Trace, Quinn, and me are pretty handy with the iron as well. I doubt you have anything to fear from a couple of white men and a bunch of ragged, shirttail Mexicans. We can run them off, real quick."

Kate worried the problem like a dog worries a bone. "Well, if they do mean us harm, I'm sure they'll show their hand sooner or later."

"We'll be ready when they do," Frank said.

Kate shook her beautiful head. "Frank, why do I feel so uneasy? And don't say it's because of the gray hair."

"I wouldn't dream of it. How about Buffalo Bill? He's a handful."

"No, I don't think so." Kate sighed and got to her feet. "It's . . . it's like trouble is just going to drop out of the sky. Have you ever had that feeling?"

Frank was inclined to say, "No I haven't," but he decided a small lie was in order. "All the time, Kate, but it usually passes after a while."

"I certainly hope so," Kate said. But she seemed very unsure that it would.

CHAPTER SIX

It was a half-wild Northern Cheyenne named Cloud Passing who brought the balloonist down to earth. In all his forty years the Indian had never seen such a thing in the sky and he decided that it bore a closer look.

Three days after he'd arrived with Buffalo Bill, Cloud Passing was exercising his favorite pony on the range when the bright red balloon hove into sight and scudded across the sky, borne by a south wind. The Cheyenne figured that the flying creature presented an immediate danger and he raised his .44-40 Winchester, drew a bead on the strange, devouring beast, and cut loose.

The bullet splintered through the bottom of the basket, *spaaanged!* off the hydrogen cylinder, and plowed a nasty trench in the flesh an inch above Josiah Mosely's left knee. Despite the glancing hit, the cylinder punctured in two places and rapidly lost gas. The balloon lost height, and the basket wildly rocked back and forth, forcing Mosely to drop to the floor. He clung to the wicker and hoped his death would be a merciful one.

Cloud Passing watched the flying monster hit the grass, bounce, and then scamper across the flat range, sometimes at ground level, more often as not a few feet in the air. His hunting instincts aroused, the Cheyenne galloped after the now running creature as he would a stampeding buffalo. He fired round after round from the shoulder, mercifully at the canopy, and yipped his hunting song.

Despite the bucking, careening basket Josiah Mosely was aware of a crazed Indian galloping alongside the balloon, shooting into the envelope.

"Git the hell away from here!" he yelled, hauling himself above the basket rim.

The Indian stared at him and his eyes got big. He racked the Winchester, aimed at Mosely, and pulled the trigger. *Click.* The rifle was empty. Controlling his galloping pony with considerable skill, the Cheyenne reversed the rifle and used it like a club to swing at Mosely's head.

And then an unforeseen disaster.

Cloud Passing missed Mosely and, off balance, he leaned over too far, toppled from his pony, and fell headfirst into the basket. Sharing a few square feet with a bloodthirsty savage, his guns in carpetbags out of reach, did not appeal to Mosely. As the Cheyenne fell inside, the youngster jumped out, dropped about ten feet, and hit the ground with a thud.

Dragged behind the wind-driven balloon, Cloud Passing hurtled at breakneck speed across the flat, a prairie equivalent of the Nantucket sleigh ride so feared by the old whaling men. The Cheyenne had never traveled at such a pace, even on Buffalo Bill's steam train, and he yipped and screamed his delight, his long hair whipping behind him in the wind blast every time the balloon soared high into the air. Cloud Passing held onto the rim of the basket and, grinning, willed the flying creature to go faster.

The two horsemen were not pleased to see Josiah Mosely, and the one with the hard blue eyes was the most belligerent. "Was it you doing all that shooting?" he said.

"Hell no," Mosely said. "It was some crazy Indian."

"Was he shooting at you?" the long-haired man on the beautiful white horse said.

"Hell yeah," Mosely said. "Look at my damned leg."

Neither horseman seemed impressed by the young man's wound, and the older man said, "He wasn't one of my Indians, was he?"

"I don't know," Mosely said. "Who are you?"

"Buffalo Bill Cody, young man, and this here is Frank Cobb, and I want to hear some respect in your tone. You didn't harm him, did you?"

"Who?"

"My Indian."

"I don't know whose Indian he is. I do know that he shot my balloon out of the sky and then tried his best to murder me."

Bill nodded. "Sounds like one of mine all right. Where is he?"

Mosely pointed south. "That way. He's riding the balloon and is probably in Mexico by now."

"What's this damned balloon you keep talking about?" Frank Cobb said.

"I rode in one before, up Kansas way," Bill Cody said. "It was an interesting experience, but I'll tell you about it later. Meantime I'm going after my Indian."

"I'll join you," Frank said. Then to Mosely, "What the hell is your name, youngster?" After Mosely gave his name, Frank said, "Get up behind me. I'm keeping you close."

"I can't ride a horse," Mosely said.

"Just git up and hold on," Frank said, and then, mimicking Mosely's high tenor, "'I can't ride a horse.' Damn it, boy, everybody in the world can ride a hoss."

"I must have been marked absent when they were giving the lessons," Mosely said.

Bill said, "Boy, for a pilgrim you're one uppity cuss. Be warned. Out this way sass can get you shot quicker'n scat."

A dead cottonwood and a sudden drop in the wind snagged the balloon and held it in place. Cloud Passing jumped out of the basket, his heart thumping in his chest. Still excited by the ride, he pulled his knife and did some kind of whooping, prancing dance around the wreckage.

He was still dancing when Frank Cobb and Bill Cody showed up twenty minutes later. Josiah Mosely had fallen off Frank's horse a mile back and completed the journey on foot, carrying his recovered carpetbags and rubbing a bruised butt.

Bill Cody drew rein and said, "Yup, he's one of mine, all right. That there is Cloud Passing, and he's one mean, nasty Indian. He's a Northern Cheyenne Dog Soldier and he says he put a bullet in Tom Custer at the Big Horn massacre." Bill shook his head. "Damn it all, Frank, it's gonna to take me all day to get him calmed down."

Frank Cobb swung out of the saddle and waited until Mosely arrived. "He the Indian who tried to kill you?" he said.

Mosely nodded. "Yes, that's him all right."

Frank nodded and his eyes moved to Bill Cody. "The law says I have to hang him from the cottonwood, Bill," he said. "Sorry."

"I understand," Bill said. "In Texas when an Indian tries to murder a white man it's a hanging offense. It's the same all over. Only thing is, I set store by that Indian, Frank. Most of the real mean Cheyenne are dead."

Frank drew his Colt and took the coiled rope from his saddle. "You know the law. Then let's get it done."

"No!" Josiah Mosely yelled. "You can't do that. What's wrong with you people? You just can't hang a man."

"I can and I will," Frank said. "He shot at you and wounded you. His guilt is clear."

"It was an accident," Mosely said. "The Indian

thought he was shooting at a big red bird, not a white man."

Frank's eyes hardened, not a good thing to see. "You told us the Cheyenne tried to murder you and now you say he didn't. Either you're lying, or you're trying to cover for the Indian. Which way does the pickle squirt?"

"I was angry when I said he tried to kill me," Mosely said. His celluloid collar had sprung away from its front stud and his round glasses were dusty so that he had to peer at Frank. "I made that part up."

"How did you get the leg wound?" Bill said.

"A bullet came up through the basket, bounced off the hydrogen cylinder, and then hit me." Mosely flexed his leg. "See, it doesn't even hurt."

"I bet it hurts like hell," Frank said. He looked up at Bill Cody, who was still mounted. "What's your opinion on this situation?"

Cloud Passing had stopped dancing and, his head craned forward, he watched the proceedings with interest. He had enough English to realize that the man with the steel eyes wanted to hang him, the little man with the bloody knee was trying to save him, and Buffalo Bill didn't care either way. The Cheyenne had lost his rifle and had only his knife, but he was determined to put up a fight. Hanging was a white man's way to kill a warrior, and Cloud Passing despised it.

"Hell, I reckon we give the Indian the benefit of the doubt, Frank," Bill said. "The kid is right, Cloud Passing thought the balloon was a big bird and took a pot at it."

Frank considered that, but a man of his time and place, he said, "Then so be it. Bill, I'm releasing the

Indian into your custody. But if he even so much as threatens a white man again I'll string him up. Are you in agreement with that?"

Bill doffed his hat. "Frank, we've made a gentlemen's bargain, and I will stand by it. Now go poke the Indian with a stick or something. I want to know if he's safe to handle."

Frank swung into the saddle. "He's your Indian, Bill," he said. "You poke him your ownself."

After he settled his plumed hat back on his head, Bill Cody said, "Young feller—what's your name again?

"I didn't put it out, but it's Josiah Mosely."

Bill said, "Ah, Josiah, as fine a king of Judea as ever was." He glared sternly at Mosely. "Do you read your Bible, boy?"

"When I have the chance I sure do," Mosely said.

"Good. Then you ain't afeerd of having your suspenders cut since you're most certainly headed for heaven an' all. Go poke that Cheyenne with a stick, see if he's tame enough to return to civilized folks."

"Mr. Cody, I've already had one brush with the Indian, and I don't fancy another," Mosely said.

Frank Cobb said, "Get up behind me, boy." And then to the worried-looking Bill, "One time I heard tell that you can tame a wild Indian by grinning at him. Why don't you give it a try?"

CHAPTER SEVEN

Buffalo Bill Cody accepted a glass of whiskey from Kate Kerrigan and said, "Thank you, dear lady. I need this after my terrible ordeal."

"You mean with the Cheyenne warrior Frank told me about?" Kate said. "I'm so glad it didn't come to a hanging. On principle, I'm against hanging people unless they really deserve it."

"It was dreadful, just a dreadful experience," Bill said.

"Do tell, poor, brave Mr. Cody," Kate said. She picked up the glass of ruby wine a maid had just poured for her. "Now you have me intrigued."

Bill gulped his bourbon and looked hopefully at Kate. "Winifred, another drink for Mr. Cody, please," she said to the maid. "I think at the moment he is feeling rather low."

"Low, indeed," Bill said, cradling his refilled glass as though it was a fragile child. "Of all the languages of all the world, low describes Bill Cody best."

It was time for prompting. "So, what happened?" Kate said.

A log dropped in the fireplace and sent up a shower of orange sparks, and Winifred lit another oil lamp against the growing darkness.

"I grinned at Cloud Passing, that's my Indian's name, for two solid hours by my watch," Bill said.

"Grinned at him, Mr. Cody?" Kate said. Her hair flowed like molten copper over the alabaster swell of her breasts, and the emeralds in her ears flashed green fire. The smell of her expensive French perfume drifted in the air like a breath of paradise.

"Yes, dear lady, grinned at him, on the advice of Frank Cobb," Bill said.

Kate frowned. "Frank told you to do that?"

"Yes. He said it's a natural fact that grinning at a wild Indian can calm him down *tout suite*, as the French fur trappers say."

"Hmm," Kate said. Then, "Winifred, remind me to have a word with Mr. Cobb at the first available opportunity. And then what happened, Mr. Cody?"

"Cloud Passing sat down."

"Sat down, Mr. Cody?" Kate said.

"Yes, dear lady, he sat down and wouldn't move."

"And what did you do, Mr. Cody?"

"Poked him with a stick."

"With a stick, Mr. Cody?"

"A cottonwood stick."

"And then what happened, Mr. Cody?" Kate said.

"The Indian went wild again, way wilder than before. He waved his knife and sang his scalping song and I thought I'd have to shoot him."

"Shoot him, Mr. Cody? Kate said.

"I reckoned it might come to that, the waste of a good Indian, but I gave grinning another try, and after an hour or so Cloud Passing finally calmed down. Fact is he calmed down so much he stretched out and went to sleep. I think the excitement of the day was just too much for him."

"And where is Mr. Cloud Passing now, Mr. Cody?" Kate said.

"He's in the kitchen tent, dear lady, quiet as a church mouse after one of the cooks gave him a pan of cornbread. Cloud Passing is right partial to cornbread."

"I'm glad it's all over now, Mr. Cody," Kate said. "It troubled me most singularly to see you so distressed."

"And I thank you for that, Kate." Bill said. "I think I'll feel better if I—" he held up his glass.

"Of course," Kate said. "Winifred, another whiskey for Mr. Cody." She smiled. "Should I offer one to Mr. Cloud Passing?"

Bill Cody shook his head. "Never give firewater to an Indian, dear lady, especially a Cheyenne Dog Soldier. They get drunk very quickly, and then bad things happen."

"Ah, words of wisdom from Mr. Cody," Kate said. "Winifred, did you pay attention to that?" The maid dropped a little curtsey and said, "Yes, ma'am."

"I'm full of them," Bill said.

"You're full of what, Mr. Cody?" Kate said.

"Words of wisdom, dear lady," Bill said. "Words of wisdom."

"You can bed down here for tonight," Frank Cobb said. "I told Mrs. Kerrigan that the bunkhouse has a space, but she said you're a guest and must sleep in a guest room. You don't walk in your sleep, do you?"

"Not that I'm aware," Josiah Mosely said.

"Good, because sleepwalking around these parts can get you shot, and so can snoring. Wes Hardin once told me he shot a man for snoring, but I think he was joshing me."

Mosely smiled. "You don't like me much, Frank, do you?"

"Like or not like doesn't come into it. I'm suspicious of any man who trespasses on KK range in a flying machine."

"It's a balloon," Mosely said. "I'm sure one day there will be flying machines, but not in our lifetime."

"Good, because I don't hold with stuff like that. Man was intended to stay put on the ground and ride. That's why God gave us horses."

"Oh, is that why," Mosely said, upending a carpetbag on the bed. "I've always wondered about that."

"Well, now you know," Frank said. Then, "What the hell! That's a British Bulldog revolver. I've only seen them in hardware stores."

Mosely said, "I know what it is. I have two of them. They belonged to a man named Lancelot Purdon. He taught me the rainmaker's profession."

"Did he teach you how to shoot them?"

"No. Professor Purdon never shot guns."

Frank picked up the revolver and said, "This is a .44 caliber and—by thunder it's loaded! Hell, if you pull the trigger by mistake, this could put a real bad hurting on you, Mosely." Frank unloaded the Bulldog and dropped the rounds one by one onto the bed. He said, "Where's the other one?" Mosely retrieved the gun from its carpetbag and handed it over. Frank unloaded that one and laid both on the bedside table. "Keep the shells separate from the gun and never the twain shall meet," he said. "Play around with these and you stand a good chance of blowing off a finger, or worse."

"I'll bear that in mind, Frank," Mosely said. "I guess those are dangerous weapons."

"In the wrong hands, and I mean in the hands of someone like you, they're downright dangerous," Frank said. "And if, God forbid, you ever took to carrying them, some wannabe gunman will take it into his head to crawl your hump and call you out. Then it's bang, bang and you're dead as a six-card poker hand. You understand me, boy?"

"Perfectly. I'll keep the guns in the bags from now on," Mosely said.

Frank worried the bone of contention a little longer. "Wrap them in an oily cloth and pass them down to your grandchildren," he said. "Don't be tempted to shoot them, that's a good way for a pilgrim to invite disaster, maybe shoot off one of his toes."

"Oily cloth, don't shoot, disaster, and give them to my grandchildren. Got it," Mosely said, blinking behind his glasses.

Frank shook his head. "I'll never understand how rubes like you who don't have the sense to spit downwind manage to survive on the frontier."

CHAPTER EIGHT

Kate Kerrigan was not impressed by Annie Oakley. She thought the girl's square chin made her look mannish, as did her mannerisms and strident Yankee voice. The buckskin dresses Bill Cody made her wear did nothing for her and only accentuated her boy's figure. Nor, it seemed, was Annie particularly enamored of Kate, eyeing her blue silk dress with its plunging neckline and huge bustle and the tiny hat balanced on top of her piled-up hair with vague disapproval. After exchanging a few pleasantries, none of them sincere, Kate was glad when the girl said she had pressing business elsewhere and left Kate to her leisurely promenade around Bill Cody's vast tent city.

It seemed that everyone was busy. Cowboys mended tack or exercised horses, and maintenance men touched up the paint of the show's battle-scarred stagecoach and wagons and made repairs as necessary. Men with steaming buckets and stained shovels patrolled the restless buffalo enclosure and others lifted, carried, or pushed and pulled boxes, grain sacks, and other burdens like ants in a stepped-on nest. The noise was constant and loud, a blacksmith's anvil clanged, human voices, hoarse from shouting, mingled with animal sounds, and somewhere one of the brass band's musicians practiced on a trombone. The entire fifteen-acre area smelled of manure, aged canvas, trampled grass, cigar smoke, and the occasional drift of perfume from the women's tents.

Kate was enthralled and her shining emerald eyes missed nothing.

"Mr. Cody, what in the world is that delicious smell?" Kate said. She'd raised her parasol against the sun and the fringe around the rim cast a lacy pattern of light and shadow across her beautiful cheekbones. "I declare, it's making me quite hungry."

"Pea soup, dear lady, the specialty of Mr. Random Clark, formerly of Her Majesty's Royal Navy and now my chief cook," Bill said. "When Random was a navy cook aboard the ironclad *HMS Invincible* he had the great honor of serving a bowl of pea soup to the German Kaiser Wilhelm the First. The grateful monarch declared it to be the best soup he'd ever tasted and awarded Random the Prussian Service to the Monarch Medal, third class. Needless to say Random is very proud of both his soup and his medal." Bill took Kate's elbow. "Would you care to sample a bowl?"

Kate shook her head. "No. I fear I'd be imposing."

Bill, never one to pass up the chance of a sweeping bow, did so and then said, "Dear lady, your imposition would be a sweet distraction. Let us proceed to the dining tent."

Random Clark was a small, wiry man with a few strands of hair combed across a bald pate, and he walked with a mariner's rolling gait. His pea soup—

he handed Kate the bowl like an angel presenting the Holy Grail to Sir Galahad—tasted even better than it smelled, and Kate decided that if she ever had a Kerrigan Medal third class, she'd award it to the ham bone and dried pea maestro.

"Yes, it was excellent. I do admire people who can cook, Mr. Cody," Kate Kerrigan said as they continued their tour. "I don't cook and never have. Through-out my life others have gladly taken that onerous chore from me. Most willingly, I should say, which I always found somewhat surprising. I do bake a fine sponge cake, though. But I've told you that already, have I not?"

"Yes you have, dear lady, and I look forward to partaking of that rare delicacy at the first available opportunity."

"And so you will, as you say, very soon for tea and cake," Kate said. "Come spring there will be no time for baking, I fear. The Kerrigan Ranch will ship more than ten thousand head of cattle to the Union Stock Yards next year and that means much hard work for everybody."

"Then we must make my participation in your tea a matter of the utmost priority," Bill said. He stopped and cupped a hand to his ear. "Hark! Do you hear that?"

Kate listened and her ears picked up a steady thud—thud—thud—

"Do tell, Mr. Cody," she said. "That is a most singular sound."

"This way and you'll see for yourself," Bill said.

He led Kate past a large storage tent and then they turned into an area of open ground. A young woman wearing a short red skirt, laced corset, black fishnet stockings, and red knee-high boots stood facing a man who had his back to a large wooden wheel painted a bright orange color. A small black boy stood beside the wheel and grinned at Kate. Next to the woman was a folding camp table that bore a large assortment of knives, including some wicked-looking bowies.

Bill Cody bowed and said, "Mrs. Kate Kerrigan, may I introduce you to Miss Ingrid Hult, and yonder pinned against the wheel is her partner Ducking Jim Benson. Ingrid, a Swedish lass from the great state of Kansas, is our knife thrower and Jim is her target."

"Target? I hope not," Kate said.

"I throw to miss, Mrs. Kerrigan," Ingrid said, smiling.

Liking the pretty, blue-eyed girl immediately, Kate said, "Please, call me Kate."

"Then you must call me Ingrid."

"May I see a demonstration of your skill?" Kate said.

Bill said, "Ingrid, do you mind?"

"Not at all, Mr. Cody," the girl said. And then, "Jim, are you ready to duck?"

Benson, a personable young man with a shock of black, unruly hair and an easy grin, looked at Kate and said, "How can I refuse the request from such a beautiful guest?"

Ingrid liked Bill Cody and it showed, probably because he was ahead of his time, paying the women in his show the same wages as the men.

The small black boy fastened straps to Benson's

wrists and legs and then spun the wheel so that the man rotated at a fairly brisk pace.

Ingrid picked up a handful of throwing knives and quickly outlined Benson's shape, concluding with a blade between his legs an inch under his crotch, calculated to make every man in an audience wince.

After Ingrid turned and dropped a little curtsey, Kate, thrilled, applauded and exclaimed, "Huzzah!"

But a more daring encore followed. The boy removed the knives from the wheel and then set Benson turning again. This time Ingrid used large bowie knives, designed for slashing and sticking, not throwing. But again she effortlessly silhouetted Benson's slim figure and the one between his thighs made Bill glance at his buckskinned crotch to make sure all his parts were still intact.

Again Kate clapped and her huzzahs were even more enthusiastic. The girl had revealed amazing skill with the knife.

"Kate, would you care to try the wheel?" Ingrid said. "I promise I'll do my best to miss you."

Kate smiled and shook her head. "I'd rather not. I think my spinning around on a wheel would be most unseemly. To say nothing of being outright dangerous."

"Ah, correct on both counts," Ingrid said. Her eyes were very blue. The black boy brought back the knives, and Ingrid selected one with a beautiful staghorn handle. "This is for you, Kate, a little souvenir of your visit to Buffalo Bill's Wild West."

Kate was touched, thanked Ingrid profusely, and invited her to the ranch for tea and sponge cake just as soon as she had some spare time. The girl said she would come and was already looking forward to it and then went back to practicing.

"There's still more to see, Kate," Bill Cody said. "If you'd care to continue our little promenade."

"I declare, I think I've had quite enough excitement for one day, Mr. Cody," Kate said.

"Then I'll escort you to your carriage," Bill said. He smiled, "Perhaps you'll find some time to practice knife throwing, if one of your servants can be induced to volunteer to be the target."

Kate laughed. "Trust me, none of my servants will volunteer, but I might be able to talk Frank Cobb into it or one of my sons, though somehow I doubt it."

CHAPTER NINE

A hundred and twenty miles south of Bill Cody's encampment lay the ruined Spanish mission of Cristo el Salvador, destroyed by Comanches two decades before Kate Kerrigan and her family entered Texas.

Two men emerged from the sand and brush country riding at a walk on tired horses. Both men looked weary, dusty, and trail-worn, and they stared straight ahead at the mission like pilgrims seeing the Grail. But there was nothing of religion in the minds of Bat Boswell and his brother Sky. They wanted whiskey, food, and a woman if there was one to be had.

Killing the man they hunted would come later.

A Winchester across his chest, Slide McKenzie stood and watched the riders come. A lanky, loose-geared man with eyes the color of swamp mud, McKenzie formed no judgments. The riders could be Texas Rangers or outlaws on the scout. They could be anybody.

When the men were within talking distance McKenzie said, "Howdy boys." Then as a joke, "Welcome to church."

The riders drew rein and looked beyond McKenzie to the mission. Three of its walls still stood and almost all of its tile roof, though much damaged in places. The forecourt swarmed with Mexicans, mostly men and children, but a few young women walked back and forth barefooted, their ample hips swaying under long, colorful skirts. The smell of spices and frying meat hung in the air, and the odor of ancient sandstone warming in the noon sun. Bat Boswell's gaze searched the mission forecourt but he saw no other white men, only the skinny drink of water in front of him with the rifle and long Yankee face.

"We need grub, whiskey if you got it, and maybe a woman," Boswell said.

McKenzie grinned. "The first two we got aplenty if you'll substitute mescal for whiskey," he said. "As for the third, all the women here are married or betrothed." Bat and his brother exchanged glances and then Sky said, his words flat, "Like that ever troubled us before."

The riders swung out of the saddle, tall men in canvas slickers. Both had sweeping dragoon mustaches, short-cropped yellow hair, and carried holstered Colts. The Boswell boys were Texans, born to the feud and the reckoning. After an early stint in the bank-robbing profession they became lawmen in several cow towns but now worked as guns for hire. The brothers were drinking buddies with John Wesley Hardin and had killed men in the vicious Sutton-Taylor scrap. For a spell they ran with Wild Bill Longley and that hard crowd, but Bill and Sky never could get along and their association had ended less than amicably.

Between them Bat and Sky had gunned nineteen white men. A pair of fine-looking fellows as they were, the Boswell brothers had time after time proved themselves to be brutal thugs and pitiless killers.

"Name's Slide McKenzie," the lanky man said.

"Means nothing to me," Bat said. "I'm Bat Boswell and this is my brother Sky."

"Right pleased to make your acquaintance," McKenzie said.

"No, you're not," Bat said. "And I don't blame you none."

McKenzie stepped to the side to let the men and their horses pass, but then he said to Bat's broad back, "I don't want no trouble."

Boswell turned his head, grinning, and said, "Then stay the hell out of our way."

"Just sayin' that I want . . . no trouble . . ." McKenzie said, but he was talking into dead air.

The Boswell brothers stopped and surveyed the crowded plaza in front of the mission. "Plenty of señoritas, seems like," Sky said. "Some of them are pretty enough, I guess."

Bat nodded. "And señoras." He smiled. "A woman can come later. We'll eat and have a drink first."

Near Bat, and his reason for stopping, a Mexican couple and their three children sat at a makeshift table and had begun to share a meal of fried beef and peppers and tortillas. The woman looked to be fifty but was probably in her early twenties, made old before her time by poverty and grindingly hard work. She held a tortilla in her hand, filled it with meat and peppers, and made ready to hand it to her husband, a skinny little peon who couldn't have weighed more than eighty pounds.

Bat intercepted the tortilla and snatched it from the woman's hand. He nodded in Sky's direction. "Make another for him."

The señora didn't know a word of English, but Boswell's meaning was clear. Without a sound, her face impassive, she piled meat and peppers onto another tortilla and handed it to Sky. There was very little left in the bowl when she finished. Her husband stared, shocked, at his family's food that was now vanishing down the throats of the two gringo gunmen and he jumped to his feet, yelling his anger. The Mexican's name was Sebastiono. He was tiny but he was game . . . . and he was a dead man.

Bat Boswell stopped chewing, his mouth full of beef, and he stared at the enraged little peon for several long moments before he drew his Colt and shot him in the chest. The .45 bullet punched two huge holes in Sebastian's frail body, entrance and exit, and he fell dead without a sound.

Sky Boswell glanced at the dead man and said, "Bat, what the hell was that about?"

"Beats me," Bat said, holstering his revolver. "I guess he was trying to impress his woman."

Sky shook his head. "What a damned fool." He looked briefly at the Mexican's wife and children, who'd thrown themselves on his body, then spat out the food in his mouth. "This grub tastes like sawdust. Let's go find mescal."

Slide McKenzie stepped beside the Boswell brothers. He had his Winchester in his hands and a worried expression on his face. He looked around at the growing crowd of hostile of Mexicans and said, "You boys better come with me."

Bat drew his gun. "The greasers want to step over their own dead?"

"They just might," McKenzie said. "Come with me into the mission." Then, "There's been enough killing here for one day. I need these people and a heap more like them."

Sky Boswell grinned. "Bat, you want to drop a few? Calm them down some."

Bat rubbed his stubbled chin, his eyes on the crowd that was slowly shuffling closer like a stalking animal. Most of the men had knives and those that didn't carried clubs of one kind or another. The smell of gunsmoke and rising dust hung in the air.

"Get into the mission," McKenzie said. "Bullets won't calm them but I can."

"Sky, we'll do as he says," Bat said. "Damn it, we can't kill them all."

McKenzie smiled, "Wise move, gentlemen," he said.

"Go to hell," Bat Boswell said.

CHAPTER TEN

"These are my own personal quarters," Slide McKenzie said, a note of pride in his voice. "This was the study of the first abbot, Ademar de la Cerda. He was murdered by Comanches when the mission was burned in 1767 and he's now a saint."

"He lived in a pigsty," Bat Boswell said, looking around him.

He grabbed the bottle of mescal and poured for himself and his brother. McKenzie had an earthenware cup on the table in front of him but Bat ignored it.

"Is that locked?" he said, nodding in the direction of the ancient door set into the crude brick wall to his right.

"Yes it's locked. Probably hasn't been opened in a hundred years," McKenzie said.

"So the only way the Mexicans can come at us is through the main door in front of me, huh?"

"Yes. That's the only way, and as you can see, the roof above us is solid."

"Good. Then if we need to we can pile the greasers up in the doorway."

"They won't attack," McKenzie said. "I told them that if you were harmed I would not lead them north." He smiled, revealing bad teeth. "They think I'm some kind of Moses who'll take them to the Promised Land."

"You?" Sky Boswell said, contempt souring his face. "You ain't Moses. You ain't nothing."

"Maybe so, but the Mexicans don't think I'm nothing," McKenzie said. "They'll make me thousands, a fortune. Study on that for a spell."

"You're full of crap," Sky said.

"Hold on," his brother said. "I want to hear him out. How can a bunch of raggedy-assed greasers make you a fortune?"

"Real easily, and you can share if'n you throw in with me," McKenzie said. "I may need a couple of guns to back my play."

"Bat, we're here to kill a man, remember?" Sky said. "We got priorities."

"Who's the man?" McKenzie said. "Anybody I might know?"

"His name is Josiah Mosely," Bat said. "You ever hear of a gun by that name?"

McKenzie shook his head. "Can't say as I have. He do wrong by you?"

"He killed a cousin of ours up in the Brokeoff Mountains county of the New Mexico Territory," Bat said. "Gal that owns a saloon that way says Mosely took off in a hot-air balloon."

"What the hell is that?" McKenzie said.

"It's a balloon full of hot air, just like you," Sky said, grinning.

Bat said, "It flies in the air and can carry a man far.

The gal we spoke to says Boswell headed south for Texas." The gunman's right hand white-knuckled around his cup. "Our cousin went by the name Jesse Tobin. He wasn't much, but he was kin, and there must be a reckoning."

"Hell, man, he could be anywhere," McKenzie said. "A flying man like that."

"The woman told us the balloon was damaged and wouldn't fly far," Bat said. "She said it would come down in West Texas."

McKenzie grinned, or tried to. He had a way of stretching his mouth and then allowing it snap back into place like a contracting rubber band.

"If the flying machine came down to earth in West Texas, it landed on the Kerrigan ranch," he said.

"How the hell are you so sure?" Bat said.

"Because Kate Kerrigan owns most of West Texas. And listen up, if you throw in with me, she's the gal that will make all three of us rich."

Sky Boswell said, "How do you figure that?"

"Blackmail," McKenzie said. "I can wring money out of her until she's parted with every last cent she has."

"What the hell has this to do with cousin Jesse?" Sky said.

"Everything," McKenzie said. "If the balloon thing came down in this part of West Texas the only place for a hundred miles around where a man could find help is the Kerrigan Ranch. That Mosely feller is either still there or Kate Kerrigan knows which way he went."

"Mighty thin," Sky said.

"Could be, but how successful has your search been so far?" McKenzie said.

Sky opened his mouth to speak but Bat talked over him. "What's this blackmail idea of yours, McKenzie?"

"There's been a drought and famine in central Mexico," the man answered. "They say in Durango alone five thousand have died of starvation in the past few weeks."

"What's that to me?" Bat said.

"Maybe a great deal," McKenzie said. "The word's gotten around that a white man, me, is promising to lead Mexicans to a better place, a land flowing with milk and honey, as the Good Book says."

"I'm still not catching your drift," Bat said. A fat black fly droned around the room and a rat rustled in a shadowed corner. Beams of dusty light angled from four small, rectangular windows cut into the top of the outside wall and illuminated the monkish cell with a dull saffron glow.

Slide McKenzie poured mescal into the three cups and then said, "Within a week I can have ten thousand people gathered here and—"

Sky said, "That's a heap of greasers."

McKenzie nodded. "Damn right it is, especially if you're a rancher and they're fanning out across your range like locusts. You know how much damage ten thousand hungry people could do to the Kerrigan Ranch? How many cattle they'd slaughter? Hell, it would be like the Battle of Gettysburg."

"You're a slick-talking man, McKenzie, but I still don't see what's in it for me and Sky," Bat said.

"That's where the blackmail comes in," McKenzie said. "I tell Kate Kerrigan that this disaster can be avoided quite simply. All she has to do is pay me a hundred thousand dollars and I'll keep the Mexicans away. But that's only the start. Come the spring roundup I'll squeeze her again . . . and again . . . and finally I'll take her ranch from her."

"And when she comes looking for you with a dozen riders and a rope you'll need protection," Bat said.

"Right. That's where you and your brothers come into the picture. But Kate Kerrigan won't come hunting me with a hanging posse, not if she values her range. If I have to light a shuck in a hurry I'll take ten thousand with me and head straight for her big mansion."

Bat looked at his brother. "What do you think?"

Sky said, "I think we do what we came here to do in the first place and that's the reckoning for Jesse. He's lying cold in his grave, his spirit unavenged, and this fool wants to take us on a wild goose chase. We don't make war on ranchers, Bat. Hell, they're our bread and butter."

Bat Boswell studied on that for a few silent moments and then said, "We want half of what you get from the Kerrigan woman."

"Damn it, Bat," Sky said.

"Half, McKenzie," Bat said.

McKenzie's mouth stretched. "Done and done, Bat. And now that we're partners call me Slide."

"McKenzie, you try to sell us out and I'll kill you. Understand?"

"Sure, Bat, sure. We're partners, now and for always."

"You're a sorry piece of trash, McKenzie, and we ain't partners, now and never," Bat said. "Just you make sure you keep your end of the bargain."

"And if there's killing to be done?" McKenzie said.

"Me and Sky will do it. Now get out there and find us a woman, the younger the better."

"No more killing, Bat," McKenzie said. "Them Mexicans are worked up as it is."

"Hell, man, we want to screw her, not shoot her," Sky Boswell said.

CHAPTER ELEVEN

"Boy, you got a screw loose in your thinking assembly," Frank Cobb said. "You'll never find a gas . . . a gas whatever you call it out there on the range."

"Hydrogen cylinder it's called, and I have to find it or I'm stuck here," Josiah Mosely said. "The Indian shot up the one I was using, and I've only got that one spare."

"Why don't you ask Mrs. Kerrigan to sell you a hoss?" Frank said. "Hoss will take you anywhere you want to go."

"I don't have any money and, besides, you know I can't ride."

"What about the red balloon thing?"

"You mean the envelope?"

"It's torn to shreds."

"Not completely. Even though the envelope is made of silk it can be repaired with some time and effort."

Frank shook his head. "All right, you can take the buckboard, but bring it back in one piece. If you damage the wagon or the horse I swear I'll take it out of your hide."

"I can drive a wagon, Mr. Cobb. I won't damage it."

"See you don't," Frank said.

As he did every morning just after sunup Frank turned on his heel and walked in the direction of the bunkhouse to assign the hands their chores for the day. The air smelled fresh of winter grass as the new day came in clean, but there was a spatter of rain in the north wind and the raw iron tang of the coming winter cold.

Josiah Mosely hitched a grade mare to the buckboard and swung south, following the route of the errant balloon. As it happened, the flat land revealed the whereabouts of the hydrogen cylinder surprisingly quickly, after less than an hour's search. The envelope was tangled around the dead, bone-white cottonwood and badly ripped, like a tattered scarlet dress covering a skeleton. But the basket was more or less intact and that cheered Mosely considerably. He loaded the basket and the ragged envelope into the buckboard and then headed back in the direction of the Kerrigan ranch house.

Mosely decided to make a detour that took him close to Buffalo Bill's tent city, a decision that would lead to a chain of events he could not foresee . . . a winter of murder and terror that threatened to destroy the Wild West show and involve Kate Kerrigan in the hunt for a killer.

Josiah Mosely halted the buckboard and kicked on the brake. He removed his round glasses, polished them on a piece of yellow cloth he took from his pocket, and rubbed away the grit they'd picked up on the trail. Once he replaced the glasses he blinked and then surveyed the endless rows of canvas tents on the grass, like a fleet of weathered men o' war under full sail on a green sea. Now and then a blanket-wrapped Indian stepped into his line of vision and once he saw a pretty girl stop, reach under the neckline of her blouse, and make an adjustment to some intimate garment.

Mosely was thrilled. Savage Indians, pretty girls with their hands in secret places, the aroma of animals, tame and wild, and the fine, savory odors from the cooking tent. In all his life, from ground or sky level, he'd never seen or smelled the like.

"What the hell are you doing, four eyes?"

Mosely turned and saw three men facing him. They looked like cowboys but bore no resemblance to the bearded, mud-spattered waddies he'd seen around the Kerrigan place. The trio were scrubbed up and dressed as neat as whiskey drummers in expensive range duds, fancy boots, and wide-brimmed white hats that no working puncher could afford. Mosely figured they looked like actors playing the parts of cowboys, and then it dawned on him that that's exactly what they were, except at one time they'd probably worked as real punchers.

Then the biggest of the three, a tall redheaded man with massive shoulders, spoke again. "I asked you a question, mister."

Mosely smiled. "Just watching the circus."

"Circus?" the redhead said. "You calling Buffalo Bill's Wild West a circus?"

"I saw a circus one time," Mosely said. "This looks pretty much the same."

The big man's eyes opened wide and his mouth stretched in a grimace. "Git the hell down from there, boy," he said. "Seems to me you need some schooling in manners."

"You're not one to school anybody," Mosely said, his anger flaring. "I think, sir, you have the makings of a bully and a braggart."

Now the redhead exploded, and he did a little dance of rage. "Git the hell down from there!" he yelled. His companions grinned and one of them said, "Spank his butt, Davy."

"I will not bandy words with fools," Mosely said. He let off the wagon brake and started to roll forward. The man called Davy was big and he was fast. He covered the distance to the wagon in three quick steps and dragged Mosely from the seat. Mosely had sand and in a desperate attempt to regain his balance he tried to push the cowboy away from him. As immobile as a full-grown loblolly pine, Davy didn't budge. Grinning, he backhanded Mosely across the face and then landed a punch to his belly. The young man groaned and started to fall, but Davy held him upright and pulled his face so close to his own he hit Mosely with his spittle as he said, "What were you looking at, boy? Say it. Say Buffalo Bill's Wild West."

Gasping his words, Mosely said, "A circus . . . circus . . ."

Davy turned his head and said to his companions, "You boys want a piece of this?"

There are bullies in every walk of life, and that day Josiah Mosely was unfortunate enough to run into three of them. As the two others stepped toward him, he knew he was in for a terrible beating, and all because a trio of lowlifes wanted some fun. It was unfair, Mosely decided. But sometimes the fates that hound a man don't give a damn if a thing is fair or not.

Davy hauled Mosely to his feet and held him in place as a hard-faced youngster he called Andy cocked his fist, his glittering blue eyes fixed on Mosely's chin. His punch never landed.

A hickory ax handle crashed down on Andy's forearm with the force of a ten-ton drop hammer, shattering the ulna and radius bones like matchwood. Andy screamed, but his shrieking cry of mortal agony was drowned out by the cougar screech war cry of a Cheyenne Dog Soldier.

Cloud Passing charged among the three toughs like a buzz saw, striking out with the ax handle like a war club, the thud-thud-thud of wood striking bone as loud as a bass drum. Andy had backed out of the fight, clutching his splintered arm, grimacing in pain. Both the other cowboys were down. Davy, his head bloody, writhed and chawed up the ground, the second, a bearded towhead, lay on his back, squealing like a piglet trapped under a gate as he tried in vain to ward off the Indian's smashing blows.

"No!" Mosely yelled. "You're killing them."

Despite feeling groggy from the beating he'd taken, the young man stepped between Cloud Passing and the downed men. Mosely stared into the black fire of the Indian's eyes and said, "It's over. They've had enough."

Cheyenne warriors were notional, and Cloud Passing

proved it by making no argument. He lowered the ax handle and said, "Mose-ly, you are my friend." He nodded. "Yes, it is done."

But no one ever said a Cheyenne Dog Soldier was not one to carry a grudge. As the hurting towhead crawled away Cloud Passing kicked him hard in the butt.

Josiah Mosely didn't see it coming and neither did the Indian.

Suddenly a net sailed through the air like a gigantic bat and settled over Cloud Passing. The rope attached to the net jerked tight and the Indian fell on his back. As he struggled, hopelessly tangled, four big, club-wielding roustabouts pounced on the outraged Cheyenne and one of them, as Irish as the pigs of Docherty, said, "Lie still, ye damned Hindoo, or I'll break every bane in your body."

"Lafferty, belay that." Bill Cody stepped into the cursing, kicking fray and said, "He's the best damned Indian I've got, and I don't want him hurt."

His club poised, Lafferty said, "Then what do we do with him, your honor?"

Bill thought for a moment, then said, "Put him in the cage with the black bear. That will quiet him down." Bill's eyes moved to his hurting, battered cowboys and he shook his head. "Then collect all the parts of those three and see if you can assemble one whole cowboy out of them." Bill threw back his head, spread his arms, and said to the uncaring sky, "Lord almighty, times are coming down hard enough. I sure as hell don't need this."

As he and the other roustabouts dragged Cloud

Passing to his feet, Lafferty said, "Say a prayer to the holy Saint Jude, your honor."

"Who is he?" Bill said.

"The patron saint of lost causes and hopeless cases," Lafferty said.

CHAPTER TWELVE

"You've no call to do that, Kate," Frank Cobb said, his scowl betraying his irritation. "I'll take Mosely down to the bunkhouse and Doc Finney can patch him up."

Kate Kerrigan's left eyebrow arched. "Really? I knew Buff Finney was a top hand, but I didn't realize he was also a physician."

"He isn't. But when he was a kid he worked for a boxing promoter over New Orleans way and was teached how to patch up cuts and bruises."

"He was teached, Frank? Surely you mean he was taught?" Kate said.

"Well, whatever it is, Mosely ain't badly hurt. Let Doc do it."

Josiah Mosely's battered face moved stiffly as he said, "Frank is right, Mrs. Kerrigan. This is no task for a lady."

"As far as I know, patching up wounded menfolk has always been the task of ladies," Kate said. "Now hold still. This will sting like the dickens."

Frank shook his head. "You're babying the boy, Kate. He has to be a man and learn to stand up for himself sometime."

"I had an unfortunate experience with the three toughs who attacked poor Mr. Mosely," Kate said. "They are—"

Frank was instantly alert, his face an odd mix of concern and anger. "What kind of experience?"

Kate smiled. "Nothing too serious. Just talk."

"You sure that's all it was?"

"Yes, I'm sure. And as far as I can tell, they've already been punished enough. Frank Butler, Annie Oakley's husband, says one of the cowboys has a broken arm, and the others are in a bad way. Bill's wild Indian is caged up with a bear, and Frank says the bear doesn't much care for his company."

Mosely said, "The Indian thinks he owes me because I wouldn't let you hang him, Frank."

"Yeah, well, in future, maybe you should learn to stand on your own two feet and fight back, Mosely," Frank said. "You can't always count on Indians saving your hide."

"Mr. Mosely, a word to the wise—the Indian had left the Cody compound and was trespassing on my range, so Frank had the right to hang him," Kate said. "But I'm glad he did not. As for the question of saving your hide, several of my riders, including Frank and my son Trace, are expert hands with the revolver. I'm sure any one of them would be pleased to teach you to shoot."

"Sure, I'll teach you," Frank said. "So long as you

pony up with the money for the cartridges. A box of a hundred rounds doesn't come cheap."

Mosely said, "You are both very kind, but I think I'll leave the shooting to others more suited for it."

Frank nodded. "For once I agree with you, boy. You'll never be a shootist. I can tell by looking at you and them little hands of yours. Besides, it takes sand to swap lead with a man, and in my book you just don't cut it."

Mosely was patched up, his face covered in iodine and small bandages, and Jazmin Salas, Kate's cook, ended further conversation when she crossed the kitchen floor with a tray of coffee and sandwiches.

But Kate thought she saw hurt in Mosely's eyes and she had the last word. "Don't take what Frank says to heart, Josiah. Not every man is cut out to be a revolver fighter."

Dinner that evening was to be a grand affair.

Jazmine Salas, with help from the assistant cook and scullery maids, had prepared a meal that Kate was confident would be to Bill Cody's taste. The menu was simple, yet, to Kate's mind at least, as sophisticated as any served in the nation that night. She studied the bill of fare for the tenth time that evening and decided it was crackerjack.

SAVORY
   Angels on Horseback
SOUP
   Scotch Broth *à la* Queen Victoria

FISH
   Baked Texas Trout
POULTRY
   Pheasant Mandarin
MEAT
   Veal Escallops with Mushroom
VEGETABLE
   Winter carrots Vichy and Potatoes *à la
   Parisienne*
DESSERT
   Peach Cobbler with Caramel Sauce

But not everyone would have the peach dessert. A privileged few would receive a piece of the coveted Sponge Cake à la Kate Kerrigan.

That evening the lamps were turned up all over the Kerrigan house from the downstairs servants' quarters to the upstairs family rooms where Kate was entertaining Buffalo Bill Cody, Annie Oakley and her husband Frank Butler, several of the show's top riders, and Ingrid Hult and her assistant Ducking Jim Benson. Her tall sons Trace and Quinn were in attendance at the dinner, as were her teenage daughters Ivy and Shannon, pretty girls who got more than their fair share of attention from Bill's young cowboys and from Ducking Jim, who surprised everyone with his fine tenor voice when he sang "So Pretty a Face" and "The Gondolier's Song," then music hall favorites. Kate, wearing an evening dress of sapphire satin, sat at the head of the dining table, Bill on her right, Frank Cobb on her left. Earlier, after she'd ministered to Josiah Mosely, she'd baked the sponge cake, only one since the effort had left her quite used up. There were fourteen diners, excluding herself, at the table, and a single sponge cake for dessert would not go far, so she limited the treat to Buffalo Bill, Mr. and Mrs. Butler, Ingrid Hult and Ducking Jim and Frank Cobb. Frank offered—rather too quickly, Kate thought—to forgo his piece and surrender it to someone else, perhaps one of the girls. He said he'd content himself with Jazmin Salas's peach cobbler with caramel sauce, but Kate would not hear of it. She noted his crushed expression and said, "Frank, your most gallant sacrifice is much appreciated, and as a reward I'll make sure you receive the largest piece of cake." But Frank looked more disheartened than ever and Kate was very pleased with him. One of the finer traits of a gentleman is to make sacrifices for others, and Frank did seem so very disappointed that his chivalrous *beau gest* had been foiled.

Josiah Mosely did not attend the dinner, though as a guest under her roof Kate made it clear that he was more than welcome. Mosely had begged off, citing his battered, iodine-stained face as an excuse, and Kate had not pressed the matter.

As he snuck out of the house into the cold moonlight that night Mosely had other, more important things on his mind than fancy grub.

CHAPTER THIRTEEN

Night and darkness transformed Bill Cody's encampment. Lit from within by oil lamps, as far as the eye could see the tents glowed like Chinese lanterns and people flickered back and forth in shadow. The horse lines lay to the west beyond the camping area and to the north was the tract set aside for the wagons and animal exhibits. That lot was poorly lit, and Josiah Mosely stood and studied the layout for long time, but he saw no sign of human activity. He reckoned that's where the bear would be held, along with its unwelcome houseguest.

Mosely, a hammer and chisel in hand, angled to his right through the mother-of-pearl moonlight. He stopped in his tracks. *What the hell is that sound behind me?* Footsteps! And too close. Within clubbing distance close.

"Who's there?" Mosely whispered. "Identify yourself and state your intentions."

A few moments silence and then, "Don't shoot, mister."

It was a child's voice.

"Who are you?" Mosely said.

"My name is Peter. But folks call me Pete."

"I'm Josiah. Are you with the Wild West show?"

"No. Mrs. Kerrigan took me in after the cholera killed my ma and pa."

"She adopted you?"

"Kinda. Kate says I'm her ward."

"What are you doing out here, Pete?"

The boy kicked the grass at his feet. "Ivy and Shannon wouldn't let me come to dinner with them. Shannon is mean. She told me I was a grubby little wretch and to eat in the kitchen."

Mosely smiled. "Girls who think they're all grown up tend to say mean things about small boys."

"Where are you headed, Josiah?" Pete said.

"Nowhere special. It's getting late. You'd better go home now."

The boy closely studied Mosely's face in the moonlight and then his eyes dropped to the hammer and chisel in his hand. "I can keep watch," he said. "I'm real good at that. Shannon says I'm her mother's spy."

Mosely said, "Hmm . . . I think you'll see what you see and then fess up."

"I won't, Josiah. Cross my heart and hope to die, stick a needle in my eye."

Mosely thought about it and then said, "All right, I can use another pair of eyes. But afterward you keep your mouth shut, you hear?"

"I crossed my heart," Pete said. "What are we gonna do, huh?"

"Free an Indian."

"The one in the bear's cage?"

"Yeah, that's him."

"Mr. Cobb says his name is Cloud Passing," Pete said. "I wanted to take him a piece of cake from Mrs. Jazmin's kitchen, but she said the bear would take it. And she said that . . . Shy— Shy—"

"Cheyenne," Mosely said.

"Yeah, that's it. She said Cheyenne warriors are full of tricks and deviltry and little boys like me should stay away from them."

Mosely smiled. "Then aren't you afraid to help me?"

Pete shook his head. "Mr. Cobb says that nothing scares me and he says that's how a boy should be."

Mosely nodded. "Every now and then Mr. Cobb says a wise thing. All right, Pete. Are we ready?"

"I am if you are," the boy said. He reached into his pocket and produced a handful of yellow crumbs that smelled like lemon cake. "I was on my way to give the Indian this when I met you. Now I'll give it to him later."

The boy called Pete stepped next to Josiah Mosely like a shadow as they made their careful way toward the bear wagon. Somewhere out in the darkness a penned-up buffalo bull grunted and closer a woman called out in her sleep. A roosting owl, drawn to the camp by the prospect of rodents, hooted, its wide-shouldered silhouette silvered by moonlight. Mosely's feet made little sound and the boy's none at all.

"There," Pete whispered. He pointed to his right. "Next to the yellow wagon."

Mosely's eyes scanned the gloom. The bright wagon was visible and beyond it lay the vague shape of the bear cage. Mosely stopped and listened. Only the owl scraped the silence with its apologetic hoot and nothing moved.

"Let's go," Mosely said.

"You have a gun?" Pete said.

"Not with me," Mosely said.

All the boy's disappointment was summed up in one word, "Oh."

Mosely smiled. "Next time I'll remember to bring them."

Pete said, "How many have you got?"

"Two."

"Can I have one?"

"Sure, when you're older. Now let's get this done."

"What are we gonna do?"

"Save an Indian from a bear and the gallows is what we're gonna do."

There are exceptions to every rule, but by nature the black bear is more genial than the grizzly and slower to irritation. However, when the grizz decides to attack he'll often just beat you up and then leave you alone—but not the black bear. If ol' Ephraim gets angry enough to strike he won't stop until he kills you. He gives no second chances. Therefore, Josiah Mosely was right to be wary as he approached the caged wagon where Cloud Passing squatted at one end, the bear at the other. Both seemed asleep, and the feral smell of wild animal and wilder man hung heavy in the air.

Remembering Bill Cody's advice to poke a Cheyenne to gauge his mood, Mosely prodded Cloud

Passing with the butt end of his hammer. The Indian woke instantly, his black eyes flashing. Then he saw Mosely and smiled.

Mosely nodded. "I'm getting you out of here, understand? You catching my lingo?"

Whether the Cheyenne understood English didn't matter. Mosely's intent was clear when he attacked the hinge that held the huge iron padlock in place. It took only a few minutes to lever the hinge away from the somewhat rotted wood, and Mosely swung the door wide.

"Get out of there," he said.

Cloud Passing didn't hesitate. He scrambled outside and to Mosely's horror so did the bear. But the animal showed no hostile intent and stuck close to Cloud Passing. Mosely swore it was making calf's eyes at him. From behind him he heard Pete say, "Josiah. Somebody's coming!"

"Light a shuck, Indian, and take your bear with you," Mosely said. Then, "And for God's sake be quiet. Not a sound, understand?"

Josiah Mosely had been around white men for too long and he hadn't spent any time with Indians.

Rejoicing in his newfound freedom, Cloud Passing threw back his head and let rip with his cougar war cry, a shrill shriek that shattered the night into a million shards of sound.

"Damn it!" Mosely yelled.

"Hey, what's going on there?" a man hollered.

The bear roared.

Cloud Passing launched into a wailing, yipping, foot-pounding dance.

Mosely grabbed Pete by the wrist and took to his heels.

A pistol shot. Then another.

From the cover of darkness Mosely saw the Indian run toward the tents. The bear launched into her bouncing ball lope and headed in the opposite direction toward her cage, deciding that there were safer places to be that night than on the vamoose with a human who was even wilder than she was.

Josiah Mosely spent the next fifteen minutes searching for Cloud Passing, but there was no sign of the man. He had vanished into the night. Mosely walked to the edge of the tents and peered into the darkness but saw nothing. He turned and stepped right into a Winchester muzzle that settled neatly between his eyeglasses. "Raise your hands, feller, or I'll blow your brains out."

Mosely blinked and beheld the pretty but somewhat mannish features of Annie Oakley, the one they called Little Miss Sure Shot. He raised his hands.

"You've played hob and damn near spoiled Kate Kerrigan's dinner," Annie said. She wore a green evening dress that didn't become her. "Now there's a half-broke Cheyenne on the loose and apart from Sitting Bull he's the best Indian we ever had."

"I won't see any man caged," Mosely said.

"You'll see yourself caged when Mr. Cody gets through with you," Annie said. She looked down at Pete. "And youngster, if you kick my shins one more time I'll put you over my knee and paddle you."

She moved the rifle from the bridge of Mosely's nose, tossed it into her left hand, and shoved the muzzle into his belly. "You come with me. Bill is on his way." Annie grabbed Pete by the ear and twisted. "You too, you little twerp," she said.

Even the charms of Mr. Dickens's sublime work *The Old Curiosity Shop* could not hold Kate Kerrigan's attention. She closed the book, laid it on the bedside table beside the little carved bone owl she treasured, and let her mind dwell on Peter. The boy was always getting into mischief, but this time it was more serious. Bill Cody was really upset over the disappearance of his Indian, and he also claimed that the bear was so traumatized by the experience she would not eat. Around the encampment people hinted darkly that freeing Cloud Passing was a hanging offense and one of Bill's riders, a former lawman, suggested that up in the New Mexico Territory there was a notorious desperado by the name of Joseph Morley or Marley who went by the handle *The Chuska Kid.* "The accused might well be the same man," the former lawman said, and everyone agreed that he was very wise and called a spade a spade.

Of course Peter was only a boy, and Bill said he'd been led astray by Josiah Mosely, perhaps aka The Chuska Kid, and that he'd leave his punishment up to Kate, as though life hadn't punished the child enough already.

Kate lay back on the pillow, her hair spreading like liquid fire across the ivory silk. She closed her eyes, dark eyelashes fanning across her cheekbones, and remembered a different time and place, the trail drive to Dodge City and her first meeting with another boy so like Peter, a boy she'd named Sam Chisholm. Holy Mother, had it been four years already? It seemed like just yesterday . . . or perhaps the day before. . . .

CHAPTER FOURTEEN

Heat lightning flashed in the sky as Frank Cobb stepped up to the fire. "Cattle are restless," he said. "Something out there is spooking them."

Kate Kerrigan stared into the surrounding darkness. "Wolves or a cougar maybe?"

"Maybe," Frank said. He wore his belt gun, the first time he'd buckled it on since the herd left Texas. He poured himself coffee, stood, and listened into the night.

In the distance the nighthawk waddie sang tunelessly to the unquiet herd.

Well come along boys and listen to my tale,
I'll tell you of my troubles on the old Chisholm Trail.
Come a ti-yi-yippee yip-pee yea,
Come a ti-yi-yippee yea.

Firelight made the shadows flicker and touched Kate's hair with red-gold flame when she moved her head. "Frank, are we in trouble?" she said. "I have a feeling . . ."

"Trouble? I don't know," Frank said. He tossed away the dregs of his coffee and dropped the tin cup by the fire. "The buckskin mare is a good night horse. I reckon I'll throw a saddle on her and ride herd for a spell. The croaking frog you hear out there is Deuce Baker. He's a steady hand, but I reckon tonight he could use some help."

"Be careful, Frank," Kate said, rising to her feet.

Frank Cobb nodded. "Depend on it."

The herd was strung out along a narrow valley with good grass and a few trees. There were several springs, two of them with sweet water, although the third and widest smelled strongly of sulfur and the cattle gave it a wide berth.

Kate was tired out from a rigors of the trail, but she knew there would be no sleep that night. Normally the cattle would have bedded down by now, but they were still on their feet, shuffling restlessly, a dust cloud rising above their backs like a yellow mist. She stepped away from the fire and stared into gloom. There was no moon, and Kate had lost sight of Frank and Deuce Baker, who were out there somewhere, invisible in the darkness.

"It's late. You should be in your blankets, ma'am."

Kate turned and saw Lem Winston the trail cook. Lem always looked like a rather grubby snowman, and tonight was no different. The flour did that, and trail dust.

"The cattle are restless," Kate said, echoing what Frank had said earlier. "I don't feel like sleeping."

Winston looked around at the punchers snoring

under their blankets. "You should take a lesson from them boys. They could sleep their way through Judgment Day."

"Then I hope I don't have to wake them," Kate said.

"Heat lightning spooks a herd sometimes," Winston said. "Seen it a time or two." Then, after a moment's thought, "But they won't run."

Kate smiled. "How can you be so sure, Lem?"

"The night is bothering them, too dark, too quiet. The cattle are jumpy all right, but they're tired and they'll settle."

"Mr. Cobb says there's something out there," Kate said. "He says maybe a cougar."

Winston nodded. "Maybe so, he's right." He turned his head and his eyes swept the towering ramparts of the darkness. "Yup, maybe so," he said again.

"What do you think it could be, Lem?" Kate said, the firelight touching her face with its rosy glow.

"Cougar. Bear. Coyotes. All kinds of critters roam the big flat. It's hard to say." The cook smiled. "Wait right there, ma'am. I got something real special for you." Normally a soft-spoken man, Cobb's voice sounded loud in the stillness.

Winston stumped away on his peg leg. He'd lost his left leg under the knee while he was still in his teens, the result of a rattlesnake bite that had gone gangrenous. He returned, holding something white in his hand.

"Aimed to give you this earlier, ma'am," he said. "But right now seems as good a time as any, you being so worried an' all." Shyly, Winston held out the white object. "It's a gift, like. It's made out of buffalo bone and I engraved it myself."

Kate took the object and smiled. It was a beautiful little owl about two inches tall. On top of its head was a carved loop representing the moon and through that ran a thin silver chain.

"Lem, it's beautiful," Kate said.

"One time a Comanche woman told me that the owl is a bird of good omen because it's the guardian of the night," Winston said. "The owl will protect you, Mrs. Kerrigan, and bring you luck."

"Then I must wear it at once," Kate said. She held out the chain. "Will you, please?"

Kate turned her back and the cook fastened the chain at the nape of her slender neck. "There," she said, turning to the cook again. "Now I am well protected. Lem, it's very pretty."

Winston gave a gap-toothed smile. "I'm glad you like it," he said.

Then, something strange . . .

"Listen," the cook said. "Now just listen to that."

From somewhere very close an owl hooted, asking its eternal question of the night.

"The owl is already guarding you, Mrs. Kerrigan," Winston said. "It's telling you something."

"Telling me what?"

"That I do not know."

Kate smiled, or tried to. "I guess I'll find out, huh?"

"That would be my opinion," Winston said. But he looked worried.

The long night passed without incident. The herd eventually settled, and by dawn most of the cattle were resting. But Lem Wilson kept his voice low as he wakened the hands instead of his usual bellow of, "Come and get it or I'll throw it out!"

Deuce Baker rode in, and when Kate questioned him he said no, he hadn't seen Frank Cobb, and yes, it was odd that he was still out with the herd.

Kate said, "Did anything happen that might have delayed Mr. Cobb?"

"I don't think so, ma'am," Baker said. "But the cattle were moving around so much it was hard to tell. Maybe Mr. Cobb went after a cougar or a lobo wolf."

"Perhaps," Kate said. She smiled. "You'd better go get your breakfast, Deuce. You look all used up."

After the young puncher left, Kate stood to eat her bacon and beans, her eyes scanning the distance for any sign of Frank. He rode in half an hour later when the hands were already out with the herd.

He touched his hat to Kate, swung out of the saddle, and helped himself to coffee. He didn't speak until he'd built and lit a cigarette and then he said though a cloud of exhaled smoke, "We lost fifty head, maybe more." He saw the question on Kate's face and said, "Rustlers. I count four of them."

"You tracked them?" Kate said.

Frank nodded. "A fair piece. I'm going after them."

"Frank, you look tired," Kate said.

"I reckon." He saw Lem Winston and called him over, then, "Mr. Winston, you go back a ways with most of the hands. Who's the best with the iron? Don't say Hank Lowery. Since he got religion he's sworn off gunfighting, or so he says."

One look into Frank's grim, strained face and Winston knew better than to ask questions. "Mrs. Kerrigan's son is good with the rifle," he said.

"I need Trace to stay with the herd," Frank said. "Who else?"

"Well, there's Dave Roche. He can draw mighty quick, and they say he killed a man over Abilene way a couple of years back. He's a wild kid, Texas born and raised, but—"

"He's hard to handle," Frank said. "Yeah, I know him. He'll do. Deuce, go get Roche, tell him to come in. You'll take his place at swing." He saw the consternation on the young waddie's face and said, "I'll get somebody else to ride night herd tonight."

The prospect of a good night's sleep cheered the youngster considerably, and he left in search of Roche.

"Frank, can this be resolved without gunplay?" Kate said.

"Sure, if the rustlers are willing to return our cattle. But I'm not counting on it."

"You said there were four of them. You and Dave Roche will be two," Kate said. "We can hold the herd here and you can take more men."

Frank said, "Kate, we need to push on. We're already at least a day behind half a dozen other outfits. First cows in Dodge bring the best prices. You know that. Besides, I need shootists, not punchers who only use their revolvers to string fence wire. A bunch of dead waddies won't get the herd to the stockyards."

"You sure about Hank—"

"He won't fight."

Kate said, "All right, if he won't fight I will. I'm going with you."

"No, you're not," Frank said.

A frown gathered between Kate's eyebrows, never a

good sign. "Are you giving me orders, Mr. Cobb?" she said.

"Kate, we'll riding into trouble, probably gun trouble," Frank said. "A gunfight is no place for a woman."

"But it is this woman's place," Kate said. "You seem to have forgotten that I'm the owner of the KK ranch. Those are my cattle that were rustled. If I was a man would you expect me to go with you?"

"Yeah, of course. But—"

"But because I'm a woman I can't handle trouble? Is that it?"

Frank looked into Kate's eyes, which were full of green fire. He chose his words carefully. "Kate, I know that you've killed men before. Three of them in New York when you were just a slip of a girl."

"They raped my sister, and she later died giving birth to a stillborn child," Kate said. "I shot all three because back then I was angry and I'm angry now. Fifty cows may not seem like much, but they are mine, and I will not have what's mine stolen by anyone. What do you want me to do, Frank? Ride point with the chuck wagon with not a care in the world while you do my dirty work and put your life in danger?"

"Kate, I don't want you to get hurt," Frank said.

"It comes with the job. I ride for the brand the same as you do." Kate raised a silencing hand. "No buts, Frank, I am going with you, and there's an end to it."

"I admire your determination and your pluck, Kate, but by times you're a headstrong woman," Frank said.

"In other words, I'm a stubborn bitch," Kate said. "Is that it?"

Frank shook his head. "I've no answer to your question, Kate. I'm riding wide around that one."

He was spared further comment when Dave Roche rode in and said, "You want to see me, boss?"

"Rustlers ran off fifty head last night," Frank said. "I'm taking them back." Roche made no answer and his young face revealed nothing. "By their tracks, I reckon there are four men involved," Frank said. "You think you can handle it?"

Roche was a lanky youngster with bright blue eyes, yellow hair and a mouth a little too thin and hard for his nineteen years. He belted his Colt high, horseman style, on his right hip and its worn walnut handle revealed that it was a working gun and not just cowboy fashion. He said, "I ride for the brand."

Frank nodded. There was nothing more needed to be said.

Kate stepped into the silence. "I'll be riding with you, Dave," she said.

The puncher's eyes slid to Frank, but his expression didn't change.

Then realization hit Frank Cobb like a slap upside the head. Kate was stubborn all right, pigheaded even, but, by God, right then he was proud of her.

CHAPTER FIFTEEN

Tracks left by fifty cows and four riders leave an easy trail to follow, and by mid-morning Kate and the men came on a creek that flowed due south and seemed to have its origin in rolling hills thick with piñon, juniper, and here and there stands of ponderosa pine. The rising sun cast shadows on the grass and the air smelled fresh of the new day.

Dave Roche had followed the northward course of the stream and now he rode back to Kate and Frank and said, "Looks like they stopped to water the cattle about a quarter mile from here. Both banks are well broken down. I reckon cows have used that part of the creek before."

"Then their cabin is likely to be close," Frank said.

"That would be my thinking," Roche said.

Frank looked at Roche and then Kate. "We ready for this?" he said.

The young puncher grinned and nodded, and Kate slid her Winchester from the boot. "Say the word, Frank," she said.

"I reckon everything has already been said, Kate. Let's ride."

Roche led the way along the creek bank. After half a mile the stream looped to the east around a cottonwood and then came up on a short stretch of piñon and juniper that opened onto a grassy meadow where dusty cattle grazed. All wore the KK brand.

A cabin lay on the northernmost edge of the meadow, a low structure with a sagging roof and a rickety porch out front. A pole corral holding five horses stood nearby and there were several outbuildings. Even from a distance it was a rundown, two-by-twice outfit that told a tale of lazy, shiftless occupants who kept their place together with baling wire and twine.

As Kate and the others rode closer through the grazing cows a greasy man with a huge belly stepped out of the cabin door and threw a pan of dirty water into the dust outside. He looked up, saw the riders coming, and ducked back inside. A few moments later he reappeared, this time wearing a gun, and was joined on the porch by three others, big, bearded, long-haired men, all of them armed.

The men watched the KK riders come, Frank Cobb in the lead. When he was within fifty feet of the cabin the big-bellied man yelled, "That's far enough."

Frank ignored that and didn't draw rein until he, Kate, and Roche were ten feet from the porch. It was draw-fighting distance and the rustlers knew it.

"What the hell do you want?" the man with the belly said.

Kate answered, smiling. "There appears to have been a misunderstanding. It seems you lifted some of our cows by mistake and we're here to take them off your hands."

"That was no mistake, lady," big belly said. "We're poor, hungry folks, and we need them cows. Fact is, we need them so bad we'll probably come back and help ourselves to more."

Frank's scanned the men on the porch, taking their measure.

The big-bellied man and two others just like him wore guns. But their cartridge belts and holsters were of poor quality, and the Colts hung too low, awkward and unhandy. They were men who used guns but they would not be fast on the draw and shoot. But the fourth man was different. As tall as the others, he was lean, narrow-faced with a great beak of a nose and hooded black eyes that were set too close together. He wore a gray frock coat, a collarless white shirt, and a flat-brimmed, low-crowned hat. His bone-handled Colt rode high, between the wrist and elbow of his right arm, and his gun leather was of good quality, obviously of Texas manufacture.

Frank pegged him as a pistolero. He'd be fast and at close range deadly.

Beside him Kate spoke again. "I don't wish to resort to violence, so this is your last warning. Return my cattle now or face the consequences."

A younger man, slack-mouthed, his hair falling over his shoulders in lank brown strands, said, "All right, enough talk. You two men ride out of here while you still can." His eyes slimed like slugs over Kate's breasts, and a smile touched his thick lips. "But the redheaded woman stays. I'm claiming her. She's my lady now, understand?"

When he looked back on things, Frank Cobb couldn't rightly figure how events might have gone from there. No doubt a general draw and shoot with a mighty uncertain outcome.

But it was young, reckless Dave Roche who had summed up the opposition and decided to deal the cards.

Schooled by his CSA veteran father in the ways of horseback fighters like William Quantrill, Bloody Bill Anderson, and the incomparable John Mosby, Roche's instinct and training was to strike hard, strike fast, and come a-shooting.

Roche kicked his horse into a startled gallop, let loose a rebel yell, and charged directly at the men on the porch. He'd read the same signs as Frank had, and as his mount jumped onto the porch Roche fired at the big-nosed draw fighter, then turned and shot at one of the other rustlers.

Overcoming his initial surprise, Frank drew and entered the fight. Roche's horse rampaged on the narrow porch, rearing, its steel-shod hooves flying. The draw fighter, who'd taken a bullet, shot into Roche's horse and the animal went down, violently throwing the young puncher out of the saddle. Frank fired at the gunman, missed. Fired again. Hit hard, the draw fighter grimaced and fell back off balance. He crashed through the cabin window in a shattering shower of splintered wood and glass.

Two of the rustlers were still on their feet, and the man with lank hair fired at Frank. He hurried the shot and missed. Frank didn't. Angered by what the man had said about Kate, he aimed for center chest, fired, and as his Colt rose in recoil, fired again. Two hits, either one a killing shot. Frank's first bullet crashed into the man's chest, and the second hit high on his forehead and killed him instantly.

Kate, her Winchester up and ready, saw the surviving rustler bolt from the carnage on the porch and break for the trees. She laid her sights between the man's shoulder blades and took up the slack on the trigger. But then she drew a deep breath and lowered the rifle. The man was scared and running from the fight, and she could not bring herself to shoot him in the back.

Frank Cobb was less merciful.

He swung his horse and galloped after the fleeing rustler. The man was just a few yards from the trees when he turned and saw Frank on him like the wrath of God. The rustler threw up his arms and screamed for mercy, but Frank drew rein, fired from his rearing horse, and pumped two fast shots into the man's belly and chest.

Kate watched the rustler double up around his bullet wounds and then fall flat on his face, dead when he hit the ground. Frank rode back at a walk, reloading his Colt from his cartridge belt. The battle had taken only a couple of minutes and gray gunsmoke drifted over the bodies of dead men.

Dave Roche retrieved his fallen Colt, stepped around his dead horse, and walked into the cabin. After a few moments a gunshot racketed from inside, and then Roche appeared at the door again, holstering his gun. He saw Frank and said, "The dude in the frock coat wasn't quite dead but he is now."

Frank nodded. "I reckon."

Then by way of explanation, Roche said, "I was right partial to the zebra dun he shot."

"Seems like," Frank said.

Kate said, "Frank, drag the bodies into the cabin, and then set it on fire. I don't want outlaws to use it again, ever."

"You didn't take the shot, Kate," Frank said. His voice was neutral, neither accusing nor questioning.

"No. No I didn't," Kate said.

Frank nodded and then said, "All right, Dave, you heard the lady. We've got some burning to do."

As Kate and the others rode away from the cabin, a column of smoke from the blazing cabin rose into the sky behind them.

Pushing fifty head of cattle and four horses across broken country, the day was shading into evening by the time Kate reached the herd. Still smarting at being left behind, Trace Kerrigan demanded to know what had happened.

Used up and in no mood to recount the events of the day, Kate said, "Ask Frank."

Looking sour, Trace went in search of Frank Cobb. Kate stepped to the fire and poured herself much-needed coffee. A young puncher tossed wood on the fire and as sparks rose in a scarlet fountain, she said, "How is the herd?"

"Bedded down on good grass, Mrs. Kerrigan," the puncher said. "They settled in right well tonight."

Kate nodded her thanks and the waddie, uncomfortable at being too near the boss, walked away toward the remuda, building a smoke as he went.

"You hungry, Mrs. Kerrigan?"

Kate turned as Lem Winston stepped to her side. He held a tin plate of food, the tines of a fork buried in the beef and beans. Kate wasn't hungry, the violent deaths she'd witnessed weighing on her; but she smiled and said, "That's very thoughtful of you, Lem." She took the plate and said, "Thank you."

An experienced range cook like Winston could gauge how hungry a person was and he said, "Eat a little, as much as you can. It will give you strength."

Kate nodded and pretended to eat. Then Dave Roche stepped up and said, "What's about some supper, Mr. Winston? Damn it all, I'm starving here."

"Here, Dave, take this," Kate said, handing the puncher her plate.

"You don't want it, Mrs. Kerrigan?" Roche said, surprised.

"No. I've had enough."

"Well, I'm sure hungry," Roche said. He grinned and began to shovel food into his mouth.

Just hours before the young man had killed two men, one of them who was already wounded, helpless, and out of the fight, and Kate marveled at that. She'd also watched Frank kill a fleeing man, a merciless act that didn't trouble him in the least. If she'd questioned him he would have said, "Hell, I had the drop on him, Kate. What did you expect me to do?"

Kate looked around her and then watched Roche and Frank eat like hungry wolves as though all the shooting, killings, and burning had never happened.

She sighed deeply. Though she admired their reckless courage, would she ever truly understand the ways of Western men?

CHAPTER SIXTEEN

Kate Kerrigan sought her blankets early, hurried though a rosary, closed her eyes, and let sleep take her. An hour passed, then another . . . and then a commotion woke her and she sat bolt upright, as did the punchers sleeping around the guttering fire.

"What the hell?" a man said.

His answer was Lem Winston's angry shout of, "Stop! Thief!"

Kate caught a glimpse of what looked like a boy running from the chuck wagon, and then she heard his startled yelp as he ran into Frank Cobb. Grabbing the boy by the scruff of his ragged shirt, Frank marched him to the wagon, where Winston waited, holding a wooden spoon like a club.

"This your thief, Mr. Winston?" Frank said.

The cook shook the spoon in front of the boy's face. "That's him. Little bandit tried to rob me."

Frank grinned. "Want me to shoot him?"

Kate's voice cut through the flickering night. "Frank, you'll scare the child," she said.

"The big lug doesn't scare me," the boy said, struggling to break from Frank's grasp.

The kid looked to be about ten years old, under-sized, undernourished, and ragged. He had a mop of straw-colored hair, brown eyes, and a pugnacious expression on his homely face.

"Did you try to steal our food?" Kate said.

"Yeah, I did," the boy said. "I'm hungry."

"When did you last eat?" Kate said.

"I dunno. Four, five days."

"No wonder you're hungry," Kate said. "What's your name and how old are you?"

"Nobody ever give me a name. I think I'm eleven, but I don't know for sure."

"Eleven?" Frank said. "Then you must have been the runt of the litter, huh?"

The boy again tried to wrench free of Frank and in the struggle his shirt rode up his back. "Hell, look at that," Lem Winston said.

Kate let out a shocked little gasp and said, "What happened to you?"

"Nothing," the boy said.

"Someone beat you, and beat you badly," Kate said. "Your back and your arms are covered in red welts."

"Yeah, well, old man Baggot done that," the boy said. "Said I gave him sass." He looked at Kate. "You'd sass as well if his pigs ate better than you did."

"Who is this Baggot?" Winston said. "Speak up now, and take that surly look off your face when you talk to Mrs. Kerrigan. I will not tolerate a surly boy, or a secretive one."

"He's a farmer," the boy said. "My pa was a farmer, or tried to be, but he never made a go of it. Came one day my ma hung herself from the rafters of the barn, and Pa gave up on the farm and on me. He sold me to Baggot for ten dollars and a jug of whiskey and then he went away. I've never seen him since."

"When was this?" Kate said.

"A year ago on last Christmas Eve. Baggot beat me that very night and I spit in his eye." The boy managed a tight smile. "And then he beat me again with a hay rake, much harder."

"And now you're hungry?" Kate said.

"Right now I'd rather be eating than talking," the boy said.

"I'll feed him," Winston said. "You like beans and cornbread, boy?"

"Right now I'd like anything that comes on a plate," the boy said.

"I'll call him Sam," Kate said. "I've always been partial to that name."

Frank Cobb watched the boy ravenously wolf down food, and raised an eyebrow in amazement. "How can anybody eat like that?" he said. "Look at him."

"He's hungry," Kate said.

"Must be. I've never seen the like," Frank said. "Hey, slow down there, boy. You'll give yourself a belly-ache or choke, whatever comes first."

The kid ignored that and continued to eat, gorging his way through a whole round of cornbread and a vast mound of beans. When he was finally satisfied, he lay on the ground by the fire and within moments was asleep.

Frank said, "What do we do with him, Kate? This

boy doesn't belong on a trail drive. You heard him, he's a sodbuster's son."

"We can't leave him here, Frank," Kate said. "We'll have to take him with us."

"You've already got Hank Lowery, Kate," Frank said. "Do you really want to take on another passenger?"

Kate frowned. "Hank pulls his freight."

Frank made no comment on that, knowing Kate had the right of it.

"Sam can help Lem Winston," Kate said. "He's a smart boy, and he'll make himself useful."

Frank smiled. "Kate, you can't save everybody you meet. I mean Lowery, trying to deny that he's a shootist, and now this boy."

"I can save some of them," Kate said. "At least the ones who come to me for help."

"You're a good woman, Kate," Frank said. "I just hope that one day Lowery or this nameless kid won't turn on you."

"He has a name. His name is Sam Chisholm. Sam because I like that name and Chisholm—"

"Because of the trail," Frank said.

"Exactly."

"If he was still alive I'm sure old Jesse would be mighty pleased to hear that," Frank said.

The boy spent the next three days helping Lem Winston, fetching water and firewood, and he showed some flair as a biscuit shooter, a talent that pleased Winston so much he predicted that young Sam could look forward to a bright future as a range cook.

But on the fourth day when Lem Winston went to roust Sam from sleep the boy was gone. The thin light of dawn had not yet chased away the late-lingering stars when Winston raised the hue and cry. Kate rose from her blankets and joined in the search of the area around camp but there was no sign of the boy.

"It's like he just vanished off the face of the earth," Winston told Kate. "Mr. Cobb says he probably headed south, but he's not sure."

When Frank returned to camp he said, "I've pulled the hands off the search, Kate. The kid's gone for good."

"I thought he might stay," Kate said. Disappointment shadowed her face. "He seemed to have settled down."

"With a boy like that you can never tell," Frank said. "He was a wild one, and they never stay long in one place." He smiled. "Pity. I was starting to like him."

"Me too," Kate said. "I'll miss him."

CHAPTER SEVENTEEN

Three days after the boy called Sam vanished a black man rode into camp at suppertime. He carried a Colt on his right hip and had a Winchester rifle in the boot under his knee.

The man sat his horse as courtesy demanded and said, "Smelled your coffee from a ways off. I could sure use a cup."

Kate said, "Light and set and make yourself to home. Are you hungry?"

The man had a good, open smile under his great dragoon mustache. "Missing my last three meals, or is it six? I can't quite recollect"

"We set a modest table, I'm afraid," Kate said. "But if beef and beans are to your liking, then you're welcome to join us for supper."

"Best offer I've had all day, ma'am," the man said. He swung out of the saddle with considerable elegance and then touched the brim of his hat and said, "I'm a Deputy United States Marshal for the Indian Territory by authority of District Judge Isaac Parker.

My name is Bass Reeves, ma'am, and I'm right glad to make your acquaintance."

"I'm Mrs. Kate Kerrigan, and this is Frank Cobb, my segundo," Kate said. "Pleased to meet you, Deputy Reeves."

Reeves took Kate's extended hand. For a long moment his gaze lingered on Frank, taking his measure, and then he nodded. "Likewise. Glad to meet you both."

Later as Reeves sat by the fire and ate, Kate said, "Mr. Reeves, did you by any chance see a boy in your travels, thin, about ten years old with a mop of yellow hair?"

"Kin of your'n, ma'am?" the lawman said.

"No. He stayed with us for a while. Just a few days and then he suddenly left."

"I buried a boy like that," Reeves said, his fork poised between his plate and mouth.

Kate looked stricken. "Buried him? When?"

"About two weeks ago."

"Then it can't be the same boy," Kate said.

"Maybe not, but the description matches," Reeves said.

Frank said, "How did the boy die?"

Reeves's expression didn't change, the face of a man who'd seen violent death in all its forms. "Beaten to death. Something inside him broke."

"Who would do such a thing?" Kate said.

"Farmer by the name of Lucius Baggot," Reeves said. "He knew I planned to arrest him for the boy's murder, and he came at me with a scattergun."

"And you killed him?" Frank said.

Reeves shrugged. "Like I said, he came at me with a scattergun."

Kate and Frank exchanged glances and Kate said, "Where . . ." Something caught in her throat and she tried again. "Where did you bury him, Mr. Reeves?"

"On a ridge about three miles west of here. I made a cross out of wood I took from the Baggot cabin and I said the words over him. I did my best for the boy, ma'am."

Frank saw the horror in Kate's face and said, "Must be a different boy, Kate. It can't be Sam."

But he saw by Kate's desolate look that she thought otherwise.

Bass Reeves, a perceptive man, said, "Mrs. Kerrigan, sometimes in the West strange things happen that can't be explained. One time I heard that the souls of murdered people can't rest and they wander the earth in search of justice. Could be the boy who came to your wagon was long dead but his soul was not at peace."

No!" Kate said. "I've made my mind up and that's not how it was, that's not how it was at all. The boy who came here was named Sam Chisholm and he's still alive and well. He'll grow up tall and strong and marry a pretty girl and make his mark and build a fine life for himself." She smiled and nodded. "Yes, that's how it will be."

"Then I reckon you're right, Mrs. Kerrigan. If you say so then that's exactly how it's going to be," Bass Reeves said.

* * *

Kate Kerrigan opened her eyes and stared at the shadowed ceiling. Bill Cody was right. The boy, the one called Peter, must be punished for his part in freeing the Indian. She would do it tomorrow . . . a hug, a please-don't-do-that-again, and a second hug.

Kate smiled, her mind made up. She'd punish Peter tomorrow and now she'd say her prayers and wouldn't think about it any further.

After all, tomorrow was another day.

BOOK TWO
The Murdering Savage

CHAPTER EIGHTEEN

On the morning of the horrific murder and scalping that terrorized Bill Cody's encampment, a man rode onto the Kerrigan spread with blackmail on his mind. The man's name was Slide McKenzie and he demanded a hundred thousand dollars, payable in cash, or he'd destroy everything Kate had worked for.

"If you don't pay up, the angel of death will descend on this ranch and destroy every blade of grass and slaughter every cow that now stands on its pastures," McKenzie said.

As she always did with strangers, Kate had met McKenzie in her parlor and now she stared at him with incredulous eyes. "Are you making a joke? If you are I don't find it funny," she said.

"No joke, missy," McKenzie said. He smiled, sure of himself, as slick as polished ice. "The money or total destruction. The choice is yours."

Kate rose from her chair and yanked on the scarlet pull that hug alongside the fireplace. After a few moments the parlor maid, pretty in her black dress and starched white apron, stepped inside and said, "You rang for me, ma'am?"

"Yes, Winifred. Go tell my sons and Mr. Cobb to come here at once."

"Mr. Quinn and Mr. Cobb are out on the range, ma'am, but Mr. Trace is to home," the girl said.

"Then go fetch him," Kate said.

After the maid left, McKenzie threw himself into a chair and said, "Aren't you gonna offer me a drink, Mrs. Kerrigan? Ain't that a common courtesy among high society folks like you?"

His swamp water eyes slimed over Kate's body, shapely in her day attire of striped, pale blue cotton blouse with a high collar, and leg-of-mutton sleeves. Her simple white skirt was made of sturdy cotton twill, short enough to reveal high-heeled ankle boots that matched the shade of her blouse.

"You're a fine-looking woman, Mrs. Kerrigan," McKenzie said. "If you're nice to me maybe I can lower my price a little." And then, because he was what Trace Kerrigan would later call, "lowlife white trash," he added, "Say by two dollars."

Two dollars was the going price of a hog farm whore, and Kate was aware of the implication, but she ignored the remark and said, "Don't sit in my presence unless I ask you to, McKenzie. On your feet or I'll have my hands horsewhip the hide off you."

McKenzie was livid, but he stood and said, "I'll remember this. Soon you'll come crawling to me on your hands and knees begging for mercy. Well, little Miss High and Mighty, you won't get any. Lay to that."

The door opened, and Trace Kerrigan stepped

inside grinning. But then his eyes moved from his mother to McKenzie and the grin slipped and vanished. "What's the trouble, Ma?" he said.

Now twenty years old, Trace had inherited his late father's height and wide shoulders. He'd lost out in the handsomeness stakes to his brother Quinn, but his quick, easy smile, outgoing personality, and good nature were enough to set female hearts aflutter.

"This . . . creature . . . is demanding I give him a hundred thousand dollars," Kate said. "His name is McKenzie, and he says if I don't do as he says he'll harm the Kerrigan ranch."

"Harm? Who the hell said anything about harm? I said destroy, lady. I'll lay it to waste." McKenzie smirked as he said that last.

Most dictionaries define *smirk* as a smile that suggest self-satisfaction, smugness, or even pleasure at someone else's unhappiness or distress. Usually a smirk is enough to get a man knuckled, but that morning Trace badly wanted to draw his gun and put a bullet into McKenzie's belly.

"And you told him to go to hell, Ma," Trace said.

"I haven't told him anything yet," Kate said.

Trace nodded. "Then I will. Mister, you go to hell. If you object to my saying that, then shuck iron and get to your work."

McKenzie held his vest open. "I ain't heeled, sonny,"

"Trace, that's enough," Kate said. "I will not have violence under my roof." Then, "Before I have you thrown out, McKenzie, what is the nature of the destruction you threaten to visit on the KK?"

The smirk again. "Mexicans."

Kate was surprised. "You mean the Mexican army?"

"No, I mean Mexican peasants, thousands, tens of thousands, hungry for land and hungrier for beef. One word from me and they flood north into the Promised Land, and by that I mean the Kerrigan range. When they get through here all that will be left is a wasteland. Catch my drift?"

Trace said, "McKenzie—"

"Call me Slide, since me and your ma are gonna to be such good friends, an' all."

Trace's smile was thin. "All right, Slide, here's something to think about—you're not going to make it back to whatever rock you crawled from under because I'm going to kill you."

McKenzie looked sly, like a fox contemplating a chicken coop. "Figured you might come around to saying that, sonny. But killing me won't make any difference. If I don't make it back to the Rio Grande alive my associates will wait a week or two and then start the Mexicans north." The man grinned. "You can't win fer losing, huh, sonny?"

It looked to Kate that the hotheaded Trace would draw, no matter the consequences, but she'd weighed McKenzie's threat and decided it should be investigated. Now, playing for time, she said, "Even if I believed you, it will take me a while to accumulate that much money." Feeling Trace's outraged glare burning into the side of her face, Kate said, "I don't keep a hundred thousand dollars in my safe."

"You got a week, seven days, lady," McKenzie said. "I'll be back on the eighth day, and I'll expect my money to be here waiting for me."

"I'll see what I can do," Kate said.

McKenzie shook his head. "Don't tell me you'll see what you can do. Just do it."

"Very well. You can go now, McKenzie," Kate said.

"If you don't have the cash then have the deed to your ranch," the man said. "One is as good as t'other."

Beside her Trace tensed, but Kate gave him a warning sidelong glance. "Get out of my house, McKenzie, now," she said. "I can't stand the stink of you."

"Seven days, lady," McKenzie said as he walked to the door, hastening his step as Trace moved to go after him.

"Trace, wait," Kate said. She waited until McKenzie slammed the parlor door shut and then said, "Take two of the hands with you and follow McKenzie's trail. I want to know what's happening down there on the Rio Grande. As far as I'm concerned, everything north of the river is KK range and if there are Mexicans there, we'll move them."

"Thousands, ma? Tens of thousands?" Trace said.

Kate nodded. "Yes, I know. We may need a little help from the army."

"Damn it, Ma, we'll need a lot of help from the army."

"Please, Trace, no profanity," Kate said. "Now go see what's stirring up those people. I want to know what hold McKenzie has over them."

"If it comes down to it, will you really pay McKenzie?" Trace said.

"We're Kerrigans, Trace. We meet force with force, and we pay tribute to no one."

"I'm glad to hear that, Ma," Trace said, grinning. "For a moment there I thought—"

"I was playing for time," Kate said. "You thought I could be intimidated, and that surprises me. Trace, your mother doesn't scare easily. In fact, Kate Kerrigan doesn't scare worth a damn." She smiled. "And I'll say an extra rosary tonight to atone for the cussword."

CHAPTER NINETEEN

An hour later Trace Kerrigan rode out with a couple of steady hands and took up McKenzie's trail.

Kate stood at an upstairs window and watched them go, fearful for her son and what he might encounter between the ranch and the Rio Grande. Slide McKenzie had upset her more than she'd let Trace know. Although she felt capable of handling any emergency, shooting down Mexican peasants fleeing yet another famine was not to her liking. A couple of months before she'd been told by her driver, Shorty Hawkins, who heard it from a Texas Ranger who'd stopped by the ranch for a meal, that there was already starvation in the states of Sonora, Chihuahua, Coahuila, and Durango, and at least three thousand deaths, mostly children and old people. At the time Kate had determined to do what she could to help, but President Porfirio Díaz's government forbade her to cross the Rio Grande, telling her, *Mexico puede hacerse cargo de su propio* . . . Mexico can take care of its own.

There the matter had ended, but now, if the vile Slide McKenzie was telling the truth, the affair was right back on her front doorstep.

A tap-tap on the door and a moment later the parlor maid stepped inside. The girl's face was pale, and she looked to be in shock. "Ma'am, there's been a murder," Winifred said. "Mr. Cody said for you to come at once."

"Is he downstairs?" Kate said.

"No, ma'am, Mr. Cody is staying by the body. He sent one of his bronc riders to tell you."

"Help me get changed, Winifred. Is Mr. Cobb back yet?"

"No ma'am." Then, "Do you wish me to get Flossie?"

Flossie was the lady's maid, and therefore the only one who was allowed to help Kate with her wardrobe.

"No, Flossie will be indisposed for a few days," Kate said. "In the meantime you will act as lady's maid."

As Winifred helped her undress, Kate's sense of unease grew. First McKenzie's threats and now this murder. It was promising to be a dreadful day. She changed from her day dress into a fringed, buckskin skirt, blue shirt with full sleeves, a wide belt decorated with silver conchos, and riding boots. Unless out riding, Kate never carried a gun around the ranch, but it was a measure of her anxiety that she took a Remington derringer from a dresser drawer and slipped it into her skirt pocket. The derringer was a gift from Kerry Clooney, the Scarlet Harlot, who had carried the little .41 in a garter under her trademark red dresses during all her Western adventures. After Kerry, a lovely Irish girl, shot an abusive suitor to death in Dodge, Kate had saved her from a hanging. "The pistol will bring you luck, Kate, me darlin'," Kerry had told her, and now as Kate patted the Remington into place she figured she'd need all the good luck she could get.

"An unlucky day for Buffalo Bill's Wild West, Kate," Bill Cody said. "I haven't seen the like since my days as a cavalry scout in the crusade against the murderous savage." Bill struck a tragic pose, placed the back of his hand against his forehead, and said, "Oh, what these eyes have seen."

"Where is the body?" Kate said.

Bill was aghast, or pretended to be. "Kate, such womanly eyes as yours should not behold such a scene of horror. I think it's best I describe it, well, in not too much detail, and let you draw your conclusions from there."

"I've probably seen worse, Mr. Cody. Please lead the way."

"You are determined?"

"I am resolved, sir."

"Then I'll take you to the scene of the crime."

"Who was the victim?" Kate said.

"One of my riders and sharpshooters, a former cowboy who had an arrogant way about him that not all liked, myself included."

"Ah, then you have many suspects, Mr. Cody?"

"No, dear lady. Not many. Just one." Bill scowled. "As you will soon see."

* * *

The body lay between two rows of tents, but a blood trail indicated that the man had been stabbed elsewhere and although fatally wounded he'd crawled a fair distance before dying. Bill Cody insisted that there should be hot coffee available at all times in the dining tent, and a cup lay on the ground near the stove where the huge pot simmered day and night. The cowboy, probably unable to sleep because of the pain of his shattered forearm, had been stabbed when he'd gone in for coffee, but whether or not he'd also been scalped in the tent Bill didn't know.

"The scalp is gone, Kate, so there's no way of telling," he said.

The dead man had a quirt looped around his wrist and Kate recognized him as one of the three cowboys who'd stripped her with their eyes during her last visit to the encampment and had later attacked Josiah Mosely. The other two stood near the body and were loudly demanding of the stunned onlookers that the murdering savage named Cloud Passing should be tracked down and hung from the nearest tree.

"Who found the body?" Kate said.

One of the cowboys, a redhead with wide shoulders, said, "Me and Buck Nolan did. Andy wasn't in his bunk this morning and we went looking for him. This is how we found him."

"What time was it?" Kate said.

The redhead grinned. "What the hell is it to you, little lady?"

"Because this is my ground and you're on it," Kate said, the crease appearing between her eyebrows warning that she was mad clean through. "I asked you what time it was when you found the body."

"Answer Mrs. Kerrigan," Bill Cody said. "And mind your manners, Davy Hoyle."

"Just before first light," the cowboy said. "What the hell does it matter? We all know who killed him and then took his scalp. It was that damned Indian, Cloud Passing. We had some trouble with him, and this was his way of getting back at us. With that broken arm Andy couldn't even defend himself."

"Yes, I heard about that trouble," Kate said. "And besides Cloud Passing there are a lot of Indians in this camp who might carry a grudge." The knife still protruded from the dead man's back, and Kate asked if anyone recognized it.

"Yes, I recognize it," Ingrid Hult said as she made her way though the crowd. "One of my bowie knives is missing."

"Is it the murder weapon?" Kate said.

Ingrid bent over and looked closer, and after a moment she said, "Yes, that's it. That's my bowie. It's a Sheffield knife with a stag and brass handle and there's not too many of them around."

Kate kneeled beside the body and after a while said, "Unless the murderer carried two knives, one for stabbing and another for scalping, he used the bowie twice."

"What difference does it make?" Davy Hoyle said. "The Indian stabbed Andy Porter, scalped him, and then stabbed him again."

"Perhaps," Kate said. "Can one of you men get the deceased's shirt off?"

The garment was stiff with congealed blood and there were no volunteers.

"I see," Kate said. "Then I'll do it myself." She

ripped open the back of the dead man's tattered shirt and stared at not one, but many wounds.

Kate looked up at Bill Cody and said, "This man was killed in a frenzy of hate. I count eight stab wounds, and there could be more." As though to make up for his unwillingness to help with the gory shirt, Bill took a knee beside the corpse and said, "Look at Andy's head, Kate. Seems like the murderer tried to take his hair but couldn't finish the job."

A flap of scalp was peeled back from the dead cowboy's forehead and removed but part of it was still attached to the base of the skull. "Wouldn't a Cheyenne warrior have done it better?" Kate said.

Bill Cody nodded. "I would say. Unless Cloud Passing was interrupted."

"You're convinced he is the killer?" Kate said.

"The evidence points that way."

"Yes, you're right," Kate said. "I'm afraid it does. It points right at Cloud Passing."

"Didn't I just get through telling you that?" Hoyle said, his face flushed with anger.

"Yes, you did," Kate said. "Bill, I'd like to take a look in the dining tent."

Davy grew even angrier. "You already know all you need to know, lady," he said. Then, turning to the on-lookers behind him, "Come on, you men, let's get a posse together and go find that murdering savage."

A cheer rose and a dozen men, most of them young cowboys and former cavalry troopers ready for any diversion, joined Hoyle as he stormed away, waving the others after him. A few blanket-wrapped Indians watched with stone faces and said nothing.

"Mr. Cody, aren't you going to stop them?" Kate said.

Bill shook his head. "Kate, once them Texas boys have taken on a hanging mind-set there's nothing on God's green earth that can stop them, short of a company of Rangers with a howitzer. Besides, if Cloud Passing doesn't want to be found he won't be. Catch my drift?"

"Then let's hope you're right," Kate said. "Now we'll take a look in the dining tent."

"Lot of blood in there, Kate," Bill said.

"I'm aware of that," Kate said.

CHAPTER TWENTY

Kate Kerrigan rose to her feet. "Judging by the blood, Andy was killed right here on this spot," she said. "Then I think someone tried to scalp him, but couldn't complete it because the act disgusted him."

"How do you figure that?" Bill Cody said.

"Step over there to the right side of the tent opening," Kate said.

Bill looked puzzled but he did as Kate said. He stood by the tent entrance and his nose wrinkled. "Hell, somebody puked here. In the dining tent, damn it."

"Look down at your feet," Kate said.

Bill did and then leaped back as though he'd stepped on hot coals. "There's vomit all over," he said.

"As I said, Mr. Cody, somebody tried to scalp Andy Porter but gave up because it made him sick. But he dragged the body out of the tent, and that I don't understand. Why not just leave him here?"

"Andy might have crawled out," Bill said.

"With a broken arm and eight knife wounds in his back?" Kate said. "I very much doubt it."

Bill stared at Kate as though he wished to say something, but was reluctant to put voice to his thoughts.

Kate smiled. "Out with it, Mr. Cody."

"The trouble Cloud Passing had with Andy Porter and them, I was told your houseguest was involved," Bill said.

"Josiah Mosely? Yes. Apparently the three cowboys thought it would be fun to assault him. He was being beaten quite badly before Cloud Passing intervened and saved him."

"What do we know about Mosely?" Bill said.

"He's a rainmaker, but you knew that already."

"Something strange about that feller," Bill said. "Something hidden, and it's dark. I saw the same thing in Hickok, a haunted, murky place within him that no one could touch."

"This is true," Kate said. She smiled. "Then it seems that we've got some sleuthing to do. We'll turn ourselves into a regular pair of Pinkertons, get to the bottom of this mystery, and bring the guilty party to justice."

"Perhaps . . . if Cloud Passing lives that long," Bill said.

Kate's carriage was close to her house when she spotted Josiah Mosely. The young man was obviously headed toward the Bill Cody encampment, and she ordered Shorty Hawkins to halt. Never the most trusting of men, the puncher pulled his Colt from the waistband and laid it on the seat beside him. He eyed Mosely with active dislike.

Mosely nodded and said, "Mrs. Kerrigan, ma'am. I heard about the murder."

"Your name was mentioned. Mr. Mosely," Kate said. "Bill Cody thinks you belong on the list of suspects."

"I didn't kill Andy Porter," Mosely said.

Shorty's face, as freckled as a bird's egg, was belligerent. "Here, how come you knew it was Porter?" he said.

"Because the news is all over the ranch," Mosely said. "The murder is the only thing people around here want to talk about."

"But you're on your way to the camp," Kate said. "Do you need to learn more?"

"I need to know if Cloud Passing is still alive," Mosely said. "I owe him, and I haven't been beholden to a man since Professor Purdon."

"Purdon? Oh yes, he taught you the rainmaker's trade, I believe," Kate said.

"And other things, like how to be a balloonist and a gentleman," Mosely said.

"Very commendable, I'm sure," Kate said. Then, "Right now there's a posse out searching for Cloud Passing."

"I know. That's why I want to be there when they bring him in. I won't stand by and let him be lynched."

"Hell, man, what are you going to do?" Shorty said. "Try to talk a hemp posse out of it? It don't work. One time I seen a feller try to talk his way out of a hanging. The vigilantes listened to him, real polite, and then hung him anyway."

The little puncher had spoken out of turn but his point was a valid one, and Kate let his rudeness go. "You can't reason with a lynch mob, Mr. Mosely," she said.

"I'll tell them I'll go to the law and identify every man jack of them as a murderer," Mosely said.

"Yup, that'll scare 'em sure enough," Shorty said. "Mister, your guitar ain't tuned right."

"Shorty, that's quite enough," Kate said. "Mr. Mosely, you'd better come back to the ranch with me. You still haven't recovered from the beating you took and Shorty is right, you can't singlehandedly stop a hanging posse."

"You heeled?" Shorty said.

Mosely shook his head. "No."

The puncher picked up the revolver. "You used a Colt's gun afore?"

"No," Mosely said.

"Then get yourself one. All you have to do is walk up to a man, shove the muzzle in his belly, and pull the trigger." Shorty looked wise. "You'll get good results, I guarantee."

"He'll do no such thing," Kate said. "Step up here beside me, Mr. Mosely. You're going back to the ranch with me. Shouldn't you be working on repairing your balloon thing?"

"Yes, yes, I should," Mosely said.

"Well then, get to it," Kate said. "There will be time enough to intervene when and if Cloud Passing is caught."

"That might be too late," Mosely said.

"Then if that's the case there is nothing you or anyone else can do, Mr. Mosely," Kate said. "You will return to the ranch with us—now."

Josiah Mosely considered that and then seemed

to realize the hopelessness of his situation. Without another word he stepped into the carriage.

"Drive on," Kate said.

Later that day as the bright afternoon faded into evening Davy Hoyle led a tired, dispirited posse back to Bill Cody's encampment. They had ridden far, covered a lot of ground, but had seen no sign of the renegade Cheyenne named Cloud Passing.

CHAPTER TWENTY-ONE

The ruined mission lay on the bend of a creek and was surrounded by trees, mostly cottonwoods, wild oak, mesquite, and here and there an isolated juniper.

Trace Kerrigan sat his saddle and swept the area with his field glasses. Because of the trees the mission was mostly hidden but what caught and held Trace's interest lay to the east of the ruin, an extensive campground that sprawled along the north bank of the Rio Grande. Greasy smoke columns from hundreds of mesquite fires rose into the air and joined together in a black murk that hung above the river like a fog. Trace calculated that a thousand people were living there, if living was the right word for what could only be a crowded, miserable existence. The bivouac looked like the encampment of a routed army, starving, defeated, and demoralized.

"Who the hell are those people and what are they doing there?" one of the punchers, a man named Zeke Cowley, asked, echoing Trace's own train of thought.

"Mexican by the look of them," Trace said. He passed the glasses to Cowley. "Here, take a look.

The puncher studied the camp for long moments and then lowered the glasses and said, "Mexicans all right, a passel of them. Looks like a Saturday night crowd at a cockfight."

"Let me see," the other puncher said. His name was Caleb Dowd, such a sour, stingy man that no one ever sought out his company. But he was a top hand and quick with the Colt. Dowd said, the glasses still to his eyes, "Ain't Miz Kerrigan claimed all the land south to the river?"

"Yeah, now it's KK range," Trace said. "Come summer we'll run cattle down that way."

Dowd handed the glasses back. "Well, them Messkins are on it and they don't look like they plan to move any time soon."

"How we gonna play this, boss?" Cowley said to Trace. He looked worried.

"I was told to follow Slide McKenzie and check his story about the Mexicans," Trace said. "Well, it seems like he told the truth. McKenzie has some kind of hold over those people, and I'd sure like to find out what it is."

"I got an idea," Dowd said, his eyes hard. "I don't reckon Bill Cody has any love for greasers. We could ask him to jine up with the KK and together we'll run them jumping beans back across the river." Dowd scratched the stubble on his neck. "Gun a few if we have to so the rest get the message."

"What do you think, boss?" Zeke Cowley said. "Is it a plan?"

"It's nothing my mother would want the KK ranch involved in, and Bill Cody wouldn't go for it, either," Trace said. "Hell, he's got vaqueros riding in his show."

He stared at the ceramic blue of the sky where a few puffy clouds drifted and after a while said, "I can't leave it here, boys. I want to go talk to McKenzie and help him see the error of his ways."

"Hang the son of a bitch," Dowd said.

Trace nodded, smiling. "Caleb, now that sounds like a plan."

"Seen you plain from a ways off," Slide McKenzie said. "Did your mama wash your face and then set you to following me?"

Trace ignored that and studied the ruined mission. Much of the building still stood, though in a tumbledown state, and the roof had collapsed. An iron bell, much rusted, still hung in an alcove above the doorway, and it clinked softly in the prairie wind.

"We need to talk, McKenzie," Trace said.

"Talk about what?" the man said. "I stated my business, and me and your ma discussed terms. There's nothing more to talk about."

"I can drill him just fine from here, boss," Caleb Dowd said. "You just give me the nod."

"You don't scare me none, boy," McKenzie said. "Now turn them horses around and get out of here before you get hurt."

"McKenzie, the Kerrigans don't pay tribute to anyone," Trace said. "This is KK range, and I want you and your Mexicans off it pretty damned quick."

"Tribute, is it?" McKenzie said. "I call it fair warning. If I lead this hungry mob north, a thousand more just like them, do you know what will happen to Mrs. Kerrigan's precious ranch? It will mean the utter destruction of everything she holds dear." The man grinned. "Bear in mind what I told your ma, boy . . . within a few months there won't be a blade of grass or a cow left. Kate Kerrigan will shed salt tears and sup sorrow with the spoon of grief and wish she'd paid me my hundred thousand dollars."

"Well, that rips it," Caleb Dowd said, a man with a hair-trigger temper.

He went for his gun . . . but never made it.

A shotgun blast shattered Dowd's spine and blew him out of the saddle. The puncher hit the ground just as Trace and Zeke Cowley swung their horses around to meet the threat.

"Don't reach for the iron. We still got three barrels for the two of you."

This from a tall, hard-faced man who stood next to another who could have been his twin. Both wore canvas slickers and carried Greener scatterguns.

Trace knew it was death to draw on that pair, and Cowley was in the same frame of mind. He kept his hands on the saddle horn, well away from his holstered Colt.

McKenzie stepped to Trace's side, a revolver in his hand. "Unbuckle the gun belt and let it fall. Then step down from there," he said. He looked at Cowley. "You too, cowboy." The man read something in Trace's eyes and said, "We got the drop on you, Kerrigan. Do what I said or you're a dead man."

Trace was up against a stacked deck and he knew it. His gun belt thudded to the ground and so did Cowley's.

"Now step down, real easy," McKenzie said. He saw

one of the tall men stare at him, his lean face framing a question. "He's Kate Kerrigan's son, Bat."

The man nodded. "Yes, you told me about him. He ain't so much."

"Yeah he is," McKenzie said. "He's my ace in the hole. Kate Kerrigan may not pay to stop an invasion of her land, but she'll ante up to get her son back alive."

"You got it all figured, Slide," Sky Boswell said. "I never took you to be that smart."

McKenzie smiled. "Hell, I was born at night, but it wasn't last night. Like I told you, Sky, you boys stick with me and you'll get rich."

Boswell pointed the shotgun muzzle at Trace. "What do you want done with them?"

"There's an old wine cellar under the mission," McKenzie said. "We'll keep them there, give me some time to study on things."

"Where's the death angel?" Bat Boswell said.

"I got it in a safe place," McKenzie said.

"Take no chances. Maybe these boys were coming after it."

"They don't know about the angel, do you Kerrigan? You've never met Santa Muerte."

"I don't know what the hell you're talking about, McKenzie," Trace said.

"Well, you'll find out soon enough," the man said.

And Bat Boswell laughed.

CHAPTER TWENTY-TWO

A flight of worn limestone steps led down to the wine cellar, a small, dark L-shaped room lit only by the oil lamp Slide McKenzie left on an upturned barrel that once held ale. Against the walls a few broken, slanted shelves showed where bottles had been stacked, and Zeke Cowley idly calculated that during its heyday a century before, the place must have held enough beer and wine to keep a man happily drunk for fifty years. Rats rustled in the cobwebbed corners where the blind, eight-eyed spiders lived, and the air smelled dry and musty like mummy dust.

Trace Kerrigan had made a circuit of the room examining the walls and roof and now he again sat on the floor beside Cowley. "Nothing?" the puncher said.

"Nothing. The place is as tight as a drum," Trace said.

"So all we can do is wait," Cowley said.

"About the size of it unless we can jump McKenzie when he comes in to feed us."

"If he feeds us, you mean."

"Yeah, and I guess it's a big if."

Cowley was quiet for a while. He stared at the feeble flame guttering in the oil lamp and then spoke in semidarkness, his voice sounding hollow in the close confines of the cellar. "Can the Mexicans do all those things McKenzie is talking about? Can they destroy the range?"

"I reckon so, Zeke," Trace said. "If there's enough of them."

"The army can drive them off though," the puncher said.

"It could," Trace said. "But by that time it will be too late for the KK. What's taken Kate Kerrigan years to build can be destroyed in a matter of months. The range is as fragile as a beautiful woman. Overgrazing can destroy it and so can a long spell of dry weather or a cold winter. Thousands of people camping on KK grass, forced by famine to kill and eat our cattle, would be its death knell."

Cowley smiled. "Buffalo Bill is doing that very thing and the grass is dying."

Trace nodded. "I know, but it's only ten acres of graze and given time it will recover. But from the New Mexico border to the Rio Grande, imagine a wasteland covered with campsites." Trace shook his head. "The range would never come back from that. As my ma says, it's the stuff of nightmares."

"Damn it, boss, there's got to be some way we can push them back across the river," Cowley said.

"Like you said, Zeke, we'd need an army and as of now we don't have one of those." Trace was silent for a while, then, his chin set and determined, "However this thing plays out, I'll make sure Slide McKenzie doesn't profit. I'll hunt him down and kill him, no matter how long it takes."

Cowley nodded. "And I'll ride with you, boss. Caleb Dowd didn't stack up to much, but we both rode for the brand. That makes a difference to a man when the time for the reckoning comes."

"Be glad to have you along, Zeke," Trace said.

Trace estimated that three hours had passed since he and Cowley had been thrown into the cellar at gunpoint, when the door opened, allowing a rectangular shaft of daylight to penetrate the gloom. Then Slide McKenzie's voice. "Kerrigan, send up the puncher."

Trace's temper flared. "Damn you, McKenzie, if you want him come and get him."

The Boswell brothers pushed McKenzie aside and stood on the stairs, Winchesters at the ready. "Send up the drover or we'll kill both of you," Bat said.

"I'll go, boss," Cowley said. "Them boys mean business."

Trace hung his head in defeat. Unarmed, he was helpless before the Boswell guns. He sat silently as Cowley mounted the stairs and the door slammed shut behind him.

CHAPTER TWENTY-THREE

The letter Kate Kerrigan held in her hands was from her bankers, assuring her that her investment in the British White Star shipping line had paid large dividends and justified the risk she'd taken in helping to fund the upstart company. Also mentioned was the standing invitation from the White Star directors inviting Mrs. Kerrigan, all expenses paid of course, to undertake an Atlantic crossing on their just completed new passenger liner the *Oceanic*, which set new standards for first-class comfort. The invitation was not without its attractions, and Kate filed it away for future consideration. There followed a long and somewhat boring list of financial returns on other investments, mostly railroads, apartment buildings, mills, several hotels, a Philadelphia bank, and, dear to her heart, a small millinery company in Dublin. An addendum contained a record of monies paid to the various orphanages and poorhouses that Kate supported.

All in all, she was happy with her various business dealings, but the threat from Slide McKenzie hung over her like a dark cloud. If she lost the KK, everything else, all her investments and charities, would go belly up.

Someone tapped on the door. Kate closed her desk and said, "Come in."

Old Moses Rice, the butler, stepped into the office. "Zeke Cowley is back, Miz Kerrigan. Mr. Trace ain't with him. Zeke says he's got a message for you."

Kate's heart lurched in her breast as she said, "Send him in, Moses."

Cowley came in with his hat in his hands and a crestfallen look on his homely young face. Before the puncher could speak Kate said, "Is my son all right?"

"He was when I left him, ma'am," Cowley said.

Kate rose to her feet, her dress rustling. "What has happened, Zeke? Tell me."

Stumbling through what he had to say, the puncher recounted how he and Trace had tracked Slide McKenzie only to be captured by the man and his two henchmen. "They shot Caleb Dowd, ma'am," Cowley said. "Blew him out of the saddle with a Greener scattergun."

"Caleb Dowd is dead?" Kate said, too shocked to believe the evidence of her own ears.

"I'm afraid so, ma'am," Cowley said. "And now Mr. Trace is being held prisoner." The young cowboy turned his hat in nervous fingers and said, "That McKenzie feller told me I was to give you a message, ma'am. He said he'd hold Mr. Trace prisoner until he gets his money. If he don't get it, the money that is, or if anybody attempts a rescue, he'll personally scatter Mr. Trace's brains with a shotgun. That's what he said, Mrs. Kerrigan."

The threat was vicious and cut like a knife, but Kate kept her composure, unwilling to let the hired help see her agitation. "Thank you, Zeke," she said. "Young man, you look all used up. When you go downstairs ask Mr. Rice to take you into the kitchen for coffee and brandy. Tell him I said it was all right." She forced herself to smile. "Don't worry, everything will turn out just fine."

Cowley didn't share her optimism. "I sure hope so, Mrs. Kerrigan," he said.

"Are you sure, Zeke?" Frank Cobb said. "I mean are you dead certain?"

"You can bet the farm on it, Mr. Cobb. They're brothers, and afore I rode out they told me they were Bat and Sky Boswell."

"Tall fellers, well set up, usually wear canvas slickers?" Frank said.

"That about pegs them," Cowley said.

Frank shook his head. "What the hell are the Boswells doing in West Texas? They never leave the New Mexico Territory. Right now they got all the business they need up in Lincoln County."

"They look like hired guns to me," Cowley said.

"They're bounty hunters," Frank said. "If the Boswells are carrying a dodger with your name on it, you might as well buy a coffin and wait for them in the graveyard because it's all over for you."

"It was the one called Sky who done for Caleb," Zeke said. "I seen his face, and by and by I heard his name to go with it."

"That's the Boswells all right," Frank said. "They're partial to Parker or Greener scatterguns for close work."

"Mr. Cobb, you reckon Slide McKenzie would really kill Trace Kerrigan?"

"Yeah, he would. And if he didn't want to do the job himself the Boswell brothers would be happy to oblige. Those boys ain't too fussy about who they kill."

Frank drained his coffee cup and stood. At the other end of the kitchen Jazmin Salas and the assistant cook were busy preparing supper, chicken and dumplings by the smell of it. "Go easy on the brandy, Zeke," he said. "It can sneak up on a man if he's not used to it."

"Sure thing, Mr. Cobb," Zeke said. "I'll be careful."

Frank wasn't sure but he thought he detected the young puncher slurring his words. After he spoke with Kate he'd return and chase the kid back to the bunkhouse. As he stepped to the kitchen door Zeke Cowley's voice stopped him. "I forgot something, Mr. Cobb. It probably ain't important."

"Let me hear it anyway," Frank said.

"One of them Boswell boys, the one they call Bat, asked me if I'd heard of a ranny by the name of Josiah Mosely in these parts. I said I sure did and I said that he was stopping over at the KK ranch. I asked him why he wanted to know about Josiah Mosely, and he said I was to mind my own damned business or he'd shut my trap permanent. Well, I shut my trap all right until now. Wait a minute . . . if Mosely knows the Boswells could he be in cahoots with them and McKenzie?"

"I don't know," Frank said. "But, by God, I aim to find out."

* * *

"Should we attempt a rescue?" Kate Kerrigan said.

Frank Cobb shook his head. "We'd be bucking the odds, and the chances are you'd end up with a dead son."

That hit Kate like a rock through a glass window. Her confidence shattered, she said, "Please, Frank, tell me that there is a way to get Trace back home alive."

"If we were dealing only with Slide McKenzie, right now I'd gather the hands and say let's ride. But the Boswell brothers are killers, violent men to be reckoned with. Kate, I don't want to scare you any more than you already are, but the first shot the Boswells fire will be the one that kills Trace."

Kate sat back in her chair, her eyes closed, and not for the first time Frank Cobb thought that she was the most beautiful woman he'd ever seen. To watch her like this, frightened and vulnerable, tore at him.

Then, after long, silent moments, Kate said, "When McKenzie comes for his money I'll have it ready for him."

Frank reached out and laid his hand on hers. "Kate, I—"

"There's no argument, Frank. I value my son's life much more than money," Kate said. "That's the bottom line, Frank, end of story, all she wrote."

"And it will be the end of the Kate Kerrigan ranch."

Kate nodded. "Yes, the end of everything, and so be it." She smiled. "Please leave me now, Frank. I'd really like to spend some time alone."

* * *

Josiah Mosely walked away from Kate's parlor door on silent feet. He's been on his way to the kitchen in search of coffee, and it had not been his intention to eavesdrop, but when he'd heard Kate say she wanted her son home alive he'd stopped and listened. He didn't know Trace very well, but what he knew of the young man he liked. Kate's conversation with Frank Cobb made it clear that Trace was being held for ransom and that she was willing to sell her ranch to pay for it.

Footsteps on the other side of the door made Mosely move quickly away, but Frank Cobb saw him and said, "Come here, you. I want to talk."

"About what?" Mosely said.

"About the Boswell brothers. Are they kin of yours?"

"Never heard of them."

Frank grabbed the young man's arm and moved away from the parlor door and into the foyer. "Bat and Sky Boswell," he said. "You sure you don't know them?"

"With names like that I wouldn't be likely to forget them, now would I?" Mosely said.

"I don't know, Mosely. You tell me."

"And I've told you already, I've never heard of the gentlemen."

"Bat and Sky Boswell are not gentlemen, they're killers. How come they wanted to know if you were this neck of the woods?"

"I haven't a clue."

"All right, then, I'll give you a clue—the Boswell brothers are hired guns and bounty hunters. Are you on the scout?"

"What does that mean?"

"Are you running from the law?"

"Not as far as I know," Mosely said. Then, his irritation obvious, "Do you mind telling me what this is all about?"

Frank stared long and hard at Mosely, summing him up, and it was obvious he wasn't impressed by what he saw. A small, frail-looking young man in a threadbare black ditto suit, wire-rimmed eyeglasses aslant on his round face, he did not cut a heroic figure.

"Come with me to the kitchen, Mosely," Frank said. "I want a cup of coffee, and by now I bet there's a drunk puncher on the floor who needs to be carried to the bunkhouse."

CHAPTER TWENTY-FOUR

When Frank Cobb and Josiah Mosely stepped into the kitchen, Zeke Cowley was already gone. "Shorty Hawkins and another puncher carried him out of here," Jazmin Salas said. "Zeke was feeling no pain. Coffee's in the pot, and I have some bear sign left from breakfast over there on the counter."

"Jazmin, if you weren't already married, I'd wed you myself," Frank said, hugging the cook. "You make the best bear sign in the West, if not the entire world."

"If I was single I wouldn't marry you," Jazmin said. "Vaqueros make *muy mal* husbands, and they smell of cow and horse dung all the time."

"In Mexican *muy mal* means very bad," Mosely said. "And smelling of cow and horse dung . . . I guess she's talking about you, Frank."

Frank shook his head. "For a man that doesn't go heeled you sure have a big mouth, Mosely. Now where's that bear sign?"

By the time Frank had drank three cups of coffee and ate six bear sign, Josiah Mosely knew about Slide

McKenzie's threats and the arrival of the Boswell brothers.

"I'm not involved in any of that," Mosely said. "And I've never met Bat and Sky Boswell and I have no wish to."

Frank rubbed sugar from his mouth with the back of his hand and then said, "No, I guess I don't think you are involved. If I did, I'd have shot you by this time."

"Well, that's reassuring," Mosely said.

"Why in God's name would two of the West's most dangerous guns be interested in a puny little runt like you?" Frank said. "That part I just can't figure."

"I don't know," Mosely said. "It's a complete mystery to me."

"I think you do know, but you aren't telling. Do the Boswells have a sister? Did you knock her up and then make a run for the hills?"

"That didn't happen," Mosely said.

"Then what did?"

The young man hesitated and then said, "I don't know."

But right then he did know and with terrible certainty.

The Boswells were hunting him because he killed Jessie Tobin, him and three others, Marty Hawley, Dene Brett, and Floris Lusk, the names ringing loud in his memory like the tolling of a bell. One of them, or all of them, was kin to the Boswells, men born to the feud, and only his death would square the account. For a moment Mosely considered telling Frank Cobb what had happened back in the New Mexico

Territory, but then came the stark realization that the man would not believe him. He could hear Frank now, *"A little runt like you killed four gunmen in a shooting scrape? Boy, you sure know how to spin a windy."*

Mosely remained silent and let Frank do the talking.

"I won't let Kate pay ransom money to Slide McKenzie and ruin herself," Frank said. "If it comes down to it, I'll ride down to the Rio Grande and brace him and the Boswells."

"How can you do that without Trace getting killed?" Mosely said.

"I can't say yet. But I'm working on it."

"Are you as good with a gun as the Boswell brothers?"

"Maybe. I don't rightly know."

"It would be one against three," Mosely said. "I'd say that's a good way to get yourself killed."

"I ride for the brand," Frank said. "I knew the risks when I signed on."

Josiah Mosely visited his room and then left the house and walked north, away from the ranch, toward the stand of wild oak and juniper where he'd left the wreckage of his balloon. He carried a small bag of tools and it was his intention to work on repairing the envelope until it became too dark to see. The afternoon chill held the promise of winter, and a few white clouds stood out in stark relief against the pale blue sky. Away from the house and the Cody encampment,

Mosely walked in silence, the only sound the steady *swish* of his feet through the dry prairie grass.

The balloon's basket was wedged between a couple of trees, its burner and hydrogen cylinder hidden in brush. The shredded silk envelope was inside the basket, and most of the tools Mosely carried were for sewing it together again.

He walked into the oaks, stepped to the basket, and then looked inside.

Josiah's Mosely's yelp of alarm sent panicked crows flapping out of the oaks and brought Bill Cody galloping to the scene on his white charger.

Bill drew rein and said to the trembling Mosely, "My dear young man, I was riding past when I heard your terrible cry of distress. Never, and I say this without a hint of braggadocio, never let it be said that Bill Cody ever ignored a fellow human being in trouble, especially"—he gave a little bow from the saddle—"Josiah Mosely the famed balloonist and rainmaker."

"In . . . in . . ." Mosely took a deep breath. "In the basket," he said, jabbing a trembling forefinger in its direction.

Bill swung out of the saddle, drew his Colt, and walked to the basket with a purposeful stride. He peered inside, reached down, and pulled up Cloud Passing by the scruff of his neck. "So this is where you've been hiding, you rascal," he said.

The Indian said something in Cheyenne that Mosely didn't understand, but he saw Bill Cody nod. "He says he ran away because he feared he'd be blamed for the death of the cowboy."

"Did he kill him?" Mosely said. "Did he stab and then scalp Andy Porter? Ask him that."

Bill spoke in Cheyenne again, and the Indian replied at length, waving his hands around in considerable agitation. When the man stopped Mosely said, "Well?"

"He says he didn't do it," Bill said. "And he says he's hungry and needs grub and a blanket. He also says that you're his friend and will not betray him to the white men who hunt him."

"I don't have any food," Mosely said. "Or a blanket."

"Nor do I," Bill said. Then, "Mr. Mosely, it has now occurred to me that fate has drawn us together for a reason. And that reason is to care for this poor Indian and save him from the lynch mob's noose."

"Maybe he did stab the puncher," Mosely said.

"No, he did not. I am convinced that a white man made it look like an Indian killing so that Cloud Passing would get the blame." Bill took a step back and stared at the Indian who still stood in the basket. "Behold the noble savage, the best damned horse Indian I ever had."

"What do we do with him?" Mosely said.

"For now, nothing. Mr. Mosely you will smuggle him food and a warm blanket, and he will sleep in the bosom of your flying machine until the real murderer of Andy Porter is caught."

"Mr. Cody, that could take forever," Mosely said, his face distressed. "I need to repair the balloon envelope and pursue my rainmaking profession."

"Then this is an ideal arrangement," Bill said. He shoved his Colt back in the holster. "Repair the envelope? Does that mean there's sewing involved?"

"A lot of sewing."

"Then you're in luck, my dear Mosely. Cloud Passing can help you. Cheyenne men are excellent sewers. Some say even better than their womenfolk, and that is high praise indeed."

"The cowboys will find him here for sure, and we'll both get hung," Mosely said. "I'm real uneasy about this, Mr. Cody."

"Nonsense, my boy," Bill said. "This spot is well hidden among the trees and even I, the greatest scout on the frontier, couldn't see you as I rode by. Only when I heard your anguished cry did I ascertain your whereabouts."

Cloud Passing said something in Cheyenne to Bill that gave him pause. But finally he smiled, pulled his knife from the sheath on his belt, and handed it to the Indian.

"Is that wise?" Mosely said.

"It shows Cloud Passing that we trust him," Bill said. "Yes, Mr. Mosely, it is wise." He stepped into the saddle, gathered up the reins, and said, "Mr. Mosely, be resolute in this endeavor until I can find the murderer we seek. In the meantime, light no fires, and keep Cloud Passing calm. Should he revert to wildness, grin at him, but don't poke him with a stick. Grinning seems to have a calming effect on the savage breast, but poking just makes him mad."

"As I recall grinning didn't work the last time," Mosely said.

"That's because I didn't grin wide enough," Bill said. "One more thing. Cloud Passing can speak passable English when he feels like it. He just don't feel like it too often."

Bill swung his horse away, made the steed rear, waved his hat to Mosely, and then galloped in the direction of his encampment.

Josiah Mosely turned and saw the Cheyenne fixedly staring at him. He tried a grin, produced only a gargoyle grimace, and Cloud Passing didn't seem impressed one way or the other.

CHAPTER TWENTY-FIVE

At nineteen, Quinn Kerrigan had reached a man's height but was yet to fill out with muscle, and this gave him a rangy look, wide in the shoulders and slim in the waist. To Kate's horror, being raised among cowboys had taught her son much about whiskey, whores, and revolver fighting, but precious little concerning literature, the arts, and the ways of an educated gentleman. As she'd once told Quinn, "I wish you to learn sportsmanship, not how to get the drop, true love, not the passing affection of whores, and above all the genteel ways of gentlefolk." Come the spring, Kate was determined to ship her younger son off to university, and Yale, Harvard, and Oxford had all been mentioned as possible choices.

For his part, Quinn hated the idea and was determined to stay in the West, setting up a future confrontation with his mother that could not be avoided.

"So why are we here, Quinn?" Frank Cobb said.

"Close the door, Frank. The walls have ears."

Frank closed the door of Quinn's room after Shorty Hawkins and a puncher named Chas Minor had entered. Like Hawkins, Minor was good with a gun and had been involved in several shooting scrapes.

Quinn spread out a large sheet of paper on a table and drew the lamp closer. "I spoke at some length to Zeke Cowley, and I drew up this plan based on what he could remember of the mission," he said. Using a pencil as a pointer, Quinn said, "See here, this is the back wall of the building and it still stands to about the height of a man. The cellar where Trace is held is on the other side of the wall, entered by a door that I think was once near the high altar and is probably locked."

Frank frowned and said, "All right, we got an *I think* and a *probably* already. Quinn, I don't like uncertainty when Trace's life is at stake."

"I understand that, Frank, but hear me out. The time when the mission is most vulnerable to attack is during the hours of darkness. My plan is to strike just before dawn from two sides, front and back, and take McKenzie and them by surprise. The frontal assault will pin McKenzie and the Boswells down while the rear party scales the wall and frees Trace from the cellar. The two forces will then join and kill or capture McKenzie and his two cohorts."

"Seems like a good plan," Zeke Cowley said.

"The trouble is that we don't know if McKenzie and the Boswell brothers sleep inside the mission," Frank said. "We could attack the front of the mission and then find them behind us. And there's another thing. We may be able to take McKenzie by surprise but not Bat and Sky Boswell. Men like them are continually on the scout. Like a pair of cougars, they sleep with one eye open and their ears tuned to what's happening around them. Night or day, light or dark, professional gunmen don't let themselves get taken by surprise." Quinn opened his mouth to speak, but Frank raised a silencing hand. "And what about the butcher's bill? With Bat and Sky Boswell in the fight, we'd have to step over our own dead to save Trace." Frank shook his head. "Kate will never go for that."

"Frank, you're good with a gun," Quinn said. "We could make it work."

Then Chas Minor, normally a taciturn man, spoke up and surprised everybody. "Seen the Boswells get their work in one time up at a settlement on the Canadian when I was wearing a deputy's badge for a spell. It was maybe three years ago, maybe less. Well, Sky killed a teamster by the name of Handy, Tom Handy he was called, after an argument over a fallen woman. Sky shoved the muzzle of his gun into Handy's belly and blew his liver out. Later that day eight bullwhackers and muleskinners, all of them armed with bowie knives and revolvers, went after Sky with a noose. Him and Bat met them boys in the street and cut loose. When the smoke cleared six teamsters were dead and two wounded. One of them died six weeks later and the other survived." Minor pulled up his shirt and revealed a red, puckered wound an inch above where the buckle of his cartridge belt would be. "The town was outraged, and I was ordered to arrest Sky Boswell for the murder of Handy. He drew down on me and cut loose before I even cleared leather. I was gut shot and I lingered in bed for the best part of a year before I could get up and walk around." Minor smiled. "The bullet is still in me, so maybe Sky will kill me eventually. The moral of this story is that the

Boswell brothers are fast, maybe the fastest that's ever been." He looked around at the others. "And that's all I got to say."

Quinn had listened in silence and now he said, revealing that Kerrigan stubbornness, "But it's still a good plan. We can make it work."

It was Quinn's bullheadedness that made Minor decide to speak again. "Maybe so, boss," Minor said. "You can take thirty punchers down there and get the job done and I'll be one of them. But I guarantee that you'll lose half of us. There's something about the Boswell brothers that's not human."

"Trace is my brother," Quinn said, his shoulders slumping. "But fifteen dead men is too steep a price to pay."

Frank Cobb laid a hand on Quinn's shoulder. "We'll find a way. Hell, there's always a way."

Quinn grabbed the map from the table, crushed it in his hands and threw it at the wall. "Damn," he said. "I can't believe a two-bit piece of trash like Slide McKenzie is leading us around by the nose. How did it happen? How the hell did we let it happen?"

"I guess I underestimated him," Frank said.

"We all underestimated him," Quinn said. "Every single one of us."

Josiah Mosely stood hidden by darkness and watched Frank Cobb and a couple of punchers leave the big house. Their faces were set, as though chiseled from granite, and all three gave off an air of defeat, walking head down like broken men.

Mosely understood. Yet another plan to rescue

Trace and the fortunes of the KK ranch had come to nothing. The young man settled his glasses straight on his nose, but they immediately drooped askew again. For the first time in his life he wished he was taller and bigger, a giant like Paul Bunyan who could stride across the range and smash Slide McKenzie and his gunmen cohorts into a pulp. But he was not Paul Bunyan. He was Josiah Mosely, an undersized, short-sighted, little runt who once got lucky in a shooting scrape . . . the kind of luck that doesn't happen twice in a man's lifetime.

CHAPTER TWENTY-SIX

Nellie Donegan liked to rise early and be first into the women's tent before the canvas bathtubs and the best towels were all taken. Dubbed by Bill Cody the *Texarkana Tornado*, Nellie was a trick rider and sharpshooter and an occasional stand-in for Annie Oakley. She hailed from the red-light Levee District of Chicago.

Nellie stepped out of her tent before first light and pulled her red silk robe closer around her neck against the morning chill. As usual a cigarette dangled from her lips and she carried the makings in her pocket. The Texas drovers were much addicted to tobacco and had passed their smoking habit on to her. The way to the bathtubs lay between the tents of the female performers and then looped around some parked wagons before straightening out again. The large bathing tent lay directly ahead of Nellie when she suddenly stopped in her tracks. There was something or somebody lying in the long grass on the north side of the worn path. The girl's first reaction was that it was a cougar waiting in ambush for anyone foolhardy enough to bathe before the dawn. But then as her sleep-blurred eyes sharpened, she made out the figure of a man lying on his back, his booted feet toward her.

Nellie pegged the fellow as a cowboy who'd had too much to drink or an unconscious roustabout, a notoriously drunken bunch.

"Hey, you," she called out. "Get to your feet. What the hell are you doing so close to the women's bath tent, you damned pervert?"

There was no response and Nellie felt a spike of alarm. Was the man dead? Had the crazy Indian returned and scalped somebody else? Raised hard in a tough town, Nellie Donegan was not a girl to go anywhere unarmed, and along with the sack of Bull Durham in her pocket, she carried a .30 caliber Marlin revolver. The girl drew the little pistol and stepped closer to the recumbent figure half hidden in the grass. The redheaded man lay on his back, his open eyes staring at a sky tinged with the lemon light of daybreak, and Nellie realized he was as dead as he was ever going to be.

She looked around and saw a man walking with a coiled rope over his shoulder. She recognized him as a roustabout named Bill, and she called his name. The laborer stepped toward her and then stopped in his tracks when he saw the body on the ground, and his eyes moved from the dead man to the gun in Nellie's hand. "That's Davy Hoyle the cowboy," he said.

"Yes, I know it is," Nellie said.

"Is he dead?"

"What do you think?"

"Hell, girl, yeah, I think he's dead. Did you shoot him?" Bill said. He was a muscular man who sported a huge mustache, and he had a bare-breasted mermaid tattoo on his left forearm.

"No, I didn't shoot him," Nellie said. "I looked and can't see a wound on him."

The roustabout kneeled beside Hoyle and then said, "Maybe he just up and died. I'll turn him over."

Nellie Donegan had seen death in most of its forms but she gasped in horror when she saw the dead man's back. His shirt, once pinstriped blue, was now scarlet, drenched with blood. The wounds in his back were numerous, wide and deep, the work of a broad-bladed knife cutting clean to the bone.

The roustabout looked at Nellie with harried black eyes. "The Indian has killed again," he said.

Buck Nolan was beyond fear. He was petrified. "First Andy Porter and now Davy Hoyle. Funerals for two of the Three Amigos and I'm the third. Mine will be next," he said.

"The Three Amigos, that's what they called you?" Kate Kerrigan said.

"Yeah. When we were punchers together back in the day, working for the Circle G, old man Louis Graham's outfit."

"Did you make any enemies then, back in the day?" Kate said.

Nolan hesitated for a few heartbeats and she thought he looked guarded, as though he was holding something back. But the young puncher said, "No, we didn't make any enemies." His anger flared. "Hell, lady, our only enemy is the damned Indian."

Bill Cody said, his voice even, "Keep a civil tongue, Buck."

"Well, we all know who murdered Andy and Dave, don't we? It was the Indian, Mr. Cody. He's your Indian, and I need your protection."

"And you'll get it," Bill said. "You need not fret on that score."

As Buck Nolan talked, Kate had been looking at the others crowded into Bill Cody's tent. Along with the roustabout foreman and a couple of riders, Annie Oakley and Ingrid Hult had shown up to represent the female members of the show. When Nolan blamed Cloud Passing all had nodded in unison, each of them convinced of his guilt. And now Kate admitted to herself that the evidence certainly pointed that way. She didn't know where the Indian was, but he was already as good as dead.

Bill Cody rose from his canvas chair—once owned by Robert E. Lee, he claimed—and said, "I have reached a couple of decisions, but first allow me to say this in answer to a few naysayers who opine that our show is doomed and will never be allowed in London town next year. When I was informed of the death of yet another cowboy I penned some verses to be read to every member of my Wild West troupe. This is to assure each one of you that no matter the setbacks, no matter the trials and tribulations, the show will and must go on."

Bill's speech brought cheers from the cowboys and polite applause from the ladies. He bowed, picked up a paper from a campaign table substituting for a desk, cleared his throat, and intoned:

The Fame of Buffalo Bill

We hear that the cowboys are wonders,
And do what no rough rider dare.
So wherever the pitch is in London
Its wild horses will drag us there.
O, fancy the scene of excitement!
O, fancy five acres of thrill,
The cowboys and Indians and horses
And the far-famed Buffalo Bill!

Applause followed, and Annie Oakley cried out, "Huzzah!" Bill bowed again and continued:

They say he's a darling, a hero,
A truly magnificent man,
With hair that falls over his shoulders,
And a face that's a picture to scan.
And then he's so strong and so daring,
Yet gentle and nice with it still—
Only fancy if all the young ladies
Go mashed upon Buffalo Bill!

More applause, several Huzzahs! and Bill bowed graciously. Then, apparently to assure his audience that an end was sight, he said, "One more verse."

The world is a wearisome desert.
The life we live is a bore;
The cheek of the apple is rosy,
But the canker-worm hides in the core.
Our hearts have a void that is aching—

That void, then, O, hasten to fill
With your mustangs and Injuns and cowboys,
And yourself, O great Buffalo Bill.

Mr. Cody was indeed a gallant and dashing frontiersman, but his poetry left a great deal to be desired. After another hearty round of applause, in which Kate joined in for politeness's sake, he bowed, smiled, and remained standing. He held up his hand for silence and said, "There are some of my competitors who would delight in my misfortune and would like nothing better than to see the Texas Rangers shut us down as a hotbed of murder and mayhem."

"For shame," Annie Oakley said.

"Indeed, dear girl, for shame," Bill said. "But that is not going to happen, because, as of this very moment"—he drew his brace of silver-plated revolvers and laid them on the desk—"I am placing Mr. Buck Nolan under my personal protection, and no safer haven can be found anywhere on earth. There will be no more murders, I can assure you."

"Hear, hear," the roustabout foreman said. But Buck Nolan did not seem impressed.

"And second, I am instituting a full investigation into the murders of Dave Hoyle and Andy Porter and I assure you the perpetrator will soon be brought to justice."

"You don't need an investigation," Nolan said. "We all know who done it. I say we search for the damned Indian and when we find him we string him up. He doesn't need a trial. Trials are for white men, not murdering savages."

"Then we must form search parties immediately," Bill said. "Let no stone remain unturned, no avenue of investigation unexplored, until we have apprehended the fugitive."

"And then hung him," Nolan said.

This statement drew cheers.

CHAPTER TWENTY-SEVEN

Hiram I. Clay's red face got redder still when Kate Kerrigan mentioned the sum of money she wanted to borrow from the Pecos River Cattleman's Association, of which Clay was the president.

"Seventy thousand dollars is a considerable sum, Kate," he said.

Kate nodded. "I know it is. I have thirty thousand on hand, but I need to borrow the rest. It has to be done quickly since my son's life is at stake."

Clay, big-bellied and florid but robust, accepted the brandy Kate handed to him, asked and was granted her permission to smoke a cigar, and then said, "You must not pay this ransom, Kate. I know that is your intention, but I must forbid it. Since this situation is of the greatest moment, the day after tomorrow I can have a hundred riders, all determined and well-armed men, outside your front door, eagerly awaiting your order to effect a rescue. We will smash this McKenzie upstart and his cohorts with overwhelming force and free young Trace from a dark and dreary dungeon." Clay raised his hand and thumped down hard on the arm of his chair. "The mailed fist, dear lady, that's the only medicine the criminal classes understand, and I include nesters of every stripe."

The big cattleman sat back and gave Kate a self-satisfied smile, as though he'd fairly presented his case and there could be no other solution.

"Mr. Clay—"

"Hiram, please."

Kate nodded. "Hiram, as soon as McKenzie and his men spot your dust cloud they will shoot my son, and many of the association's cowboys, young men with wives, children, or sweethearts, will die in the exchange of fire that follows. The cost of trying to free Trace would be counted in the bodies of dead drovers, and I am not willing to pay such a blood price."

"Kate . . . I— perhaps . . ." Clay's voice trailed away, unable to express the tangled thoughts that ran through his head. He knew Kate Kerrigan spoke the truth, unpalatable as it was.

"I've studied the problem from all angles, and there is only one answer," Kate said. "I have to pay the ransom. There is no other way."

"A solution will present itself. I am confident it will," Clay said.

"And in the meantime?" Kate said.

"Well, as for the Mexicans currently squatting on your range, I will wire General Porfirio Díaz and request that his troops remove them forcibly," Clay said. "That gentleman owes me many favors since our cattleman's association supplied his rurales with rifles, horses, and beef during his rebellion."

"And the raising of the ransom money?" Kate said.

She used her body as a perfumed, silken lure, bending forward more than was strictly necessary to push an ashtray closer to Clay. She saw his eyes drop to her deep cleavage and she marveled at the power a woman has over an ardent man.

Clay harrumphed, raised his gaze to Kate's radiantly beautiful face, and said, "Kate, it will take time to raise such a sum."

"I have less than a week left," Kate said.

"Ah, then you shall have it soon, even if I have to furnish the entire amount myself."

"I will pay after the spring gather," Kate said.

Clay smiled. "Dearest Kate, your credit is good with me and every rancher in Texas. It will be a great honor to loan you the money you need."

"Thank you, dearest Hiram. As soon as possible you must visit for tea and sponge cake," Kate said. She rose to her feet. "Now, you are a busy and important man and I have no wish to detain you longer."

Clay drained his brandy glass, rose, and kissed Kate's hand. "My accountant will be in touch, so until we meet again, my dear," he said. "Let us hope in happier circumstance when Trace is safe and sound in the, ah"—he glanced at the swelling tops of Kate's breasts—"bosom of his family."

"Dear Hiram, I will count the hours," Kate said, allowing the man to kiss her hand again.

"I wouldn't put my hopes in Hiram Clay calling in favors from Porfirio Díaz," Frank Cobb said. "Díaz has a famine on his hands, and he's dealing with a lot of unrest, not only among the peons but in the military."

Quinn Kerrigan sat on an empty cot in the bunkhouse, a cup of coffee in his hands and a lot on his mind. "I don't think Ma gives a damn about Díaz returning favors and wondering about what he'll do or not do," he said. "Once she pays the ransom for Trace, she'll be ruined, and whether or not there are Mexicans on the north bank of the Rio Grande won't matter. She told me she might head for the New Mexico Territory and start again on a quarter-section."

"You'd go with her?" Frank said.

"Of course. You?"

Frank nodded. "To hell, if that's where she wanted to go."

Quinn smiled. "I don't think hell enters into Ma's thinking." Then, his face suddenly alight, "Wait a minute . . . wait a cotton-picking minute . . . you look like him, Frank. Not in the face, but you have the black hair and the same rangy build."

"Look like who?" Frank said. Then warily, "You're not getting another of your bright ideas?"

"You look like Slide McKenzie. You could get close, real close."

"Close? You mean close to Bat and Sky Boswell?"

"Yeah. Close enough to draw down on them."

"And get my head blown off," Frank said. "Maybe I could shade one of them—and that's a big maybe—but not them both. I shoot Bat, Sky will drill me or vice versa. Depend on it."

"But it's something to think about though," Quinn said. "Wearing McKenzie's clothes, you could pass for him at a distance, and I'll be with you."

"Has Slide seen you?" Frank said.

"I don't think so," Quinn said. "Suppose I dress like a saddle tramp and ride with you. Maybe the Boswell boys will think I'm somebody McKenzie picked up on the trail. Especially if we're leading a packhorse with Ma's big steamer trunk tied to its back." Quinn's young face glowed with enthusiasm. "The Boswells might reckon McKenzie needed help to carry the money."

"And he hired a man to guard it," Frank said. "Is that right?"

"Damn sure it's right," Quinn said, clapping his hands. "It's a plan."

"It's a lousy, half-assed plan that will get us both killed," Frank said.

"So you don't like it?" Quinn said, disappointment slumping his shoulders.

"I don't want any part of it, but, God help me, I'll study on it for a spell," Frank said. "Bad as it is, and it's real bad, right now it's the only plan we have."

CHAPTER TWENTY-EIGHT

As was her habit before retiring, Kate Kerrigan threw open her bedroom window and stared out into the mother-of-pearl night illuminated by a waxing moon. Doctors said night air was bad for the lungs, but Kate did not hold with that. In the gloom she could not see her land, but for a few minutes she breathed deeply of its smell, the odor of grass, of cows and horses, and, delicate as a baby's breath, the fragrance of sagebrush and distant pine borne on the breeze. It was the smell of the living land, the land that roused the Irish in her and whispered in her ear that hers was "a rich and rare land, a fresh and fair land, a dear and rare land," this land of hers.

A long-dead Irish poet wrote that line and Kate never tired of calling it to mind.

After a while she leaned forward to close the window and her silk nightdress fluttered in the breeze as though she was about to take flight. She stopped suddenly and stared into the darkness. There! A man walking, not out for a stroll before bed but striding purposely, knowing where he was going and hurrying to get there. From the lofty viewpoint of her window Kate recognized the shadowy figure, short, slender, wearing a ditto suit and plug hat. It was Josiah Mosely, and where was he going this time of night?

Unbidden, a disturbing thought barged its way into her head: Could Josiah be the cowboy killer, bent on getting even for the beating they'd given him? Was he now hunting for Buck Nolan to make his revenge complete?

It was possible, and Kate knew she had to act to stop him. Fearing she'd lose him in the darkness, she threw on her robe, stepped into her slippers, and, as an afterthought, dropped her derringer into her pocket.

Kate hurried downstairs, moving through the dark house like a candle flame, and stepped outside. She stood for a few moments, her eyes searching into the darkness. There was no sign of Josiah Mosely. The young man had been swallowed by the night. But Kate had been around Frank Cobb enough to learn the ways and skills of the tracker, and after she scouted the area where she'd last seen Mosely she picked up his trail. But he was heading due north, away from the Cody encampment.

Puzzled, helped by the moonlight, Kate followed the man's tracks that after several hundred yards began a gradual swing to the northwest toward the tree line. Had Josiah stashed his balloon there and was going to work on it? But at night? And in the dark? It didn't add up.

Ahead of her, Kate heard an owl hoot. A few moments later the call was answered by another, farther away. But these were no owls. Mosely had signaled to someone, warning of his approach, and the hidden man—she was sure the hoot had been made by a male—had answered.

Mosely moved again and Kate followed, drawing close.

A dark cloud glided across the face of the moon, dimming the light. Kate waited, her face turned to the sky, watching as the silver-rimmed cloud slowly sailed on. The moonlight brightened . . . and solved one mystery but created another.

"Mr. Mosely," Kate said, her voice loud in the stillness, "I hope you have a good explanation for this."

Kate's words froze Josiah Mosely and Cloud Passing in place, an immobile tableau of a white man handing a bulging burlap sack to an Indian.

"Well?" Kate said, emphasizing her demand by palming the derringer.

Mosely finally found some words. "I can explain," he said.

"I think you'd better," Kate said.

"So Bill Cody believes someone else committed the murders," Kate Kerrigan said, returning the derringer to her robe pocket. "I wonder if he has anyone in mind."

"I don't think so," Josiah Mosely said. "Or if he suspects someone he's keeping it to himself."

Kate glanced at Cloud Passing, who stood aloof eating the roast beef and bread Mosely had brought him from the kitchen. "He's the obvious suspect," Kate said.

Mosely nodded. "Maybe too obvious, there's no doubt about that. Earlier today I saw a posse looking for him. We'd already brought the balloon basket and envelope deeper into the trees, and just as well, because a couple of men rode pretty close, looked around, and thankfully kept on going."

"Were they cowboys?" Kate said.

"Yes, big hats and spurred boots," Mosely said.

"You were lucky. Punchers won't walk when they don't have to. That's why they didn't dismount and search the trees. Roustabouts and others would have beat the bushes."

Mosely's voice held a tone of urgency. "Mrs. Kerrigan, you won't sell us out, will you?"

Kate shivered, the thin stuff of her night attire providing little protection against the cool night air. "I will think about this and pray for guidance," she said. "Then I'll make my decision."

"I feel responsible for Cloud Passing, and I don't want to see him hanged for something he didn't do," Mosely said.

"None of us do, except the real killer if there is one," Kate said. "Be careful, Josiah. You're dealing with a Cheyenne Dog Soldier, and from what I've been told, he can turn on you."

"He won't. Cloud Passing knows his time is over, and that's why he allows Bill Cody to exhibit him like one of his wild animals."

"I must go now," Kate said. "The night is getting decidedly cold."

"I was just bringing food to Cloud Passing," Mosely said. "I'll escort you home, Mrs. Kerrigan, since there is a killer still at large."

As she and Mosely walked through the darkness, Kate turned and saw Cloud Passing watch them go.

The thought came to her then that thanks to Buffalo Bill Cody and others like him the proud Cheyenne warrior was gone and in his place stood a cigar store Indian. Like Mosely she didn't want the man to hang—his life was already a living death.

"Mrs. Kerrigan, before we retire, could I interest you in a cup of coffee?" Josiah Mosely said.

"I am very tired," Kate said.

"I just want to talk to you," Mosely said. "It won't take long."

The young man's face was pleading, and Kate smiled and said, "Very well, then. One half cup and then I must turn in."

For the convenience of the drovers, Kate insisted that a pot of coffee simmer on the kitchen stove day and night, and she bade Mosely sit at the table while she poured a cup for them both.

Once she was seated she smiled and said, "Now Mr. Mosely, what can be so important that it's keeping me from my beauty sleep?"

The young man gathered his thoughts and said, "Mrs. Kerrigan, I'm a rainmaker who has never made it rain. I've never traveled on a steam train, never visited a big city, and I have never seen a great ocean. I have no loved ones, folks who are glad at my coming and sad at my leaving. Horses don't like me and neither do dogs and most children."

Kate's eyelids drooped as Mosely talked, but they popped wide open when he said, "I have never slept with a woman or even held one in my arms."

"Mr. Mosely," she said, "that is hardly a matter for polite discussion."

"There is nothing to discuss, Mrs. Kerrigan. Please, hear me out. I am small and skinny and not very strong, and that's why tough and rugged men like Frank Cobb can barely tolerate me. I can read and write and do my ciphers, but I can't sing a love song or make pleasant parlor conversation. To sum up, I live in this world, but I don't matter a damn."

"Mr. Mosely, I—" a flustered Kate began, but Mosely cut her off.

"I'm not seeking sympathy. I'm just telling you the truth. I'm as significant as a lit candle on the prairie during a lightning storm, and that means I'm of no consequence whatsoever. When I die no one will grieve for me because it will be like I never lived."

"Mr. Mosely, why are you telling me all this?" Kate said. "Is there anything I can do to help you?"

Mosely smiled and shook his head. "Many men would view that as an invitation."

"It's not," Kate said.

"Of course it's not, because that's not how it was intended."

"Now I really must get to bed," Kate said. "We'll talk of this again sometime."

"No, we won't, because I will not mention it again," Mosely said. "But I want to ask you to do one thing for me, a small favor. When you hear of my death, and you will, say my name out loud. Please say 'Josiah Mosely' when there are others present so they know that such a man as me once existed, that he felt the sun on his back and turned his face to the rain."

After a while Kate said, "I must go now." She rose

to her slippered feet and glided across the kitchen's flagstoned floor. When she reached the door she opened it a little, then turned and said, "Josiah Mosely I will say your name. I will say it aloud. And tonight I will pray a rosary for you." Kate dashed a tear from her eye. "Josiah, as you talked I came to believe that you and Cloud Passing were destined to meet because you are both poor, tormented creatures." She shook her beautiful head and said, "And oh, how my heart breaks for you."

After Kate left, taking the moonlight with her, Mosely sat in the dark kitchen and steeled himself for what he had to do.

CHAPTER TWENTY-NINE

"Beef and beans, Kerrigan," Slide McKenzie said. "Hell, you're eating better than the Mexicans out there."

"That's because we need you alive," Bat Boswell said. He smiled. "For the time being anyway."

The gunman stood on the stairs, a handsome man wearing a frilled white shirt and tight pants tucked into English riding boots. A tooled cartridge belt circled his slim hips, an ivory-handled Colt in the holster. Appearances were deceptive. Boswell had the savage mind of a predator, a killer without conscience, and his brother Sky matched him in every regard.

McKenzie passed a tin plate and fork to Trace and said, "Just a few more days and you'll be out of here. Unless I don't get the hundred thousand from your ma, and then you'll be dead."

"Then that's how it will be," Trace said. Looking into McKenzie's eyes was like staring into the mud of a fetid swamp. "But in the end you'll lose, McKenzie. The Mexicans camped out there will never follow a lowlife like you onto the KK range. They're human beings, and you can't use them as a weapon."

McKenzie grinned. "You're right, Kerrigan, maybe they won't follow me, but they will follow the Santa Muerte."

"What the hell are you talking about, McKenzie?" Trace said.

"I found her in this very room stashed over there in a corner. I guess the Comanche took one look and left her alone. She's like one of them Madonna statues you see in the Mexican churches, but her head is a skull. The one I got has a real skull, some gal who died hundreds of years ago, I guess. The Mexicans called it a miracle that the statue survived all these years, and I told them that Santa Muerte had come to me in a vision and swore to me that she will lead them all to the promised land." McKenzie smiled. "And they believed me. Hell, they got down on their knees and prayed. Now the word has spread deep into Mexico that a miracle was performed here and more and more folks are arriving every day."

"You idiot, McKenzie, Santa Muerte is the Angel of Death," Trace said. "She'll end up killing you. Get rid of that statue. This is a warning you should heed."

"Like I give a damn," McKenzie said. "A wooden idol worshiped by a bunch of ignorant popish peasants ain't gonna kill a good Protestant like Slide McKenzie, no sir."

"McKenzie, if the angel doesn't kill you I'll live to wring your scrawny neck," Trace said. "Depend on it."

"Big talk, kinda what I'd expect from a rich woman's son," McKenzie said. "Well let me tell you this, Kerrigan, a week from now your ma won't be so rich. Fact is, she'll have to sell her body to all comers just to buy her daily bread." McKenzie dredged up a smile from the slimy depths of his soul. "I already offered her two dollars for a screw, and she turned me down. But soon she'll be right glad to take it and beg for more."

Driven by rage, Trace threw the plate into McKenzie's face, covering him in beans and beef fat. As the man jerked back, Trace threw a powerful straight right to his chin and McKenzie went down like a poleaxed steer, a scarlet fan of blood and saliva blood spurting from his mouth. Trace, insane with anger, advanced on the man, his boots ready to cave in McKenzie's ribs and pulp his face. But he never got the chance. Something hard slammed into the right side of his head, and he found himself falling headlong into a bottomless pit of lightning-streaked darkness.

Trace Kerrigan woke to lamplight and a pounding headache.

It took an effort to open his eyes, but when he did he found himself staring into the amused face of Bat Boswell. The gunman held aloft an oil lamp that cast half his face in shadow. Trace was vaguely aware of Sky hovering in the background.

"You broke McKenzie's jaw," Bat said. "One of the Mexicans who says he's a doctor tied it up for him." The gunman's smile stretched into a grin. "The cloth is tied at the top of his head. Makes him look like a demented jackrabbit."

"Now he wants to kill you," Sky Boswell said. "And I guess all things considered that's understandable."

"Then why didn't he?" Trace said. Talking hurt his head.

"We stopped him," Bat said. "Slide wanted to go at you with a wood ax."

"Chop you up piece by piece, Kerrigan," Sky said. He shrugged. "Messy."

"Why did you stop him?" Trace said. "Out of the goodness of your hearts?"

Bat shook his head. "There's no goodness in our hearts, Kerrigan. But we're interested in your welfare on account of how you're our ace in the hole."

"McKenzie already told me that very thing," Trace said.

"This is nothing to do with McKenzie," Bat said. "Just suppose that rich mother of yours decides to hang McKenzie instead of paying him. Now where does that leave Sky and me? McKenzie told us that if he wasn't back in a reasonable amount of time we were to shoot you. But where's the profit in that? We'd waste ten cents on a cartridge, lose our meal ticket, and end up with nothing."

"So if McKenzie gets his suspenders cut you hold me for ransom, huh?" Trace said.

"Right first time. What a clever feller you are, Kerrigan. Your mother must be very proud of you. Ain't he clever, Sky?"

"As a tree full of owls," Sky said.

"Of course we won't be as greedy as McKenzie, because all that does is create ill-feeling," Bat said. "Fifty thousand will be enough for me and Sky, and we can't say fairer than that. We got a man to track down and kill, and that takes money."

"My mother will never pay a ransom," Trace said.

"I think she will," Bat said. "We'll start off by sending her the fingers of your left hand. If she doesn't pony up, we'll send the fingers of your right hand. By the time we get to your left ear I reckon Ma will figure that paying the piper is better than getting her son and heir back home one piece at a time."

Trace's anger flared. "Boswell, you and your brother are lowlife trash," he said. "You're—"

A shotgun roared and buckshot slammed into the wall above Trace Kerrigan's head, showering him with chunks of ancient plaster. He dived for the floor as Bat Boswell roared, "McKenzie, no!" Footsteps sounded on the stairs and Boswell yelled, "Sky! Stop him!"

Fearing a second shotgun blast, Trace rolled to his left behind a pile of bricks and debris that had fallen from the roof at some time in the past. McKenzie was on the stairs battling Sky for possession of the shotgun. Finally the bigger, stronger Boswell wrenched the gun from McKenzie's grasp and said, "Get the hell out of here, Slide."

McKenzie, the band around his chin tied at the top of his head like ears, saw Trace, who was slowly getting to his feet. The man made strange *gggnnnn—gggnnnn* noises though his jammed-shut teeth, and his bloodshot eyes were wild and made him look like an escapee from a mental asylum.

Sky Boswell tossed the shotgun to his brother and then hustled McKenzie out the door and slammed it shut behind him.

But although he'd been unable to form coherent words, McKenzie's meaning had been clear—Trace Kerrigan was a dead man.

CHAPTER THIRTY

Davy Hoyle was buried beside Andy Porter in the Kerrigan cemetery on the ridge overlooking Kate's mansion. Bill Cody said the eulogy and the Wild West show's young pastor, the Reverend Sam Houston Dinwiddie, led the assemblage in prayers for the dead.

"A nice sendoff, I thought," Bill said as he escorted Kate down the rise toward the house, her arm in his. He lowered his voice. "The only one absent was the Indian."

"Yes. But he's safe for the time being," Kate said. She was deeply troubled.

Bill talked on about his coming visit to Europe and his desire to meet old Queen Vic, but Kate was only half listening, enough to smile at the right times and nod. It was the unladylike behavior of Annie Oakley and Ingrid Hult that occupied her mind.

The two women had pushed through the crowd of Bill's performers and Kate's punchers to the graveside as the plain pine coffin, hammered together by one of the show's carpenters, was lowered.

Annie Oakley had started it.

To Kate's surprise the girl moved to the edge of the hole, stared down into its depths for a few moments and then kicked dirt on top of the coffin. As debris drummed onto the lid, Ingrid Hult, her face pale as though carved from marble, joined her. She raised her bright red skirt a few inches and then used the toe of her high-heeled boot to kick soil and loose rocks onto the coffin. Like Annie Oakley had done, Ingrid's act was violent, as though she'd imagined herself kicking dirt into Davy Hoyle's face.

Kate had looked around at the rest of the mourners. Beside herself, had someone else noticed? Bill Cody's head was bent, listening to the preacher's leaden words, and most of the other mourners were doing the same, although a few looked up warily at the sky where massy ramparts of gray and black clouds had gathered and distant thunder boomed.

Then, as Kate watched, the two women turned their backs on the grave and pushed their way though the crowd. A moment later a woman hooted, loudly. Kate frowned. Was that a cry of grief or a whoop of laughter? Yes, she was sure it had been laughter. It had come to Kate then that only someone who truly hated the deceased would hoot with glee at his funeral.

Kate came back to the present. "I'm sorry, Mr. Cody," she said. "I was woolgathering. What did you say?"

Bill smiled and patted Kate's hand. "Laying the dead to rest can be so trying. I asked you if you cared to come back to my camp. Random Clark, remember him?"

"I remember his wonderful pea soup," Kate said.

"Yes indeed. Well, Mr. Clark has prepared a funeral breakfast and I'd very much like you to join us."

"I'd be delighted," Kate said. "I do feel a little sharp set."

"Splendid! You know I love to show you off, Kate," Bill said. "If I had a walled garden I'd invite you inside so the roses could see you."

"And you, sir, are most gallante," Kate said. "That was a poetic thought, but I'm afraid all I'm thinking about right now is bacon and eggs."

Davy Hoyle's funeral breakfast was well attended by a somewhat rowdy crowd, but when Kate Kerrigan glanced around the tables Annie Oakley and Ingrid Hult were notably absent.

As a major shareholder in the White Star shipping line, Kate mixed business with pleasure and advised Bill Cody that when he left for England he must travel on the new *Oceanic* liner, a steamship so large she could accommodate the entire Wild West show with room to spare. Bill was extremely interested and promised that he'd have his accountant look into the dollars and cents of such a crossing.

"If it can be done, dear lady, Bill Cody will do it. The *Oceanic*, you say? Such a leviathan must be the wonder of our modern steam age."

"It is indeed, Mr. Cody, and your comfort will be assured, because I will insist that you occupy the finest first-class parlor suite available," Kate said.

"Your generosity overwhelms me, Kate," Bill said. He forked a chunk of sausage into his mouth. "I am very touched."

As casually as she could, as though it was just a way of making conversation, Kate said, "Davy Hoyle was very handsome. I suppose he was popular with the ladies?"

Bill nodded as he chewed. "He seemed to be."

"Did Annie Oakley walk out with him?"

"Oh goodness gracious no," Bill said. "Annie is a married lady. Her spouse is Frank Butler, the marksman, and one of my employees."

Kate knew she was pushing it, but Bill seemed to be engrossed in his breakfast and was only half-listening. "Ah, then the unmarried ladies like Ingrid Hult must have vied for his attention," she said.

Bill dipped a chuck of bread into an egg yolk. "No, not Ingrid. She and Jim Benson plan to get married in London next year." Bill chewed on the bread and then said, "I often saw Davy and Polly Coulter canoodling together. But I don't know how serious they were."

Kate was disappointed. She'd wanted to hear that Annie Oakley and Ingrid Hult were spurned lovers and as a result they both hated Hoyle enough to kill him. But that was obviously not the case. There must have been another reason for their graveside behavior.

Bill Cody loudly greeted a couple of young Sioux warriors who passed the table and then turned his attention to Kate again. "Polly Coulter is a trick rider and doubles as a lady in distress in the stagecoach attacked by Indians sequence. She has a wonderful scream, has Polly. You can hear it all over the arena."

"How nice for her," Kate said. She dabbed her lips with her napkin. "This was a wonderful breakfast, Mr. Cody. And now I really must be going."

"I will escort you, dear lady," Bill said.

"No need. I'd like to walk alone today. I have some thinking to do."

Bill bowed. "As you wish, Kate. And may I say that your company this morning has been a sweet distraction."

Kate gave a little curtsey. "And I enjoyed yours, as always. You won't forget about the White Star line and the *Oceanic*, now will you?"

"To travel on your bark will be the greatest experience of my life, exceeding anything I encountered on the Plains," Bill said. "But, oh, that it was your fair hand on the helm to make my happiness complete."

"I will be there in spirit," Kate said. And as a White Star shareholder, she meant that most sincerely.

The threatening thunderstorm had stalled somewhere above the Guadalupe Mountains, but the violent sky looked as though ramparts of black breakers were cresting gray before crashing onto a dismal shore. The air had thinned and smelled of ozone. Kate Kerrigan snapped open her lace parasol and then lifted her dress to avoid grass stains and worse. Now she regretted sending Shorty Hawkins home with the carriage because the rain might start before she reached her front door.

Kate was thinking how difficult it was to walk quickly across uneven ground in high-heeled ankle boots under a sky black as the wrath of God when the drum of galloping hooves behind her brought her to a halt. She turned and had to step smartly to her left as

Annie Oakley drew rein on her horse, the buckskin mare rearing as it fought the bit.

When the horse settled and stood, Kate said, "Why Mrs. Butler, what a pleasant surprise."

"This is not one of your social occasions, Mrs. Kerrigan," Annie said. She held a Winchester across the front of her saddle and the muzzle pointed casually at Kate as though it was unintentional.

"Then what can I do for you?" Kate said.

"Just one thing," the girl said. She was angry, her masculine jaw set. "Keep out of our affairs and mind your own business."

"And what business would that be?" Kate said.

"Whatever a fine lady does to occupy her time."

"I wasn't always a fine lady, you know. In fact there were times when I was no kind of lady." Kate smiled, keenly aware of the Winchester. "I was raised in the Hell's Kitchen neighborhood of New York where there were no ladies, fine or otherwise. Have you visited there? No? I'm afraid you wouldn't like it much."

"Nothing that happens in Bill Cody's camp is any of your concern," Annie said. "Take my advice and stay well away."

"Or what?" Kate said.

"Or suffer unpleasant consequences." Annie Oakley's finger was now inside the rifle's trigger guard.

"Young lady, Bill Cody's camp is on my property, so whatever happens there is very much my concern," Kate said.

"I'll tell you for the last time," Annie said. "Stick to having tea and crumpets with your rich friends and leave us the hell alone." Now the girl was making no pretenses. The Winchester pointed right at Kate's chest. "Do you understand me?"

"Perfectly," Kate said.

Annie nodded and swung the buckskin away, but she drew rein as Kate said, "One final word, Mrs. Butler, if I may. I'm afraid that what I'm about to say is not going to sound very ladylike. More Hell's Kitchen than tea and crumpets in my parlor."

"Then say it," Annie said. "I'm listening."

Kate smiled. "Mrs. Butler, I'll go wherever I please . . . and if you ever point a rifle at me again, I'll take it from you and shove it up your ass. Now, do we understand one another?"

After she got over her initial shock Annie Oakley said, "You're a hard, profane woman, Mrs. Kerrigan."

"You don't know the half of it, sister," Kate said.

CHAPTER THIRTY-ONE

The thunderstorm that had threatened all day broke over the KK ranch just before midnight. Rain drummed on the canvas of Bill Cody's tents, thunder crashed and lightning scrawled across the night sky like the signature of a demented god. The buffalo huddled together in their corral and rainwater dripped from their beards.

Buck Nolan, angry that he'd been forced to answer a call of nature on such a wild night, stepped from the latrine thumbing his suspenders over his shoulders, head bent against the rain. For security reasons he now occupied the tent next to Bill Cody's but the great frontier hero's stentorian snoring told him that he wasn't taking his guard duties too conscientiously.

Nolan ducked into his tent, removed his wet clothes, and rolled into his cot. Tired out from Davy Hoyle's funeral and the stresses of the day, he closed his eyes, and lulled by the ticking sound of the rain and rolling thunder, he closed his eyes and slept.

An intense, piercing pain deep in his chest woke Buck Nolan an hour later. He raised his head, gagging as he stared in horror at the handle of the bowie knife sticking out of his breastbone and the clenched fist that had driven it into him with so much hatred. Nolan tried to scream, shriek, cry out, but the sound drowned in his bloody throat. His eyes frantic, appalled by the manner of his death, he managed to utter a single word, "You . . ."

An open hand was placed on top of the fist. Pushed. The blade drove deeper, hewing Nolan's faltering heart asunder. The pain was a terrible, dreadful thing, but the young man was unable to voice even a groan.

Later Bill Cody would say of Buck Nolan, "The poor son of a bitch died an awful death."

And he was right.

As the assassin retrieved the bloody knife and left the tent to flee though the torrential rain-slanted darkness, Nolan gasped his last. His open eyes stared at the roof of the tent but saw nothing.

"Nobody saw anything," Bill Cody said. "Well, it was dark and rainy, so maybe that's not too surprising."

"Apart from being saddle buddies, did the three murdered punchers share anything else in common?" Kate Kerrigan said.

"Not that I'm aware of, Kate," Bill said. "I'll talk with Polly Coulter. She might know something." He drained his glass and said, "You pour good bourbon, dear lady." He rose to his feet, a tall, silver-haired and elegant man dressed in white buckskins, the fringes on the sleeves of his beaded coat a yard long. "Now

I have to get back. My people are scared, and the question on everyone's lips is 'Who's next?'"

"I don't believe that there will be more murders, Mr. Cody," Kate said. "Besides being drovers, the three dead men did have something in common. They were the ones who beat up Josiah Mosely and—"

"Were attacked by Cloud Passing," Bill said. "It always comes back to the Indian. Somebody sure wants to see that Cheyenne hang."

"Before you leave, Mr. Cody, I wish to ask you a question," Kate said.

"And I'll do my best to answer it," Bill said.

"Why did Annie Oakley warn me yesterday to keep my nose out of the investigation into the deaths of the cowboys?"

Bill Cody smiled. "She's a caring gal, is our little Annie," he said. "She told me all about that. She says her warning was for your own good since if you pried into the murders too closely the killer might make you a target."

Kate frowned. "Is that what she said?"

"Yes, she did, dear lady," Bill said. "You have a friend and protector in Annie. Now, by your gracious leave," he bent and kissed Kate's hand, "I must wrench myself from your delightful company and reassure my frightened people with my stalwart presence."

Kate smiled. "You are a most devoted employer."

"Indeed I am," Bill said, white gloved hand on chest, striking a pose.

"Please tell Mrs. Butler that I feel much safer now that she's watching over me with her Winchester," Kate said.

* * *

"It's an honor to bring you the money you need, Kate," Hiram I. Clay said. He smiled under his walrus mustache. "That's why I have twenty of my best riders camped on your doorstep."

"And why it's now under the guard of my son and my segundo," Kate said. At close to three hundred pounds Clay always looked too big for the slender furniture in Kate's parlor, but she'd steered him to the overstuffed bergère chair that she kept for large visitors, away from her Louis XIV antiques.

From behind a blue cloud of cigar smoke, Clay said, "I wired Fort Concho to appraise the commandant of the refugee situation on the Rio Grande and also informed the Mexican government, but I can't guarantee that either party will act before spring, if at all." The big rancher shook his head. "Oh, Kate, dear Kate, I wish you would reconsider. My boys are as keen as mustard to attempt the rescue of your son. Hit fast and hit hard with overwhelming force is the best medicine for the outlaw breed."

"Hiram, as I told you before, I will not roll the dice for my son's life," Kate said. "Any rescue attempt is out of the question."

"Buffalo Bill Cody is wintering on your land, Kate," Clay said. "Have you sought the advice of that gallant stalwart and my brother Freemason?"

"No I have not," Kate said. "This is my problem, not his."

"When does this McKenzie wretch come for his blood money?" Clay said.

"Four days from now."

"Hang him, Kate."

"And Trace will die."

"Impasse," Clay said.

Kate smiled. "Hiram, there's a word I don't hear every day."

The rancher said, "I learned that from Colonel William 'Pecos Bill' Shafter, the commandant at Fort Concho. It was a few years ago and he was talking to his officers about the Apaches. 'Gentlemen,' he said, 'the savages have gone to ground and we have reached an impasse.' Later I asked a young lieutenant what the word meant and he said, 'A situation in which no progress is possible.'"

"It's a ten-dollar word, all right," Kate said. "And it fits my present circumstance exactly. While my son's life hangs in the balance, no progress is possible."

Clay stared into his glass and kept his eyes lowered as he said, "None of your fellow ranchers in the Cattlemen's Association have mentioned it, but as president I fear I must."

"When will I repay the loans?" Kate said.

Now Clay looked at her. "Unpleasant though it may be, it's a question that needs answering, Kate."

"Business is business, Hiram. I will sell the KK, and if necessary my shipping and railroad shares. Everyone will be paid in full and with interest."

Clay was a picture of misery. "I had to ask, Kate. You understand?"

"I understand perfectly, Hiram. And you are right, you had to ask."

"Will you stay in Texas?" Clay said.

"I have a ten-thousand-acre tract of rangeland in

the New Mexico Territory. I can go there and start over."

"But Texas is your home."

Kate nodded and quickly turned her head away.

"Marry me, Kate," Clay said. "Let me take care of you."

Kate smiled. "I'm flattered by your offer, Hiram, but if I marry again it will be for love, not security. You're a fine man and a great catch for any woman, but I'm not in love with you."

"I'll always be here if you change your mind, Kate," Clay said.

"Thank you, Hiram," Kate said. "And for my part I will always bear that in mind."

CHAPTER THIRTY-TWO

At a time when they both had major problems to deal with, the last thing Kate Kerrigan and Bill Cody needed was the arrival of Isaiah Potts and his three moronic but vicious sons, Jerome, Franklin and Baptist, the last a homicidal menace to all humanity but especially pretty women . . . and the prettiest woman in all of West Texas was Kate Kerrigan.

Frontier trash like the Potts were attracted to isolated settlements where there was no gun-handy sheriff to keep them in line, and a tent city like Bill Cody's encampment was very much to their liking. So too was the nearby four-pillared mansion, grandly built in the symmetrical Federal style with its central entrance, deep porches, balconies, and magnificent white columns.

Isaiah Potts, a dirty, matted piece of filth who wore two clean and oiled Remingtons in holsters, took note of the mansion and the pretty lady who had stepped outside to wave good-bye to a fat man in a carriage. His son Baptist also saw the pretty lady and he flexed the fingers of both hands like a bird of prey spreading its talons, his slack mouth wet, his black eyes eager.

Potts saw the expression on his son's face and said, "We'll try the tent town first. It must have whiskey and women."

"Could be law there, Pa," Franklin said. Like his father and brothers he was an uncurried brute, bearded, thin strands of long hair falling in greasy tangles to his shoulders.

"We go in grinning, like we're visiting kinfolk," Isaiah Potts said. "Ain't no lawman gonna fault us for that."

"Pa, it don't look like a town to me," Franklin said.

"And I say it's a town," his Pa said. "You don't contradict me, boy, or I'll have the hide off your back with a whip."

"Like you ain't done that to me a hunnerd times afore," Franklin said.

Jerome, the youngest of the three and a little smarter, said, "Done that to all of us. One day we're gonna kill you, old man."

"Ain't one of you got the guts to draw on me," Potts said. "An' I got eyes in the back of my head. Remember the Louisiana swamp witch that time. She cast a spell and gave me the power and don't you ungrateful whelps forget it."

"Her name was Lorena an' I done her, recollect that, Pa?" Baptist said.

"We all done her," Potts said. He glared at his son. "You didn't have to kill her."

"Sometimes I don't know my own strength, Pa," Baptist said. "I break women real easy."

"And sometimes I don't think you're an idiot,

Baptist, I know. Now enough of this talk," Potts said. "Follow me and we'll find out what shakes the bushes in this burg."

It didn't take Isaiah Potts long to figure out that he'd made a mistake. This wasn't a tent town, it was Buffalo Bill Cody's Wild West show. Already some hardcases, punchers by the look of them, had gathered together and were giving Potts and his sons some mighty tough looks. All of them were armed, and Potts thought he recognized Luke Pettigout in the crowd, a lawman and sometimes Pinkerton agent from over Denver way. Potts, not the bravest of men, wanted no part of him or the punchers, either. There were a few women around, pretty gals, but Potts ignored them. All he wanted was to get the hell out of there.

Then Buffalo Bill himself showed, wearing two Colts, and Potts's heart sank. But the great man seemed affable enough. "What can I do for you boys?" he said. That was friendly, but Bill's hands were close to his guns. His blue eyes were taking the measure of the Potts clan, and he obviously didn't like what he saw.

Potts touched the brim of his battered top hat and said, "Me and my boys are just passin' through, Mr. Cody. Smelled your coffee, like."

"What a pity, we just ran out," Bill said. A dozen of his riders backed him.

"Then we'll be on our way," Potts said. "Read about you in the dime novels an' all them Indians and buffaloes you shot, Mr. Cody. I'm honored to meet you."

"Don't believe everything you read in the dime novels," Bill said.

"Then we'll be on our way," Potts said. He was glad to get away from there.

"Hell, Pa, I could've taken him," Baptist said. "He didn't look so tough."

"Maybe so, but what about the rest of them?" Potts said. "They'd have gunned you fer sure."

"Did you see them women, Pa?" Jerome said, his feral eyes gleaming.

"Yeah, I saw them," Potts said. "But right now I'm looking at something a sight better."

"I'm just going out for a short walk," Kate said to her butler Moses Rice, the old black man who'd made the journey west with her.

"You want me to come with you, Miz Kate?" Moses said. "I don't like you out there by yourself with a murderer on the loose."

Kate smiled. "I'll be fine. I'm not going far, and I have my derringer."

"Miz Kate, will Mr. Trace be home soon?" Moses said. "I sure miss him."

"We all do, Moses," Kate said. "Yes, he'll be home soon. Please see that Ivy and Shannon eat their lunch."

"Them young ladies ain't to home, Miz Kate," Moses said. "They said they were taking a walk to the Wild West show to talk to the buffaloes."

"To talk to Bill Cody's young cowboys, they mean," Kate said.

"I tried to stop them, but they don't listen to me," Moses said.

"The girls are quite safe, Moses," Kate said. "There will be no more murders."

The old man seemed surprised. "How are you so sure, Miz Kate?"

"Because the score has been settled," Kate said.

Moses Rice looked puzzled but said nothing.

They took them both. And the kidnap was done swiftly by experts.

Ivy Kerrigan, fifteen years old and in the first beautiful bloom of womanhood, fought desperately to save her little sister. But Isaiah Potts backhanded her across the face and threw her across his saddle. Stunned by the blow, Ivy was vaguely aware of Shannon's scream before she lapsed into unconsciousness and heard no more.

CHAPTER THIRTY-THREE

Kate Kerrigan was frantic with worry. Her daughters had not returned from the Cody encampment, and now it was mid-afternoon, and in a few hours the light would fade. Quinn and Frank Cobb were out with the hands while Bill Cody's search parties scouted the high country to the west.

Unwilling to alarm Kate, Bill had earlier told Frank about the visit of the four saddle tramps to his camp. "Luke Pettigout thought he recognized them," he said. "He says the oldest goes by the name Isaiah Potts and the other three could be his sons."

"What's he got on them?" Frank said.

"Nothing much," Bill said. "They have a reputation for petty thievery, but he believes a while back one of the sons got into some trouble in Louisiana over a woman. That's all he could tell me. But I can size up a man and I reckon all four of them are lowlife trash."

That was enough for Frank. He quickly picked up the tracks of four horses heading east and sent a rider back to report this to Kate.

The cowboy rode in on a lathered horse and an

anxious Kate met him at the front door. "You have news, Tom?" she said.

"Ma'am, we haven't found the girls yet," the puncher called Tom said. 'But unless them four turned around, their tracks head east toward the Colorado, though Mr. Cobb doesn't think they have any intention of riding that far. And if they did loop back they'll run into Cody and his riders. Mr. Cobb says we got them in a vise and we'll find them all right. Mrs. Kerrigan, we'll bring Ivy and Shannon back to you, safe and sound."

Kate read the young puncher's eyes and knew he was hiding a terrible truth from her. Bill Cody's description of the four suspects left little doubt about the fate that awaited Ivy and Shannon.

"Perhaps my daughters just wandered off somewhere," Kate said.

"Yeah, that's it, maybe that's what happened," the cowboy said.

But he didn't believe it, and neither did Kate.

It had been Quinn's idea that his mother stay home and wait for the girls.

"You should be here when they get back, Ma," he'd said.

But three hours had passed since Quinn and the others had ridden out, and Kate couldn't bear to be cooped up any longer, not when her children were in danger. She changed into riding clothes, took a .44-40 Winchester from the rack and a box of shells from the drawer. Despite Moses' protests and the wails of the distraught housemaids, she walked out the back door and headed for the barn. Kate had taken only a few steps when she heard someone call her name. She looked around her. "Who's there?"

Kate levered a round into the rifle. "I said, who's there?"

"Look up, Mrs. Kerrigan."

Josiah Mosely's shouting voice came from above her. The hot-air balloon hovered about fifty feet above the ground, Mosely and Cloud Passing looking over the side of the basket. The Indian dropped a couple of sandbag anchors, and Mosely did something with the burner that made the balloon descend slowly. When he got within talking distance he said, "Wind's from the west, Mrs. Kerrigan. We can cover a lot of ground."

After she got over her initial shock, Kate said, "How . . . I mean . . ."

"Cloud Passing repaired the envelope and we dodged hanging posses to find the burner and hydrogen cylinder," Mosely said. "She's still a bit tattered and leaking hydrogen and the basket needs repairing, but she can fly, more or less. Hurry, Mrs. Kerrigan, get on board. We're squandering daylight."

Kate said, "Mr. Mosely, I don't think . . ."

"Cloud Passing will help you into the basket," Mosely said. "You want to find your daughters, don't you? Then the balloon is your best chance."

Despite the anchors the basket floated two feet above the ground, but Cloud Passing picked up Kate as easily as he would a child and carried her to the balloon. "Hand me your rifle, Mrs. Kerrigan," Mosely said. The Indian hoisted Kate into the basket and then effortlessly climbed in himself. Cloud Passing hauled up the anchors, and the balloon soared vertically for fifty feet and then caught the upper level wind and drifted westward.

As the balloon gained altitude Kate closed her eyes and white-knuckled the rim of the basket, blaming herself for letting this happen. She should be on a horse. But Mosely seemed quite unconcerned and continually adjusted the burner or tested the wind. Cloud Passing squatted on the wicker floor and chanted what Kate was convinced was his death song. Up this high the wind blew stronger, and the balloon rocked as it kept on its westward course.

Kate opened her eyes and steeled herself to look down. How tiny her mansion looked from here, and even Bill Cody's sprawling encampment disappeared into insignificance against the backdrop of the vast landscape. For the first time Kate realized just how immense was the KK ranch. From horizon to horizon where herds of sleek cattle grazed, the fair land that stretched on forever was hers, and so too was the great arch of the Texas sky where years before Kate had reached up and grabbed a handful of stars and watched them shimmer in the palm of her hand.

"Riders below," Mosely said.

Kate followed the young man's pointing finger and saw a dozen riders kick up dust as they rode out of a sunken dry wash and then regained the flat. Holding on tight to the basket rim, Kate thought she spotted Frank Cobb's bay in the lead, but she wasn't sure. Up-turned faces followed the progress of the balloon as it glided past, and one of the riders waved. Kate feared to take a hand off the basket and didn't wave back.

"Fine wind, a trade wind," Mosely said, grinning. "We're leaving them far behind."

"Can you see anything ahead of us?" Kate said.

Mosely shook his head. "Nothing but empty range, sand, and sagebrush."

"They may be south of us," Kate said, almost frantic with worry.

"Or north of us," Mosely said. "We'll search on this course a little while longer and then I'll take her up higher and see if we can catch a wind that will take us in a different direction."

"We're at the mercy of the damned wind?" Kate said, her terrible strain erupting into anger.

"I'm afraid so, Mrs. Kerrigan," Mosely said. "You can't steer a balloon like a sailing ship."

Cloud Passing stared critically at Mosely and then shook his head. The Cheyenne didn't seem impressed by the balloon, either.

"Mr. Mosely, we must find my children," Kate said.

"I know, Mrs. Kerrigan," the young man said. "And we will."

But then disaster.

The south wind that had been blowing steadily for most of the day suddenly dropped, and the balloon hung motionless like a red inkblot on the blue parchment of the sky.

"We've lost the wind," Mosely said, stating the obvious. "I'm taking her down."

"Where are we?" Kate said.

"Somewhere in Texas," Mosely said. "That's all I know."

Even with the burner cut, the descent took the best part of five minutes, and the landing was hard. The basket hit the ground and tipped on its side, spilling its three occupants onto an area of cactus and bunchgrass.

Kate scrambled to her feet, and Mosely straightened up his spectacles and gave her a sheepish grin. "Sorry, Mrs. Kerrigan. I never was much of a hand at landing this thing."

Mosely looked like a guilty boy, like Pete when he got caught with his hand in the cookie jar, and Kate did not have the heart to chide him for almost breaking her neck. She picked up her Winchester and said, "I'll search on foot the rest of the way."

Then Cloud Passing surprised her.

His nose lifted, he tested the still air and then said, "Smoke."

"Where?" Kate said. "Wait. Yes, I can smell it. It's close."

This was rolling, hilly country mostly covered in prairie grasses, the most common bluestem and Indian grass. Half a mile to the north lay the southern edge of the cross-timbers region, where stands of wild oak, cedar, and scattered juniper prospered. It was to the tree line that Cloud Passing silently pointed.

"Let's go take a look," Kate said. "Mr. Mosely, are you armed?"

"No, I only flew the balloon," Mosely said. He stared at the ground, unwilling to say what was in his mind.

Mrs. Kerrigan, the next time I take up my revolvers will be my last.

There were revolver-fighting men, and there were others who were not. Kate didn't blame Mosely, and she didn't push him. "Then you stay here with the balloon and tell Frank Cobb where I've gone."

"Maybe you should wait until the others get here," Mosely said.

"There's no time to waste," Kate said. "Just point Frank in the right direction."

"Then take the Indian with you," Mosely said. "If they find him here, more likely than not they'll hang him just to pass the time."

It seemed that Cloud Passing knew more English than he pretended. "I go with the woman," he said.

The Cheyenne carried a bowie knife in a sheath on his belt but no other weapon. Kate took the derringer from her pocket and handed it to him. Cloud Passing stared at the little pistol and looked baffled. Kate took it from him and mimicked pulling back the hammer and pressing the trigger. The Indian smiled and nodded.

"I think he got it, Mrs. Kerrigan," Mosely said.

"I hope so," Kate said. And to Cloud Passing, "Come with me. Let's go find my daughters."

The big Dog Soldier said nothing, his face empty.

"Damn your eyes, stop this squabbling, you ill-begotten whore trash. You can fight for her," Isaiah Potts said. "But no matter who wins, remember I get the first taste."

"Guns or knives, I don't care," Baptist said. "I want both of them."

"One at a time, boy," Potts said. "And the fight for the oldest is with blades. First man cut to the bone is the loser. Use the edge, mind. I'll shoot any of ye that stick with the point."

"Why don't you get in on the fight, old man?" Baptist said.

Potts grinned, revealing few teeth and those black.

"You'd like that, Baptist, wouldn't you? Well, you'll get your chance to kill me, but not today and not over a woman. Bide your time until I find something worth fighting for, like"—he rubbed his thumb and forefinger together—"money . . . munny-munny-munny, huh, boy?"

Baptist nodded. "That time will come sooner or later, and I'm looking forward to it."

"Jerome, Franklin, you two willing to fight for the women?" Potts said.

"Damn right we are, Pa," Jerome said. "I'll take 'em both to wife."

"And I'll gut any man for them," Franklin said. "The oldest one, I never seen a woman as fine as her."

"That's because she ain't a whore, numbskull," Potts said. Then, grinning, "Yet." Potts rose from a rocking chair that continued to thump on the dirt floor after he got to his feet. "Get the lanterns and bring them two outside. Knife fights are always more lively in the dark."

While this conversation was taking place, Ivy and Shannon huddled together in a corner of the filthy cabin. Shannon was terrified and kept her eyes closed as though what she couldn't see didn't exist. But Ivy, older and more schooled in the ways of men, knew exactly what was in store for them. She held Shannon close and whispered, "Ma will come for us, you'll see."

But the girl didn't open her eyes, and she shivered in fear.

Ivy said again. "And Frank will be with her. Our knight in shining armor will ride to the rescue."

* * *

Frank Cobb ran out of tracks around the time he ran out of daylight.

"We can pick them up again at first light," he said to Quinn Kerrigan.

"Frank, I say we press on through the night," Quinn said. "Keep them on the move and give them no rest."

"Quinn, this is a big country," Frank said. "They could have swung north toward the timber or headed for the Rio Grande and Mexico. We'll wait until daybreak and pick up their tracks again."

"And what happens to my sisters in the meantime?" Quinn said.

Sick at heart, Frank Cobb had no answer for that question.

"Me, I'm riding on through the night," Quinn said. "My mind's made up, Frank."

"Then take Chas Minor with you," Frank said. "He's good with the iron."

Quinn stared at Frank for a long while and then said, "There's moonlight, but you still think I'll be wasting my time."

"You'd need a cavalry regiment to scout this big country for tracks, even in moonlight," Frank said. "And then it could be daylight before you find them."

"It can be done and I'm giving it a try," Quinn said with the stubborn certainty of youth. "If Ivy and Shannon are out there, I'll find them."

CHAPTER THIRTY-FOUR

From her hiding place in brush among the oaks Kate Kerrigan studied the ramshackle cabin in the clearing. Beside her she heard the steady breathing of Cloud Passing. It had been the Cheyenne's keen sense of smell that had led her to this place.

The cabin had a swaybacked roof, and it tilted badly to one side. Several slanted pine trunks, one end driven into the ground, supported its weight and kept the whole structure from collapsing. A pole corral holding four horses stood to the right of the cabin, and in the opposite direction a rickety windmill vainly waited for the breathless wind.

Kate pushed her Winchester out in front of her. Were the kidnappers in the cabin or was it just some squatters, perhaps a family? She dismissed that thought immediately. The horses in the corral were of good quality, probably stolen, and the saddles that straddled the top fence post cost more than any forty-a-month puncher could afford. There was no doubt in her mind that this was where her daughters were being held. Already the day was shading darker, and time was of the essence. If she was to attack, it had to be now. There was a window to the front of the cabin, and a couple of shots through the glass would shake things up. But it was too risky. She could easily hit Ivy or Shannon. Right, then she'd shoot high, where the cabin roof met the wall. That way there was less chance of harming her girls. Kate figured she could keep the kidnappers pinned down in the cabin all night if necessary until help got there. Surely Frank and the others would hear the shooting and come on at a gallop.

Kate nodded. Of course they would. They must.

She shouldered the Winchester, but Cloud Passing pushed it down and shook his head. "Woman, look," he whispered.

Kate saw that the cabin door had opened. A moment later a shaggy, ragged man stepped outside, followed by three others who were younger versions of himself. The older men lit half-a-dozen oil lamps that formed a circle around a patch of level ground. He then walked back inside the cabin and reappeared a few moments later pushing Ivy and Shannon ahead of him. The man wore a gun but the younger men were unarmed.

Kate's breath came in quick little gasps and she felt ice in her stomach. She was terrified, not for herself but for her daughters, who'd been pushed away from the circle and now stood holding onto one another and looked heartachingly young and vulnerable.

Kate quickly made up her mind.

She'd drop the older man with her first shot and then the three others. But even as she planned her play she knew she couldn't pull the trigger. At a distance of nearly a hundred yards and in failing light she wasn't a good enough rifle shot to guarantee a hit on the older man and if she missed he might panic and kill the girls. The smoke from her rifle would give her position away, and Kate knew that a gun duel with four outlaws was not a fight she could hope to win. Frustrated, afraid for her children, she lowered her head onto the stock of her rifle. Ivy and Shannon were right there, standing in front of her, and there was not a thing she could do to save them.

Beside Kate, Cloud Passing grunted and nudged her with his elbow. Kate raised her head and looked toward the cabin again. Ivy, looking scared, had crossed her arms over the top part of her camisole. Her white blouse with its lace top had been torn from her body by the older man and now he tore it into strips. As Kate watched the man knotted several of these together, making a single strip about three feet long. He stepped into the circle formed by the lamps and beckoned to a pair of the younger men to join him.

Kate's heart raced in her chest and beside her Cloud Passing chanted under his breath. The Cheyenne tensed, his black eyes intent on the men within the glowing circle of lamps. Kate guessed that Cloud Passing was singing a war song and that the warrior Dog Soldier was taking over, transforming a blanket Indian into one of the most feared fighting men on earth.

Outside the cabin the older man held up the knotted strip of cloth and the two others in the circle each grabbed an end in their left hand and drew bowies with eight-inch blades from the sheaths on their waists.

Crouched, their knives held low and ready, the combatants waited until the older man stepped out of the circle . . . and the fight was on.

At that time in the West knife fighting was based on the swordplay of the New Orleans fencing schools run by masters like the famous duelist and fencer Jose Lulla. The New Orleans style of edged-weapon combat was used effectively by James Bowie and others, but on the frontier it became a rough-and-tumble affair. Knife against knife fights did occasionally occur, but more often the blade was used in conjunction with any other weapon that came to hand, including brass knuckles, chairs, clubs, rocks, and firearms.

Schooled by their father, the Potts boys fought in the classic style, blade to blade, using the parries, attacks, and returns taught by the fencing masters.

Forbidden to use the point but revealing considerable skill with the bowie's edge, Baptist systematically cut up his brother Franklin while he escaped without a scratch. When Franklin's slashed face became a scarlet mask of blood and he could no longer see to fight, Isaiah called the match and declared Baptist the victor.

Then as Jerome stood outside the circle and practiced his fighting moves, Baptist made the mistake that would be his death.

Flushed with pride over his victory, he walked quickly toward Ivy and before the girl could react, he grabbed her and his hungry, lusting mouth sought hers. Ivy struggled and did what Franklin could not— she drew blood. Her nails raked Baptist's cheek, and the man bellowed in rage. Savagely, he backhanded Ivy across the face, and the girl staggered and fell.

Kate Kerrigan's bullet hit Baptist where his left earlobe met the side of his neck. The man screamed and fell. Cloud Passing shrieked his war cry and ran toward Jerome.

An enraged female cougar protecting her young, Kate Kerrigan advanced on Isaiah Potts, working her Winchester from the hip. In the dying light, surprised by the suddenness and ferocity of Kate's attack, Potts raised his Colt to eye level and fired. His bullet split air an inch from Kate's head and she went down on one knee, shouldered her rifle, and triggered a shot.

Cloud Passing's attack took Jerome Potts by surprise. He assumed a crouched blade-fighting position, but the Dog Soldier startled him a second time. Instead of going knife to knife as Jerome expected, Cloud Passing launched himself at the white man, his bowie raised in his hand. The Indian slammed into Jerome's chest and they both hit the dirt hard. But Cloud Passing was fast, very fast. His knife rose and fell, and the blade plunged deep behind Jerome's collarbone. It was a killing blow, and the white man knew it. He shrieked in pain and terror. He was still alive when Cloud Passing scalped him.

Kate's bullet missed Isaiah Potts, and she levered another round into the chamber of the Winchester, her body tense, expecting his bullet. But Potts, a sure-thing killer, did not have the belly for a close-range gunfight. He turned and scampered inside the cabin, the frightfully bloody Franklin close on his heels. Kate slammed a couple of shots into the cabin window, shattering glass but as far as she knew scoring no hits. Cloud Passing was a ways off prancing out a scalp dance and it would be a long time before he regained what for him was normality. But he was in great danger of being shot from the cabin and Kate yelled at him to get down. The Cheyenne ignored her and Kate shot into the cabin again to keep heads down.

Ivy and Shannon ran to her, but Kate had no time to celebrate their reunion. "Into the trees," she said. "And stay there."

"Ma . . ." Ivy began.

"Later," Kate said. "Now do as I say."

The side of Ivy's face was badly bruised, her right eye swollen shut, and Kate fired into the cabin again and again, levering the Winchester dry. She hoped she'd killed somebody.

Kate reloaded the rifle from the box of shells in her skirt pocket and then looked up and saw something that chilled her to the bone . . .

Baptist Potts was slowly getting to his feet.

The man staggered upright, saw Kate, and stumbled toward her, his knife in his hand. Kate's bullet had shattered Baptist's chin and it hung loose and bloody, a grotesque sight. He made a strange, feral sound in his throat, and his yellow eyes were filled with hate.

Kate watched him come . . . the man who had kidnapped and then struck her daughter. She raised the Winchester to her shoulder. It was now too dark to use the sights. Baptist hurried his pace. The man's face was a grotesque mask of bone and blood, a walking nightmare.

Now! Kate fired.

Hit hard, Baptist staggered, but kept to his feet. Kate fired again, racked the lever, and fired a third time. The man went down . . . and stayed down.

Kate didn't even look at his still body. She again turned her attention to the cabin.

"Hello, you out there!"

A man's voice from inside the cabin.

"What do you want?" Kate said.

"We're shot all to pieces. We want to come out."

Kate rose to her feet. "Throw down your weapons and come out with your hands up. Walk into the lamplight circle in front of the cabin where I can see you."

Cloud Passing had stopped dancing. He stood perfectly still in the moon-silvered darkness, Jerome's scalp hanging from his hand as he stared at the cabin.

"They're coming out," Kate said.

The Cheyenne turned his head to look in her direction, but he said nothing.

The cabin door opened, and Kate kept a tighter grip on the Winchester.

Isaiah Potts stepped out first, his son Franklin, bloody from head to waist, behind him. Both had their hands raised, and the older man seemed to be wounded. They walked through darkness into the orange circle of the lamplight. "We need a doctor, you bitch," Isaiah said, the last words he ever spoke.

A moment later he and his son were cut down by a steady hammer of gunfire.

Quinn Kerrigan, the gun slick Chas Minor at his

side, emerged from the gloom. Both carried smoking rifles.

"Quinn, they had surrendered," Kate said. "They were unarmed."

"Mrs. Kerrigan, we saw Miss Ivy's face," Minor said.

"They were mad dogs, Ma," Quinn said.

Kate hesitated for a moment and then said, "Well, don't do that again."

Quinn Kerrigan and Chas Minor dragged the dead Pottses into the cabin and then set it on fire. With the resilience of youth, Ivy and Shannon, riders since they could walk, mounted a couple of the dead men's horses and Kate rode another. For some reason known only to himself, Cloud Passing decided to walk, and he trotted beside Kate's mount.

Josiah Mosely was where Kate and the Cheyenne had left him, and his inflated balloon tugged on its sandbag anchors. "Heard the shooting," he said. "I'm glad you're all right. Miss Ivy, I'm sorry about your face."

Ivy managed a smile. "Thank you, Mr. Mosely. The swelling makes it look much worse than it is. I'll be fine in a couple of days."

"Ma, Frank Cobb and them will have coffee," Quinn said. "If you don't mind riding in the dark."

"Mr. Mosely, what about you?" Kate said,

"I'll take the balloon up at first light and see if I can catch a west wind," Mosely said. "I may have to scrape blue paint off the sky before I find one."

"Can you take a passenger?" Kate said.

"Of course," Mosely said.

"Then I'll fly with you," Kate said. "I need the sky to make me feel clean again."

Quinn said, "No, Ma, that balloon thing is way too dangerous."

"And that's exactly why I want to do it," Kate said. "Take my horse, and then you and the others go on. I'll catch up."

"I can't let you do that, Ma," Quinn said.

"Quinn's right, Mrs. Kerrigan, you could break your neck in that contraption," Chas Minor said.

Kate frowned. "Quinn, children don't tell their parents what they should and should not do," she said. "Mr. Minor, that also applies to employees and employers. Do you understand?"

Minor touched his hat brim. "Sure do, boss."

"Quinn?" Kate said.

"Likewise, Ma."

"Good, then it's settled," Kate said. "Mr. Mosely, we'll ascend, if that's the correct expression, at dawn and try to reach the last morning star."

CHAPTER THIRTY-FIVE

"Is it broken, Doctor?" Kate Kerrigan said.

"You're lucky, Mrs. Kerrigan. It's only a bad sprain. But you're very bruised."

Bill Cody's full-time physician Dr. Zebulon Farrell gently lowered Kate's foot to the ground and then, as he rummaged in his bag, said, "I'll wrap the ankle good and tight, but you'll need to stay off of it for at least a week." He held a rolled bandage in his hand and said, "Did you twist it walking?"

"No. I was in a hot-air balloon that made a hard landing," Kate said.

The doctor's eyebrow crawled up his forehead like a hairy caterpillar. "You mean a flying machine?"

"Yes. A balloon flying machine."

"My advice is to stay away from those in the future," Dr. Farrell said. "If God had meant us to fly, he would have given us wings. Was anyone else hurt?"

"No. The pilot is a man named Josiah Mosely, and he escaped with some cuts and bruises."

"Nevertheless I should take a look at him," the physician said. "Flying machines indeed, yet another modern fad that will kill and injure scores of people before it's all over."

After he bound up Kate's ankle, Dr. Farrell said that he could give her a sedative and something for pain. But Kate refused. She needed her mind to be sharp when Slide McKenzie came to collect his hundred thousand. Maybe there was some way out of paying his extortion money, but she very much doubted it. She was facing ruin, and she had a sprained ankle. One or the other would have been more than enough, but both at the same time was intolerable.

After the doctor left, the parlor maid opened Kate's bedroom door and said that Frank Cobb wished to talk with her.

"Show him in, Winifred," Kate said.

A moment later Frank stepped inside, his hat in his hands. "What did the pill pusher say, Kate? Is the ankle broke?"

"No," Kate said. "It's just a sprain, but Dr. Farrell told me to stay off my feet for a week."

Kate sat in a chair, her foot supported by a stool and a pile of cushions.

"Glad to hear it," Frank said. He waited long moments before he spoke again and then he said, "You did good yesterday, Kate, showed a lot of sand."

"I killed another man," Kate said.

"It's the cost of empire building, Kate. The British killed tens of thousands to build an empire on which the sun never sets, and slaughtering so many never seemed to trouble them much. Besides, those Potts boys needed killing."

"Is that what they were called?" Kate said. "Did you know them, Frank?"

"I heard rumors that they'd left the Trinity River and were headed this way, but I never set much store by it. They say old Isaiah was a cannibal, but I never set store by that, either. No matter, the world's a better place without his shadow falling on it."

"The older man had surrendered when Quinn and Minor gunned him down," Kate said. "Him and one of his sons."

Frank shrugged. "Sometimes surrendering comes just a tad too late."

"My empire will fall, Frank," Kate said. "Another couple of days and it will be no more. But my son will be alive, and that's what matters."

"Don't despair just yet, Kate," Frank said. "We'll find a way."

"I don't share your confidence," Kate said. Then, "Where is Cloud Passing?"

"Locked up. Quinn says he scalped somebody else, huh? Danced around with it."

"Yes, a man he'd killed in fair fight. Don't all Indians do that?"

"Some of them, yes."

"Cloud Passing didn't murder those cowboys, Frank."

"Most folks say he did, and the majority plans to hang him."

"It may be the last thing I do as owner of the KK, but I won't let them hang Cloud Passing," Kate said.

"Kate, face it, he's as guilty as sin," Frank said. "You have enough problems on your plate as it is, and you don't need another."

"I won't see an innocent man hang," Kate said. "And one more thing, Frank, he fought beside me last night and probably saved my life. That's not something I can forget. I can't turn my back on him now."

"Kate, there hasn't been another killing since the Indian went on the scout," Frank said. "Don't you find that strange?"

"No, I don't, because the real killer had a grudge against the three cowboys, and now his murder spree is over," Kate said. "There will be no more killings, Frank."

"I know there won't, now that the Indian is chained to a post behind Bill Cody's tent," Frank said.

"Like a wild animal?" Kate said.

Frank said, "He's a Cheyenne Dog Soldier, remember? He is a wild animal, and mighty dangerous."

"See that Cloud Passing has blankets and proper food," Kate said. "I'll get to him as soon as I can."

"The doc told you to stay off your feet for a week," Frank said. "The Indian's trial is set for three days from now. Hiram Clay will be the judge."

Kate was surprised. "I didn't know that."

"Bill Cody says he won't sit in judgment on the Indian and he passed the job to Clay," Frank said. "From what I've been told Clay has no love for the red man."

"Hiram's oldest son was a West Pointer, an officer in the Ninth Cavalry," Kate said. "In 1870 he was killed by Apaches in the New Mexico Territory. Hiram's wife never got over her son's death, and she followed him to the grave less than a year later."

"And that's why Clay is down on Indians," Frank said. "Bad news for your Cheyenne, Kate."

"There will be much happening in the next few days," Kate said. "It's a bad time to be laid up with a sprained ankle."

"I'll take care of your interests," Frank said. "Including Slide McKenzie."

"Frank, he gets the money and leaves," Kate said. "There is no negotiating on that point."

"Quinn and me have a plan," Frank said. "We think it has a good chance of working."

Kate frowned. "What kind of plan?"

"I can't tell you yet, Kate," Frank said. "Quinn wants to keep it a secret until we work out all the details."

"Will my other son's life be in danger?" Kate said.

"I'll take care of Quinn," Frank said, lowering his eye from Kate's gaze.

And Kate knew that was no answer at all.

CHAPTER THIRTY-SIX

Dr. Zebulon Farrell gave Josiah Mosely a clean bill of health. "Apart from the broken finger and some cuts and bruises you're fine," he said.

"How is Mrs. Kerrigan?" Mosely said.

"And a handsome woman she is," the physician said.

"How is her injury, Doctor?" Mosely said.

Farrell returned from a pink-tinted daydream, harrumphed, and said, "A sprained ankle. She'll be on her feet in a week or so."

"Is she angry?" Mosely said.

"With you?"

"Yes, me."

"Not in the least. That fair creature has no room in her bosom to harbor anger. Hers is a most loving nature."

"We made a hard landing," Mosely said. "The balloon scraped some treetops, and the basket hit the ground on its side."

"A dangerous business, Mr. Mosely." Dr. Farrell snapped his bag shut. "Leave the splint on the finger and come and see me in two weeks."

After the doctor left Mosely studied his injured right hand. The ring finger had fractured when he'd used his hand to break his fall, and the doctor had splinted it with a thin piece of wood and surgical tape. Farrell had left a small roll of tape as a precaution and warned, "If the existing tape gets wet from bathing and begins to fall apart, get one of the servants to put on some new strips or come see me right away."

Josiah Mosely had no intention of doing either.

The splint made it impossible to hold a revolver, and he would very soon need his gun hand. He rose and locked his bedroom door. Sometimes Kate's nosy maids barged right inside without even a knock. Mosely then sat on the bed and prepared himself for what had to be done. The middle joint of his finger was broken, but the whole digit was bruised and swollen and excruciatingly painful. Slowly, bit by bit, Mosely removed the tape, his tormented breath hissing through clenched teeth. At one point he thought he'd blacked out for a few moments, but he wasn't sure. Finally, he removed all the tape and the splint . . . and now the real agony began. Using his pocketknife Mosely cut off a foot of tape at a time and began to tightly bind the broken finger to his pinkie, gasping as shrieking agony stabbed at him. It took time. Patience. Piece of tape by piece of tape, Mosely slowly, painfully, joined the fingers together and when he finished the broken finger was bound to its neighbor in an incestuous embrace.

Mosely rose from the bed, wiped tears of pain from his face, poured himself a glass of bourbon, and gulped it down. He was trembling, and the glass rattled as he laid it back on the table. For a moment he considered lying down for a while but knew he would not rest. He had to test the hand.

Unbuckling the straps of the carpetbag with his good hand was a chore, but the throbbing ache in his fingers warned him that worse was to come. He removed the British Bulldogs and laid them side by side on the bed. He picked up a revolver in his left hand and then the other in his right. Pain slammed at him and he yelped in agony.

Mother of God, this is impossible!

He dropped the revolver and it lay on the cathedral window quilt mocking him, a deadly weapon but with its graceful curves and gleaming blue metal a thing of lethal beauty.

Mosely tried again. This time he let his thumb, forefinger, and middle finger do the work. The broken finger and pinkie were not engaged, but he couldn't shoot the hard-recoiling Bulldog like that. He grasped the gun again with all five fingers and almost cried out as he was hit time after time with jagged blades of pain, like being cut with a rusty razor. He pulled the trigger. *Click.* Again. *Click.* Again, the beautiful hammer rising and falling. *Click.* He imagined the Bulldog bucking in his hand, recoiling violently, thrashing him. But he could do it. He could use the gun. The agony would be intense, but brief, because he'd be dead very quickly.

Mosely dropped the Bulldog onto the bed and again reached for the bottle.

His right hand, his gun hand, pulsed pain and he

trembled all over, like a fearful man climbing the thirteen steps to the gallows.

Before seeking the sleep that always eluded him, Josiah Mosely took solace in Mr. Dickens's *A Tale of Two Cities.* As he'd done often in the past few days he turned to the last chapter of the novel and Sydney Carton's words before his terrible death: *It is a far, far better thing that I do, than I have ever done; it is a far, far better rest I go to than I have ever known.*

It was a noble sentiment, one that Mosely applied to himself. But when the time came could he die as bravely as Sydney Carton? He had no answer to that question. Though his future was measured in days, in hours, it remained shuttered and dark to him.

CHAPTER THIRTY-SEVEN

Cloud Passing dreamed of buffalo and he saw his Sioux woman, dead this seven years, follow the herd on a white pony. He called out to her in his dream, and she turned her head and smiled her beautiful smile at him. Her hair was as he remembered it, long and black as night, shiny as a raven's wing. Her name was *Anpaytoo* in the Dakota tongue. That meant Radiant One. She beckoned to him to come follow the mighty herd that blotted out the sun with its dust, but he was unable to move, as though bound hand and foot, and could only watch as Anpaytoo and the buffalo rode into shimmering distance and vanished from his sight.

Cloud Passing woke with a start. For a fleeting moment he thought the buffalo herd had returned, but it was only the cough of an old bull in the enclosure. The Cheyenne angrily tugged at his bonds, but he was roped securely to a timber post driven three feet into the ground. The moon rode high in the sky, spreading its light, and somewhere beyond the compound the silvered coyotes yipped. There was no sound from the sleeping camp, but Cloud Passing heard Bill Cody mutter as he turned in his cot.

The Cheyenne closed his eyes and dozed and slowly his head sank onto his chest. His warrior awareness woke him as footsteps, light and almost silent, came toward him. Cloud Passing smiled. It was the woman Bill Cody called Little Sure Shot, but her name was Annie Oakley, and she was good with a Winchester and would keep a man's lodge well supplied with meat. He would like her as a wife.

Annie wore a drab brown robe over her night attire, and she held a Green River thin-bladed knife in her hand. "How are you doing, Injun?" she said.

Wary now, Cloud Passing smiled and nodded.

"Ain't one for conversation, are you?" the girl said. "You're getting out of here. Go find your tribe or something."

Annie slashed at the ropes, and within a couple of minutes the Cheyenne was free. He rose to his feet on stiff knees and rubbed his wrists. "Now git," Annie said.

Cloud Passing stared at her, not quite understanding what was happening. The girl had freed him, but why?

"I go now?" he said.

"Yeah, beat it, scat, vamoose, disappear. You catch my drift?" Annie said.

Cloud Passing nodded, but stayed where he was.

"Injun, if you don't get the hell out of here, they'll string you up higher than an East Texas pine," Annie said. "Now light a shuck. Wait, here, take this knife."

The Cheyenne took the blade and nodded. "I go."

Without another word he turned and walked into the gloom.

"And don't ever come back, Injun," Annie whispered.

Awakened by voices, Bill Cody tossed and turned on his cot and couldn't get back to sleep. Finally, he rose, threw on his robe, and built a cigarette, a tobacco habit he'd picked up from his Texas cowboys who were much addicted to it. He stepped out of the tent, thumbed a match into flame, and lit his smoke. Now was a good time to check on the Indian. The post was still intact, but the ropes lay on the ground in pieces, and of Cloud Passing there was no sign.

Bill Cody shook his head, sighed deeply, and then finished his cigarette. He returned to his cot, quickly fell asleep, and didn't raise the alarm until he woke up five hours later.

Once again search parties were organized, but a young horse wrangler summed up the feelings of the riders when he told Bill Cody, "Getting mighty tired of this, Colonel. If I catch up with the son of a bitch I'll just put a bullet in him."

After the surly posse rode out, everybody else in a shooting or hanging frame of mind, Bill studied the ground near the post. As he expected there were tracks of booted feet and a few of Cloud Passing's moccasin prints, but what caught his attention and made him wonder was the fact that smaller feet had been there, a woman's feet. She'd worn bedroom slippers with a flat sole and heel, and her prints were barely there. Whoever she was, the woman was small and light and did not tread heavily on the earth.

Several women with the show fitted that description but why would any of them free an accused murderer and a dangerous savage to boot? Bill pensively stroked his chin and decided that nothing about this affair made any sense. Maybe the woman, whoever she was, had come to visit, to say howdy. It was a great mystery and anything was possible.

Bill was about to step back into his tent to clear some paperwork when a woman's voice stopped him. He let the tent flap drop, turned, and saw Polly Coulter. A girl saved from plainness by a mane of beautiful chestnut hair that played well in the arena, she was dressed for riding and had a revolver on her hip. Bill cut an elaborate bow and said, "May I say that you look divine this morning, Miss Polly?"

"You may say it, but you don't mean it," Polly said. "The only man who ever talked pretties to me and meant them was Davy Hoyle."

"Don't sell yourself short, dear lady," Bill said. "Do I mean divine, as in lovely, ravishing, stunning, and alluring? Why, of course I do. And Buffalo Bill Cody has never been known to tell an untruth."

Polly Coulter let that go and said, "Who cut the Indian loose?"

"That, I do not know," Bill said. "But I plan to inquire into the matter."

"The Cheyenne didn't kill Davy or Andy Porter or Buck Nolan, either," Polly said. She looked pale, like a woman who had been in considerable emotional pain for some time.

Surprised, Bill said, "Then who did? Do you know?"

"No, I don't know. But I can tell you this, the day Davy signed on with the show he was a dead man, and so were the other two. Someone had seen them, someone with an ax to grind, and from that moment they were marked men."

"And who was that someone, Polly?" Bill said. "Have you any idea at all? A woman's intuition, perhaps?"

"I told you, I don't know."

"A man? A woman?"

"Either. Maybe both," Polly said.

"Why?" Bill said. "Why kill with such savagery . . . so much blood."

"Could be the answer lies in something Davy told me one time when he'd drank too much whiskey. He said him and Andy and Buck had done something real bad that they were ashamed of, something so low down he couldn't tell me what it was."

"A killing, maybe?" Bill said.

"Like I said, he wouldn't tell me. But I'm sure whatever it was got him and the others murdered."

"Well, where do I go from here?" Bill said. "I think this mysterious business calls for a Pinkerton."

"Why don't you ask Mrs. Kerrigan?" Polly said. "She seems to know all the answers."

"Maybe so," Bill said. "But I'm damned if I know all the questions."

BOOK THREE

Descent into Hell

CHAPTER THIRTY-EIGHT

It was a bad day for Slide McKenzie.

Bat Boswell brought the appalling news after kicking McKenzie, none too gently, awake. The man sat up in his blankets and made angry, questioning noises through his clenched teeth.

"Prepare yourself for a shock, Slide," he said.

McKenzie growled, untied the knotted cloth at the top of his head and said, "What?" That one word caused him considerable pain and he winced.

"The whole damned Mexican army is camped on your doorstep," Bat said. "I think they're looking for you."

Sky Boswell grinned. "Infantry, cavalry, and cannons. They must reckon you're a mighty dangerous man."

McKenzie retied the bandage, again giving himself floppy rabbit ears. He pulled on his boots and stepped out of the mission, the Boswell brothers on his heels.

When he saw the sight that greeted him, McKenzie groaned.

Mexicans flooded across the river like Israelites

crossing the Red Sea . . . and the reason was not hard
to find. Wagons, piled high with round loaves of
bread, burlap sacks of beans, and casks of wine were
parked among soldiers who were already distributing
the provisions to the starving peons.

Slide McKenzie's eyes almost popped out of their
sockets. He ran into the mission and returned holding high the statue of the Santo Muerte. McKenzie
held the skull-topped effigy above his head, but hand-
icapped by his broken jaw, he was unable to implore
the Mexicans to come back to the land of milk and
honey. He gestured with the effigy, holding it as high
as his strength would allow, but the peons ignored
him. When it comes to a choice between bread and
beans or a wooden saint, starving people will choose
the grub every time.

But McKenzie, frantic and looking more than ever
like a deranged jackrabbit, splashed into the river,
making strangled noises in his throat as he tried to
wave the Mexicans back to dry land. But most of them
were now being fed by the soldiers, and an officer
stood on the back of a wagon and yelled a speech.
McKenzie heard cheers and yelling as the Mexicans
were assured that the famine in Chihuahua and Durango was over and they could return to their villages.

The statue of Santo Muerte dropped at his feet,
McKenzie cut a forlorn figure as he stood on the river-
bank alone. Then he lifted his head as a dozen lancers
led by a resplendent officer splashed across the Rio
Grande shallows on high-stepping horses. The officer
halted the detail and then kneed his mount closer
to McKenzie. In perfect English he said, "I should

have you shot. The people were starving, those who believed your lies."

McKenzie moved to untie his bandage but the officer said, "There is no need for that. You told the peons that you would lead them north where there was land and cattle for the taking. And you used the statue to make them believe you were an *hombre santo*, a holy man. Is that not so?"

McKenzie nodded, but his black eyes were defiant.

"The land north of here is owned by the Señora Kate Kerrigan," the officer said. "Had you taken the people there, the State of Texas would have considered it a Mexican invasion, and we would have a war on our hands. Our nation is still recovering from the corrupt rule of Benito Juárez, and the last thing we need is a war. Do you understand?"

McKenzie nodded, his swollen face surly. But unwilling to remain silent, he untied the wrapping around his jaw and said, slowly and painfully, "That's all a pack of lies, General. I never promised them anything."

"Hiram H. Clay of the Texas Cattleman's Association is a man of integrity, and it was he who alerted President Díaz by wire of the situation here on the river. It was no lie, as I've seen for myself." The officer beckoned to a lancer and said something to him. The soldier kneed his horse forward, lowered his lance, and placed its steel point against McKenzie's throat.

The officer said, "I am Colonel Martin Rios and my orders were not to kill you, McKenzie. But after this if I see you again on either side of the Rio Grande I will have you shot."

Rios swung his horse away, and the lancer followed

him, but the soldier left his calling card, a glistening ruby on McKenzie's scrawny throat.

Unwilling to suffer the pain from his unbound jaw when he tried to talk, Slide McKenzie decided to write his words. He didn't like talking to the Boswell boys anyway. He stepped into the saddle and then took a tally book and a stub of pencil from his shirt pocket. He scribbled a note and handed it to Bat.

KEEP KERRIGAN ALIVE UNTIL I GET BACK

The gunman grinned and touched his hat. "Sure will, Slide. Pity you lost so much of your bargaining power. All them Mexicans have gone with the army."

Flushed with anger, McKenzie wrote again.

I STILL HAVE KERRIGAN

Then, after Boswell read the note, McKenzie dashed off another.

I PLAN TO BREAK HIS JAW AND THEN GUN HIM

Bat Boswell nodded. "A laudable ambition, Slide. Make him suffer as you are suffering, poor thing, huh?"

McKenzie nodded.

"One more little item, Slide," Boswell said. "I mean, it's hardly worth mentioning."

McKenzie scowled his question and Bat said, "Don't come back here empty handed."

A quick scribble.

I'LL GET THE MONEY.

Sky Boswell looked up at McKenzie, his eyes icy. "And don't even think about not coming back at all."

McKenzie wrote again.

SO LONG AS KERRIGAN STILL BREATHES
I'LL BE BACK.

Bat Boswell said, "Don't worry, Slide, he'll be here when you return with the money. We'll fatten him up for you."

Sky looked at his brother. "Fatten him? There's barely enough grub left for us."

Bat shrugged. "Hell, we'll feed him his horse."

CHAPTER THIRTY-NINE

Cloud Passing jogged north through the brightening morning, heading for the only place he felt safe, the grove of oaks where he and Josiah Mosely had repaired the balloon. The morning sun slanted through the tree canopies, pinyon jays quarreled among the branches, and insects made their small music in the grass, but there was no sign of Josiah Mosely.

Cloud Passing grunted, stepped into the middle of a clearing, and hunkered down to wait. He was sure that sooner or later Mosely would show, and maybe he would bring grub.

But at that moment, his taped-up hand hidden behind his back, Josiah Mosely perched uncomfortably on the edge of a chair in Kate Kerrigan's parlor, balancing a cup of tea on his lap as he said his farewells. Kate sat in silence as her lady's maid brushed her shining, luxuriant mane, and her green eyes never left Mosely's face. His lopsided glasses and unruly hair gave him the look of a slightly deranged college professor.

Mosely spoke with a lump in his throat. "I have enjoyed my stay, Mrs. Kerrigan, but I've imposed on your hospitality long enough, and I have to be moving on."

Not long from bed, Kate's magnificent body was still warm, and Mosely fancied that he could feel its perfumed heat.

"You have not imposed on me in the least," Kate said. "In fact I have enjoyed your company and my wonderful balloon flights."

Mosely blushed and stammered, "I'm sorry about your ankle, Mrs. Kerrigan."

The horrified maid momentarily paused in her brushing since any mention by a gentleman of a lady's body part was a serious breach of etiquette, but Kate merely smiled and said, "A sprained ankle is a small price to pay for touching the sky, Mr. Mosely. Are you sure I cannot convince you to stay for just a while longer?"

"No, ma'am, my bags are packed, and I'm leaving today," Mosely said.

"Then your mind is made up. You've made many friends here, Mr. Mosely," Kate said, a small lie. "Do come back and see us." She extended her hand, and Mosely took it in his and bowed. "Will you make it rain somewhere?" Kate said. "In your red balloon?"

"Yes," Mosely said. "And I will bring the thunder and the lightning."

He and Kate stared into each other's eyes for long moments, and finally Kate said, "May God go with you, Mr. Mosely."

* * *

The balloon was tethered about a mile north of the Kerrigan mansion and tugged on its rope anchors like a Thoroughbred eager for the track. Mosely tossed his carpetbags inside and then climbed into the basket. After the straw and alcohol spirits in the burner were alight and the hydrogen heated, the envelope swelled, and he hauled in the sandbag anchors. Once aloft it was Mosely's intention to catch a south wind, but the breeze, such as it was, pushed him north at barely treetop height. About a mile ahead of him he saw something run out of the oaks. A man? Or was it a deer? The wind dropped, and the balloon scudded across the flat, the basket only five or six feet above the ground. Mosely's eyesight was not of the best, but he made out the figure of a man. Whoever he was, the man waved his arms, trying to catch Mosely's attention, and he ran back and forth, obviously trying to anticipate the balloon's errant path. The basket bounced across the grass, sometimes bounding ten feet into the air before dropping again. With his good hand Mosely held on to the basket for dear life and saw the male figure run toward him. The man wore buckskins, and his long hair streamed as he sprinted, for the basket. Now Mosely recognized him as Cloud Passing.

"No! Go away!" Mosely yelled, frantically waving his hand. "Bad Indian!"

He knew he was going to his death, but Cloud Passing had no need to die with him. It was a moral dilemma, but two events resolved it for Josiah Mosely. The first was that Cloud Passing jumped for the basket and held on to the rim, his feet dangling. The second was the arrival of a cowboy posse that was all too delighted to take potshots at the balloon and its occupants.

Mosely left the balloon to its own devices and grabbed Cloud Passing's wrists. The Cheyenne was a big man and heavy, but between Mosely's hauling and the Indian's scrambling, Cloud Passing managed to tumble into the basket. Bullets ripped into the wicker, and Mosely figured they were done for, but then the fickle prairie wind finally decided to cooperate. A random gust hurtled the balloon skyward, and when Mosely looked down the posse had shrunk into insignificance, like so many scurrying ants. Now and then he saw a puff of smoke from a rifle, but the soaring balloon was well out of range.

Cloud Passing, normally a stone-faced man, stared at Mosely and grinned from ear to ear.

"That was fun, huh?" Mosely said, irritated. "You almost got me killed, and those rannies were shooting at you, not me."

"Where we go, Mose-ly?" Cloud Passing said.

"South, if I can catch an upper-level wind."

"Then I go with you," the Cheyenne said.

Mosely shook his head. "I need to go alone. I have something I must do."

"I go," Cloud Passing said. "I no want to stay here and get hung."

"You could die, understand? I mean kick the bucket, perish, expire, turn up your toes, get your suspenders cut. Die. Catch my drift?"

"I go with you," the Indian said. Then, after a while, "Cheyenne already dead. Gone. Swept away by the wind." He smiled. "Bill Cody say that . . . *the Red Man was swept away by the wind.*"

Mosely straightened his glasses and looked into Cloud Passing's black eyes and to his surprise he saw ancient pain. "Then we're both doomed, you and I," he said.

Cloud Passing made a gesture with his hand. "Swept away by the wind, Mose-ly."

"Then we'll hope it's one that will sweep us south," Mosely said.

CHAPTER FORTY

His hat pulled low over his eyes to shade him from the relentless sun, Slide McKenzie did not see the hot-air balloon that passed over his head as it was thrown around the sky by a fitful wind. Had he noticed, he probably wouldn't have given the craft a second thought, wrapped up as he was in a cocoon of pain, fury, and greed.

It was his third day on the trail north and he held his bony mustang to a walk, his mind working.

His first thought was to pick up the ransom money and keep on riding. Now that the Mexicans were back across the Rio Grande, it was a viable option, since he wouldn't need to share with the Boswell brothers. But that meant forgoing his revenge on Trace Kerrigan and leaving angry Boswells on his back trail, a bad move. Slide forced his mouth open and spat over the side of his horse, and strands of saliva dripped from his chin. No, it was out of the question. His throbbing jaw had helped him make up his mind. Among the finds he'd discovered at the mission was an old leather glove reinforced with metal plates and spiked studs across the knuckles. It was a fearsome weapon that could shatter a man's jaw with one punch. Trace Kerrigan's jaw. He'd let the pretty boy suffer until his jaw suppurated and then he'd kill him. Slowly. The mental picture that formed in McKenzie's brain thrilled him, and suddenly the day seemed brighter and he looked forward to soon acquiring his new-found wealth.

McKenzie drew rein and tested the level of the water in his canteen. It was low, but he was on Kerrigan range and was not far from the ranch house. He tilted the canteen to his mouth and drank through clenched teeth, water running down his cheeks and chin. When he finished he rubbed his sleeve across his wet mouth then looked up and saw riders coming toward him out of the heat haze. Two of them, taking their time.

McKenzie slid a Winchester from the boot and carried it upright, the butt on his right thigh. He watched the riders come.

They were two young men, riding blood horses. McKenzie figured that one could be a Kerrigan. The other older rider had the hard-eyed, ready look of a seasoned draw fighter. That man was tense, dangerous, and he'd be almighty sudden.

Slide McKenzie nodded. And then Frank Cobb stared at his bound-up chin and said, "What the hell are you?"

"Jaw's broke," McKenzie said, tightly.

"Are you Slide McKenzie?" This from the younger man.

McKenzie nodded.

"I'm Quinn Kerrigan, Trace's brother."

McKenzie realized that he was treading on egg-
shells. Both these men had reason to kill him. He
decided to brass it out. Removing his hat, he untied
the jaw band, and said, painfully, "Mrs. Kerrigan is expecting me." He quickly retied the bandage and some
of the pain eased.

"You're a sorry piece of trash, McKenzie," Frank
said.

"I know what I am," the man said, forcing out each
word from his shattered jaw.

"Boot the rifle, now, or I'll kill you," Frank said.

McKenzie managed an insolent smile and then slid
the Winchester back into the scabbard.

"You come with us," Quinn said. "And on the way
give us an excuse to gun you."

"Not likely, Mary Ann," McKenzie said, his strangled
voice thin as a wire.

Kate Kerrigan would not meet Slide McKenzie in
her home. Helped by a couple of her maids, she made
her way downstairs and managed to hobble outside,
where a chair was provided for her. Bill Cody had
been visiting and stayed close by. Kate had told him
about McKenzie's extortion, and he vowed to shoot
the man dead "instanter."

Facing a sea of hostile faces including Frank Cobb,
Quinn, and Kate's domestic staff, McKenzie seemed
less sure of himself. Jazmin Salas's husband Marco,
the KK blacksmith, carried a huge hammer and
growled threats against McKenzie under his breath.

Slide badly wanted away from there but he couldn't talk his way out of this situation. He took out his tally book, scribbled some words, tore out the page, and handed it to Kate.

WHERE IS MY MONEY

Kate threw the paper aside and said, "If you harm my son in any way I'll hang you, McKenzie."

Writing was too slow. McKenzie said, "I want my money." He sounded like a wounded animal.

"Frank, give this trash the money sack," Kate said.

Frank Cobb picked up a stuffed flour sack and threw it into McKenzie's chest. The man grinned and nodded. Then he opened the sack and shrieked. McKenzie pulled out a handful of torn-up newspapers and waved it at Kate. Pain or no, he opened his mouth and yelled, "You'll regret this, you lying, cheating bitch!"

"It's the only money you'll get from me, you piece of human dirt," Kate said, her eyes full of green fire.

"Your son is a dead man, you hear? He's a dead man," McKenzie screamed. He groaned, clutched his martyred jaw, and sank slowly to the ground.

Kate looked at the whimpering man without pity and then said, "Mr. Cody, do you have a zoo cage for this animal?"

"I certainly have, dear lady, a coyote cage that hasn't been cleaned out in weeks," Bill said.

Kate smiled and clapped her hands, "Capital, Mr. Cody!" she said. "What crackerjack accommodation."

"Before you do I'll need his clothes," Frank Cobb said. He made a face. "But they look mighty disgusting."

Quinn grinned and said, "I'm glad it's you, Frank, and not me."

"You're my helper, remember?" Frank said. "You'll need to find some rags to wear yourself."

McKenzie's swollen face purpled with anger. His fist closed on a rock that he threw at Frank Cobb's head. Frank dodged the missile, grinned, and said, "Try that again, Slide, and we'll hang you sooner rather than later."

"Draw fighter? Damned back shooter more like," McKenzie said, every word its own separate little agony.

"You're sure a sore loser, ain't you, Slide?" Frank said.

"I haven't lost . . . not yet," McKenzie said. "I always win in the end."

By nature Slide McKenzie was a talking man and to find himself unable to string words together was a trial to him. He decided that his talking was done, at least for now.

Bill Cody stepped into the clothing breach. "Mr. Cobb, I am unaware of your reason for wishing to borrow McKenzie's sartorial splendor, but my show's seamstress can duplicate his duds. I can assure you that in consideration of a small remuneration, she'll do a first-rate job and do it quickly."

"We'll pay the lady, Mr. Cody," Kate said. "And if you care to join me later for an aperitif I can disclose my son's plan to you. It is, to say the least, fraught with danger and uncertainty, but against my better judgment I've decided to take the gamble."

"It will be my pleasure to join you later, Kate," Bill said, giving his customary bow. "And I'm sure your son Trace would want you to roll the dice rather than pay extortion money."

"I hope I'm doing the right thing," Kate said. "I'm putting a lot of faith on the speed of Frank Cobb's gun and Quinn's bravery."

"I won't let you down, Kate," Frank said. "And I won't let Trace down, either."

"I know you won't, Frank. And now I must be out of this sun," Kate said. She pointed at McKenzie. "It's time this monster was locked up where he belongs."

For his part McKenzie had been listening intently to this exchange and he realized he'd lost his ability to bargain, at least for now. But another ace in the hole might just have presented itself . . . a face in the crowd . . . perhaps someone he could intimidate into helping him.

The next morning Moses Rice was preparing young Pete Letting's breakfast when Kate hobbled into the kitchen, supported by a cane and her lady's maid. "Moses, have you seen my son and Frank Cobb?" she said. "I can't find them anywhere."

Before Moses could answer, the boy said, "They rode out already, told me not to tell anybody."

Kate frowned, accepted a chair from Flossie, and gratefully sat down. "Did you know about this, Moses?"

The old black man looked guilty. "Mr. Quinn told me that you'd get cold feet at the last minute and try to stop him, and so I wasn't to tell you until they was two hours gone."

"And are they, Moses? Are they two hours gone?" Kate said.

"They pulled out at first light, Miz Kate," Moses said. "I'm real sorry."

"And Mr. Cobb was dressed funny," Pete said, grinning.

"Eat your oatmeal, Pete," Kate said. "You're a growing boy." And to Moses, "I'm retiring to my room, Moses. Please tell Jazmin that I won't require any lunch today."

Kate's rosary was already in her hand before she and Flossie reached the stairs.

CHAPTER FORTY-ONE

Hot-air balloon flying was still in its infancy when Josiah Mosely and Cloud Passing soared skyward on what was destined to be their last adventure together. Cautious balloonists flew only when the weather was close to ideal, normal winds and clear skies. Storms were always a hazard, as were very strong winds. Both could wreck the balloon, one with lightning strikes and the other by sending the flimsy craft cartwheeling across the sky, throwing the occupants of the basket to their deaths.

Mosely was well aware of these hazards as he clawed for altitude and tried to catch a favorable wind. After vainly battling an air current that pushed the balloon north for at least twenty miles, he finally landed and anchored near a stand of wild oak.

"We'll pick up a south wind tomorrow," Mosely said. "Look at the trees."

Cloud Passing nodded but said nothing. Unlike Mosely the Cheyenne seemed content to go in whichever direction the wind blew him. They shared a supper of roast chicken and bread that Mosely had brought along in one of his carpetbags and then spent an uncomfortably cold night. At first light Mosely lit the burner and once again the balloon ascended.

This time at a height of several hundred feet they caught a favorable wind that by late afternoon was still blowing strong. When Mosely brought the balloon down he estimated that they were halfway to the mission.

"We'll get there just before nightfall tomorrow," he said. Then, "Cloud Passing, when we land you stay with the balloon, you hear? What I have to do is none of your business. I don't want you getting hurt, so be a good Indian and don't come after me." He rummaged in his bag and found a pint of whiskey. "I don't hold with Indians drinking, but tonight I'll make an exception." He offered the bottle to Cloud Passing. "Take a little nip against the cold."

To Mosely's surprise the Cheyenne refused. He rocked back and forth and from side to side and circled a forefinger near his temple. "Busthead no good for warrior. Get drunk and lose too many fights."

"I don't want you to fight," Mosely said. "You will stay with the balloon."

"Why are we here?" Cloud Passing said.

"I plan to kill men, bad men."

"Why?"

"They are enemies of my friends."

"You are not a warrior, Mose-ly. Why do this thing?"

"Because when I look back I want to spit on my life. Now I need people to remember that at least my death was noble and they will say my name with honor."

Cloud Passing said, "Ah, it is good to be brave. No

one remembers a coward. In battle the Dog Soldier stakes himself to the ground so that he cannot run away. If he is killed, his death is a noble thing. To-morrow you will you stake yourself to the ground, Mose-ly?"

"Yes. I will."

"Then I will make a song about you and sing it to my people. You will be remembered as long as there are Cheyenne left to remember."

Mosely smiled. "I didn't think you could speak English so well, so eloquently."

Cloud Passing made a face. "Faugh, the less the white man knows about the Indian the better." He grabbed the bottle from Mosely's hand and tossed it into the darkness. "Whiskey courage is just another name for cowardice."

"Ah well, no whiskey, no coffee, no food, we might as well get some sleep," Mosely said.

"I have one more thing to say to you, Mose-ly," Cloud Passing said. "Do not tell a Dog Soldier that he cannot go to war. It is like talking to winter winds."

"Then we'll die together," Mosely said.

"No, I will not die. Not in this fight," Cloud Passing said. His black eyes glittered. "But you, sky warrior, will find the noble death you seek."

The south wind that blew cold off the Chihuahuan Desert stranded the balloon where it was, on flat scrubland that offered little. Josiah Mosely and Cloud Passing kept the craft anchored, a difficult job since it constantly tugged on the ropes, eager to be airborne. Fat white clouds like a herd of sheep migrating north scudded across the sky, impossibly high, effectively roofing over Mosely's hopes of chasing friendlier winds.

He considered his options, such as they were.

He could wait with the balloon until the wind changed or leave it anchored here and make the rest of the journey on foot. After some thought, Mosely decided on the latter.

He told Cloud Passing of his decision and said, "You will stay with the balloon. I will not be back."

The Cheyenne shook his head. "You are my friend, Mose-ly. I will be with you at the end of your life and sing your death song."

Mosely knew further argument was useless. "Get the canteen," he said.

After the Indian did as he was told, Mosely took the pair of British Bulldogs from the carpetbags, checked the loads, and then hefted the revolvers in his hands. Heavy. They'd drag his pants down, but that couldn't be helped. He dropped a Bulldog into each of his pants pockets and then made a pile of the burner fuel in the bottom of the basket. He set the straw alight and stepped back, firelight reflecting red in his glasses he watched the basket and then the envelope go up in flames. After a few minutes nothing remained of the balloon but a few pieces of metal and the discarded hydrogen cylinder.

"Now we walk," Mosely said.

Cloud Passing glanced at the sky. "It is good, Mose-ly. The stars are out to show us the way."

CHAPTER FORTY-TWO

It was almost noon when a hot, dusty, and exhausted Josiah Mosely caught sight of the mission. "This is the place," he told Cloud Passing. "Unless there are two missions around here."

The Cheyenne's sharp eyes scanned the area around the ruin, and after a while he said, "Many people were here and now gone. Look like Pawnee village after long winter. Faugh! It is a dung heap."

"Then it's the place we're looking for," Mosely said. "I'm going in alone, Indian. After the shooting is over, wait a while, and if you see two white men still standing get away from here a-running. Do you understand me?"

"I will do what I will do," the Cheyenne said.

"Damn it, you can't come with me," Mosely said. "You don't even have a gun."

"This is your fight, Mose-ly, your death, and I will not be a part of it." Cloud Passing laid his hand on Mosely's thin shoulder. "I will not steal your honor this day."

Mosely smiled. "It's been good knowing you, Indian. You take care now."

He removed his plug hat, poured some water from the canteen onto his unruly hair, and then parted it in the middle with his fingers and smoothed it down flat on both sides. His glasses were lopsided as always and he left them that way. Holding his hat in his hand Mosely figured he looked like a harmless rube lost in the wilderness. It was the only edge he had.

The Cheyenne had no word in their language for good-bye, but they did let others know that they were sad to see them leave, and Cloud Passing looked down-hearted as Mosely walked away from him. After a while Mosely turned and waved, a small, insignificant figure all but lost in a vast landscape. Cloud Passing stood still, staring at Mosely, but didn't move. The Cheyenne didn't wave good-bye, either.

Josiah Mosely stopped, tested his taped-up gun hand, and found it painful and stiff but flexible enough to get the job done. He walked, holding his hat, toward the mission. The rear part of the building's roof still existed, but the mud brick walls of the façade and sides had been mostly torn down. Mosely guessed that Trace Kerrigan was somewhere under the roofed section, probably trussed up and unable to move. As he stepped closer he tossed his hat into a heap of rubble, slouched, and thrust his hand deep into his pockets, his fingers closing over the graceful, curved butts of the Bulldogs. Now that the time had come, Mosely was scared, not of dying but of dying badly. Or uselessly. Or without honor.

Three broad limestone steps led to what had been the mission door, and a fire burned on the top one, a smoking coffeepot on the coals. Mosely had his foot on the bottom step when two men appeared from somewhere inside the ruin. His heart thumped in his chest and suddenly his mouth was dry. The men were tall, slender, handsome, and wore their guns as though they were a part of them. Clad only in pants, boots, and frilled white shirts, the top buttons open revealing the tanned Vs of their broad chests, they were the sort of men Mosely once dreamed of being before he was faced with small, scrawny reality.

Bat Boswell's cold eyes studied Mosely for long moments before he grinned and said, "What the hell? Where did you come from?"

"North," Mosely said.

"You walked?"

"Part of the way." Then, to justify his being there, "My horse up and died on me."

"What the hell are you, boy?" Sky Boswell said. "One of them traveling preachers?"

"No. I'm just me."

"And that sure ain't much," Sky said.

Bat said, "Get out of here, boy. We got nothing for you."

"Hold on just a minute, what you got in them pockets?" Sky said.

"Nothing but my hands," Mosely said.

"Maybe you got a poke," Sky said. "Struck it rich somewhere, huh?"

"I have nothing."

"Then we'll take a look," Sky said.

Mosely took a step back. "I heard you were hunting me," he said.

Bat Boswell scowled. "Now who the hell would hunt a pissant pipsqueak like you?"

Mosely smelled the freshness of the morning and the welcoming tang of boiling coffee. From horizon to horizon the sky was eggshell blue and the Rio Grande glittered in the light of the rising sun. It was a good day to be alive. "Name's Josiah Mosely," he said.

The Boswell reaction was not what he expected.

Both gunmen stared at him for a moment, unbelieving, then both burst into derisive laughter. Finally, Sky recovered enough to say, "Who told you about him, boy? Who told a little runt like you about Josiah Mosely the New Mexico draw fighter? If you're he then I guess I must be the pope of Rome."

"Hell, Sky, I ought to gun the rube for telling a big windy," Bat said.

Sky nodded. "I like you, boy, you think big," he said. "But I reckon we're bound to kill you for lying to us, and that's a natural fact."

"Where is Mosely?" Bat said. "Did he put you up to this as a good joke?"

"I am he," Mosely said. "I killed them all, Hawley, Brett, Lusk, and that piece of human garbage Jesse Tobin."

For a moment the Boswell brothers were too stunned to react. And that was all the edge Mosely was going to get. He pulled the sweaty British Bulldogs from his pockets and at a range of six feet cut loose with both hands, shooting well despite the spiking agony of his broken finger.

Mosely had the element of surprise on his side and

had drawn down on two skilled gunmen who'd fatally underestimated him. He scored a center body hit on Sky and shot Bat in the right forearm just above the wrist, effectively crippling his gun hand. Sky, hit hard, gasping from shock, returned fire. Mosely took Sky's bullet in his left shoulder and a split second later another slammed into his chest. Meantime Bat held his Colt in his left, and he and Mosely fired at the same time. Mosely aimed well, a solid chest hit that penetrated deep. Bat, shooting with his weak hand, missed, fired again, and hit Mosely where the left side of his neck joined the shoulder. It was not a killing wound, but it momentarily paralyzed Mosely's arm and forced him to drop the Bulldog. Sky was down, mortally wounded, coughing up black blood. He was out of the fight and out of time.

"I'll kill you, by God!" Bat yelled as he raised his Colt to eye level.

Once again he and Mosely shot at the same time. Mosely was hit a fourth time, a glancing wound to the side of his head, but firing double action he emptied his revolver into Bat. Dying rapidly, the tall gunman dropped to one knee and gasped, "Who the hell are you?"

"Josiah Mosely. Or I was."

"You're a damned liar," Bat Boswell said. He dropped on his face, groaned once deep in his throat, and then died.

Mosely looked at the two dead men, at the carnage he'd created. "I am Josiah Mosely," he said. Suddenly the limestone step rushed up spinning, to meet him and he stumbled and then fell headlong into darkness.

* * *

Josiah Mosely woke to the concerned, bronze face of Cloud Passing. The Cheyenne held Mosely's head in his arms, and above him the sky had turned cobalt blue in the late afternoon light.

"Hell, I thought I was dead already," Mosely said, his voice barely a whisper. "I'm shot through and through."

"I saw you fall and then I came," the Cheyenne said.

"How— How long . . . have I been . . ." Mosely said.

"Not long," Cloud Passing said.

"You've been out for no more than five, six hours."

That last from another voice, a white man's voice, the voice of Trace Kerrigan.

"You're alive?" Mosely said.

"Yes. Thanks to you and Cloud Passing," Trace said. "I didn't think one man could break the cellar door down, but he did."

"Hurt shoulder, hurt back, and then saw key hanging beside door," the Cheyenne said. "That was a bad thing. Loco Indian."

"I'm glad you're safe, Trace," Mosely said. "Now I can die in peace."

"You saved my life, Josiah," Trace said. "I won't let you die."

"I'm shot all to pieces," Mosely said.

"You're such a skinny little feller the bullets didn't stay inside you," Trace said. "Now you have to keep breathing until I can get you to a doctor."

Mosely shook his head. "No, it's all up with me. This is how my hand played out."

"The hell it is," Trace said. "You're going to get well again and fly that balloon of yours."

"Cloud Passing told me I would die," Mosely said. "He's an Indian and he knows these things."

Trace glared at Cloud Passing. "Now why did you tell him something like that?" he said.

"Indian is usually right," the Cheyenne said. "But sometimes Indian is wrong. Maybe Mose-ly live. Maybe that will be."

CHAPTER FORTY-THREE

Slide McKenzie threw the tin plate of bacon and beans at the cookhouse helper who'd brought it to him. "You expect me to eat in this stinking cage?" he said. He'd untied his chin binding and his swollen jaw hurt like the dickens. To add to his misery, the plate had clanged against the bars, bounced back, and splattered him with most of his dinner.

"Suit yourself," the helper said. He was a stove-up puncher named Slattery and he didn't take sass or backtalk from any man. "You'll be mighty hungry afore I bring you another plate, lay to that."

"You go to hell," McKenzie said, but Slattery was already out of sight.

Dripping beans, McKenzie cursed as he pondered his harsh fate. How was it that bad things always happened to him? His jaw was broke. Kate Kerrigan, that damned bitch, had refused to pay the ransom money and there was a strong possibility that he'd get hung. The only bright side was that the Boswell brothers would see to it that Trace Kerrigan died, and her son's death would cause his uppity mother plenty of pain of her own.

McKenzie stayed with that thought, since it brought him a deal of pleasure, and he smiled as he once again tied up his throbbing jaw.

A few hours later, three-thirty in the afternoon by the ornate French carriage clock in Bill Cody's tent, McKenzie saw the woman he'd recognized in the crowd that morning. As she walked past the cage wagon, soap and towels in her hands, he called out to her.

"Remember me, missy," he said, each word lockjaw tight. "Ol' Slide McKenzie as ever was."

The woman stopped and her face paled. "You know me?" she said.

McKenzie untied his bandage. He was prepared to bear the pain if it offered him a chance to escape.

"I remember you just fine. And I mind that time down on the Cimarron," McKenzie said, grimacing as each word punished him. "Now what was the name of that little burg?"

"Post Oak," Ingrid Hult said.

"That's right, Post Oak. And I was bartending that day in Ryan O'Hara's saloon, remember that dive? I always figured you was a magnificent sight, the way you come into the place and just blazed away. I can't recollect the cowboy's name, but it will come back to me."

"Dooly Baker," Ingrid Hult said.

"Yeah, that's the ranny. Emptied a six-gun into ol' Dooly, huh? Six shots in the back. Dropped him like he'd been hit between the eyes with a hickory ax handle."

"What do you want from me, McKenzie?" Ingrid said.

McKenzie held his aching jaw in place as he said, "Something about rape and a suicide, wasn't it? I mean, the thing that started all the trouble. That's what I heard anyways."

"What do you want from me, McKenzie?" the woman said again.

"I want you to get me out of here."

"And if I don't?"

"I know it happened in Kansas, but murder is murder. I wonder what Bill Cody will say when I tell him what I seen that day in Post Oak? Or Mrs. Kerrigan? That lady might just hang you."

"Let me think about this, McKenzie," Ingrid said. "You've taken me by surprise."

"Don't think too long or I'll do some talking."

"I'll be back with an answer as soon as it gets dark."

"See you do. I'm not a patient man. And make sure your answer is the right one."

McKenzie watched the woman leave. Real pretty. Swings her hips nice. Hey, maybe he could parlay the killing of Dooly Baker into something besides the escape. He tied up his jaw and decided that his talking was done for a while. Now it was all up to the woman.

As he buttoned his shirt Ducking Jim Benson looked down at Ingrid Hult, who lay on her cot, the thin sheet that covered her revealing every voluptuous curve of her naked body. Ingrid was, he decided, the most beautiful woman he'd ever seen. Their love-making was a problem, but nothing that could not be solved with time, patience, and understanding. As soon as he took Ingrid in his arms she became rigid and unresponsive, something closely akin to fear in her eyes, and it tore at his heart.

"I'm so sorry, Jim, please forgive me," she told him as she'd done so many times before. And he answered her as he'd always done. First his shy smile and then, "It will take nothing but time, my angel."

"I try," Ingrid said.

"I know you do."

"The memories come back . . ." Ingrid squeezed her eyes shut. "I see the faces again, one after the other, like in a bad dream. But it wasn't a dream. It was real."

Benson sat on the cot and took the woman's hand. "We'll make it right one day soon. You'll see."

He rose to his feet. "I have to go, Ingrid."

"Jim, there's been so much killing, so much blood," Ingrid said. "Is there no other way?"

"With men like Slide McKenzie there never is another way. He slithers in the slime, and that's the only way of living he understands. Everyone lives, Ingrid, but not everyone deserves to. McKenzie is one of them."

"The man never did me any harm, until today," Ingrid said. "Perhaps I should talk to Mr. Cody, tell him everything."

"No, it's too great a risk. Bill might turn you over to the Rangers and you'd be put on trial and maybe hanged or sent to a women's prison for years," Benson said. "This time we'll do it my way."

Benson shoved a Remington revolver into his waistband and then covered it with his coat.

"Jim, are we doing the right thing?" Ingrid said. She sat up in the cot and held the sheet to her naked breasts. "In the past did I do the right thing? Vengeance is mine, I will repay, saith the Lord. That's in the Bible."

"We're both in the right," Benson said. "An eye for an eye a tooth for a tooth. It also says that right there in the Bible. Who dare judge us later and say what we did was wrong?"

Ingrid lay back on her cot. "Slide McKenzie. I didn't even know the man before today and now I will kill him."

"No, I'll kill him," Benson said. "If there is blame to be laid for his death, then let it be laid on me."

"But, Jim—"

But Benson was gone.

Ingrid Hult buried her face in her hands. It began with the death of her fourteen-year-old sister and would end with the destruction of five men, four of them by her own hand. The cowboys who had raped Kari into suicide had paid the blood price, the *wergild* as her Viking ancestors had called it, and now Slide McKenzie, who had sought to profit by it, would also die.

And what of the Indian, Cloud Passing? She had scalped the rapists and murderers, a horrible deed that had made her sick to her stomach, to shift suspicion to the Cheyenne. Ingrid would not allow the man to hang for her crimes. No, claiming the *wergild* was not a crime, it was justice. Thank God Cloud Passing was still at large, but if he was condemned to death she would speak up and absolve him of all blame . . . and die in his stead. If that must be the way of it, then so be it. She'd go to the gallows willingly knowing that her sister Kari, beautiful, laughing Kari, was avenged, and in the end that's all that mattered.

An hour later five shots smashed the quiet evening into a million shattering shards of sound and then alarmed voices cried out into the clamoring night.

Ingrid Hult buried her face in her pillow and cried bitter tears.

CHAPTER FORTY-FOUR

"Five shots at close range, Kate," Buffalo Bill Cody said. "One through the palm of his left hand as he tried to fend off the murderous balls. The wretch died like the dog he was."

Kate Kerrigan stared at the body of Slide McKenzie slumped on the bottom of the cage. A look of horror was frozen on the man's face, and the front of his shirt was black with congealed blood.

A giggle, and then, "He looks like a shotgunned bunny. What's that thing on his head?"

This from Annie Oakley who stood on tiptoe and peered over Bill Cody's shoulder.

"His jaw was broke," Bill said.

"Who broke it?" Annie said.

Bill shrugged. "Hell, I don't know."

Annie turned her attention to Kate. "One of your hands do this, empty a six-gun into him, Mrs. Kerrigan? Or did you gun him yourself? I understand his name was McKenzie, and he was trying to blackmail you."

Kate's reply was icy. "No, I did not shoot him, Mrs. Butler, and neither did any of my men."

Annie smiled. "Well, somebody sure as hell did."

"Someone with a grudge," Bill said. He very carefully studied the ground at his feet and didn't look at Kate.

"My son is still held hostage," Kate said. "McKenzie's death solves nothing."

"Then let's hope your boy Quinn and Frank Cobb can free him," Bill said. "Kate, I've thought it over and I must confess that I still favor an attack with overwhelming force."

"I've already had this discussion with Hiram Clay," Kate said. "I didn't like the plan then and I don't like it now."

"Yes, it has its risks," Bill said. "Well, Frank Cobb has a reputation of being good with a gun. If anyone can prevail, he can."

"Let us pray so, Mr. Cody," Kate said. "I'm pinning all my hope on the speed of Frank's gun. In the meantime, you have a murderer in your midst, and I suggest you make every effort to find him."

"Whoever he is, he's long gone," Annie Oakley said. "I doubt you'll ever find him."

That surprised Kate. Annie seemed very keen to derail any inquiry into the matter. To test the waters she said, "We can't pin this one on the Indian, can we?"

"Perhaps not," was all Annie Oakley said before she turned on her heel and walked away.

Then Bill Cody said, "Kate, if he was one of mine I'll find him, though McKenzie was a man who badly needed killing, so if you will forgive the expression, dear lady, who the hell cares?"

Kate smiled. "Mr. Cody, I agree with your sentiment

entirely, yet I can't help but think that the murder of the three cowboys is somehow linked to McKenzie's death."

It was Bill's turn to be surprised. "A most singular statement, Kate, but an erroneous one, I fear." He shook his silvery head. "No, McKenzie was killed by someone who hated him. He was a shady character, and I suspect a figure from his past was the culprit."

"Or his present," Kate said.

CHAPTER FORTY-FIVE

Between them, using horses and ropes, Trace Kerrigan and Cloud Passing pulled down a section of the mission wall on top of the bodies of the Boswell brothers. Trace said that all things considered, it was a better burial than they deserved, interred in what was surely still holy ground.

Josiah Mosely was in bad shape. He wasn't getting any better, as though he'd already given up the fight for life.

"We have to get him to the KK," Trace said. "Josiah needs a doctor real bad."

Cloud Passing shook his head. "Mose-ly can't ride."

"He's a small man," Trace said. "I'll take him up with me."

"He needs doctor, you say," the Indian said. "You speak the truth."

"Yeah, and he needs one soon," Trace said. "I don't want him dying on me. I won't allow it."

Pulling down the walls had taken time, and there was no alternative but to ride out under the noon sun. Trace had Mosely in front of him, holding him upright in the saddle. The man was as light as a slender twelve-year-old, and it took no great effort to support him. But after an hour the front of Trace's shirt was stained with Mosely's blood and the little man breathed in short, shallow gasps.

"Cloud Passing, we'd better stop and let him rest for a while," Trace said. "He's in a bad way."

"Hot sun no good," the Indian said. "Maybe better to wait for night and then ride."

"If Josiah doesn't get medical help soon he'll die," Trace said. "We can't afford to waste a whole day. He can rest for half an hour and then ride again."

The Cheyenne's face was grim. "He is a dead man, Kerrigan. I told you Indian sometimes wrong about such things, but that was a foolish thing to say. Look at his face. The death shadows gather like dark clouds in a rain sky."

"I told you, I'm not going to let him die," Trace said. "Now help me get him down. He'll feel better once we get him into some shade for a spell."

Mosely flopped like a rag doll as Trace and Cloud Passing lifted him from the saddle and laid him on his back in a clump of brush that afforded some protection from the merciless sun. Trace put his canteen to the young man's mouth, but Mosely turned his head away, murmured something, and refused to drink. Trace untied his bandana, wet it down, and placed it on the wounded man's forehead. It was a caring gesture but did as little good as Cloud Passing's use of his horse to block out the relentless sunlight.

Trace said to the Indian, "He's resting now, breathing easier. That's a good sign, isn't it?"

"He's dying," Cloud Passing said. "Not long now."

Anxiety spiked in Trace. "Help me get him on the horse. The sooner we reach the KK the better."

The Cheyenne made no answer. He stared beyond Trace to the north, his face both puzzled and uneasy. Trace read Cloud Passing's troubled eyes and turned. "Oh my God," he said.

His hand dropped to his gun.

"It's Trace and the Indian, got to be," Quinn Kerrigan said.

"Sure looks like it," Frank Cobb said.

He reached into his saddlebags, found his field glasses, and scanned the distance. "It's Trace and the Indian all right," Frank said. "And they don't look too friendly."

"They think you're Slide McKenzie, Frank," Quinn said. "If Trace cuts loose with a rifle we're both on a stony lonesome. He doesn't miss too often. Quick, get out of those damned duds."

The clothes to match McKenzie's outfit, black vest, dirty white shirt, and gambler's sleeve garters had been hastily tacked together to pass muster at shooting distance, and Frank ripped them off, stripping down to his vest. He'd loosely bandaged his chin and tied it at the top of his head, and this he gratefully discarded. He put the glasses to his eyes again.

Trace and the Indian still seemed wary, but were not pointing guns in their direction any longer. "I think they recognize us," Quinn said.

"I hope so," Frank said. "I don't trust the Indian and I trust Trace even less."

* * *

"Damn it, Frank, I was getting ready to shoot you right off that horse," Trace Kerrigan said. "Why did you dress up like Slide McKenzie? And you, Quinn, you look like a raggedy-assed saloon swamper."

"Well, ask your brother," Frank said. "It was his bright idea."

"We came to rescue you, Trace," Quinn said. "I figured if we looked like McKenzie and a helper—that's why we have the big money trunk on the packhorse—we could get close to the Boswells and cut loose. Hey, is that the rainmaker lying there?"

"Yes, it's Josiah Mosely. He killed the Boswells and then Cloud Passing freed me. He's shot real bad."

Frank Cobb was incredulous. "Did I hear you say that Mosely killed the Boswells?"

"As far as I can piece it together, he walked right up to them, drew, and killed them both," Trace said.

"Hell, I don't believe it," Frank said. "That's impossible."

"Believe it," Cloud Passing said. "It is how it happened."

"You saw it, Indian?" Quinn said.

"Yes, but from a distance, away from the guns. Mose-ly wanted to do this thing alone." Cloud Passing stared right at Frank. "He is a great warrior, and now he is dying, and when he is gone I will do him great honor."

Trace said, "Just so you know, Frank and Quinn, the Boswells would've pegged you as imposters way before you got within shooting distance. Even sitting a horse, Frank, you're six inches taller than McKenzie and twice as wide in the shoulders. It's kind of noticeable, and the Boswells were noticing men. They underestimated Josiah Mosely, and that was their big mistake. They wouldn't have underestimated you."

"I underestimated him myself," Frank said. "And that was my mistake."

He swung out of the saddle and took a knee beside the wounded man and used Trace's bandana to wipe the fever sweat from Mosely's face. "How you doing, pardner?" he said. "We're going to get you home to the ranch."

Mosely's eyes flickered open. He looked into Frank Cobb's face and smiled. "Tell Kate . . . tell her I loved her."

Just that and nothing else. And then all the life that was in Josiah Mosely left, and Frank reached down and gently closed his eyes. "He's gone," he said. "Damn it all, Josiah Mosely, you were a man."

Cloud Passing took a cross-legged seat on the ground, placed his forearms on his knees, and sang the Cheyenne death song for the fallen warrior.

CHAPTER FORTY-SIX

Frank Cobb, feeling a gnawing guilt for failing to respect a man who turned out to be braver than himself, arranged Josiah Mosely's funeral.

The young man was buried in the cemetery on the ridge overlooking the Kerrigan mansion, and despite Kate's protest that it was a pagan practice Frank laid Mosely's revolvers in the coffin and buried him with a dog at his feet. The dog was Slide McKenzie.

The funeral made Bill Cody uneasy. Bill, a Methodist, was only as religious as he cared or needed to be, but in common with Kate he thought the warrior burial belonged to Dark Ages and had little to do with Christianity.

But Frank was unrepentant.

When Bill took him to task, Frank said, "Josiah died a noble death, and I buried him as a fallen warrior should be buried, with his weapons and a dog at his feet. We should all aspire to such an honor."

Bill did not pursue the matter, mainly because a funeral breakfast had been laid out in Kate's kitchen and the six fried eggs, bacon, and pork sausage on his plate demanded his immediate attention.

Frank, still upset over his past treatment of Mosely, his dislike and disdain for a man who had deserved better, had little on his plate when Kate took him aside.

In a whisper she said, "Where is Cloud Passing?"

"He's holed up somewhere, Kate. He says it's a place where he and Josiah repaired the balloon."

"His life is still in great danger, Frank. Now more than ever."

"Do you care that much, Kate?" Frank said.

"He helped save my son's life, so yes, I care that much," Kate said.

"I think he's safe for now," Frank said. "Nobody with a lick of sense believes that he somehow made his way back to the camp and shot Slide McKenzie."

"Who did, Frank?" Kate said.

The segundo shook his head. "I have no idea. It's a big mystery to me."

"I think it's the same person who murdered the cowboys," Kate said.

"Could be," Frank said. "I can't say for sure. I'm not a Pinkerton."

"I'm not, either, but I still intend to find out," Kate said.

But the work of the ranch had to continue, and Kate Kerrigan was forced to shelve her investigation, at least for a while.

She sent a thousand cattle a hundred miles south to occupy the grazing land all the way to the Rio

Grande. With the chuck wagon rolled a second flatbed, this one loaded with the prefabricated walls and roof of a line cabin. Once the cabin was built her riders could keep watch on the river and warn of any further incursions by Mexicans.

A few days after the herd left for the river, a puncher reported that rustlers had struck on the west bank of the Pecos close to the New Mexico border and had made off with thirty head.

As she always did on those occasions, Kate rode with Frank and the hands and took part in a running, long-range rifle battle that resulted in no casualties on either side. The rustlers made good their escape, but the KK recovered its stolen cattle. Kate ordered the torching of several cabins located just across the border that she suspected belonged to the bandits. Despite the tearful pleas of their families, she burned the rustler cabins to the ground and confiscated eight horses, some hogs, and a Holstein milk cow. On a pine tree near one of the burned-out cabins Frank Cobb tacked up a carved wooden sign that read RUSTLERS BEWARE. Whoever the cattle thieves were, there is no record of them ever again lifting Kerrigan cattle.

Kate Kerrigan returned home to a pair of missives that intrigued her.

One was a gold-edged invitation from the White Star shipping line requesting her to cross the Atlantic on such and such a date as their guest on the new passenger liner the *Oceanic*. White Star noted that His Grace the Duke of Argyll, the richest man in

Scotland and owner of several large cattle ranches in Montana and Wyoming, would make the crossing on that date and was most anxious to meet her. The invite was for four months hence, well after the gather, and Kate decided a sea voyage might be a great adventure and was worthy of some serious thought.

The second was of greater moment since it was a note from Annie Oakley "requesting an audience at Mrs. Kerrigan's earliest convenience."

Kate read the note, read it again, and then said, "Bitch."

"How nice to see you again, Mrs. Butler," Kate Kerrigan said, smiling. "By the most fortuitous happenstance you were just in time for tea. Winifred, you may pour."

Kate waited until the tea was poured and then picked up a knife. "May I slice you a piece of cake?"

Annie nodded; she was a plain girl in a plain cotton dress with a plain manner of speaking. She stood in stark contrast to Kate's silken, exquisite beauty.

After the girl had eaten the cake and was on her second cup of tea, Kate said, "Now what can I do for you?"

"I have questions to ask," Annie said. "It's some of those questions that isn't real." She frowned, thinking. "Now what do you call them?"

"Winifred?" Kate said.

"Hypothetical questions," the parlor maid supplied.

"Yeah, that's it, Winifred," Annie said. "How did you know?"

"Winifred was once a librarian," Kate said. "She's just a mine of information."

"Well, like I said, they're . . . hypothetical questions," Annie said.

"And hopefully I'll be able to give you hypothetical answers," Kate said.

Annie sat back in her chair, lifted a leg, and clasped her knee in both hands, a most unladylike posture Kate thought.

"Suppose there were two young sisters living with their father on a farm in Kansas, the younger of them very pretty," Annie said. "Now suppose that one fine day four drovers, all of them drunk, were riding back to Texas on the Chisholm trail from Abilene and stopped by the farm to water their horses. Are you with me so far, Mrs. Kerrigan?"

"Yes, Mrs. Butler, I believe I am," Kate said.

"This is all hypothetical, you understand," Annie said.

"Yes, of course it is," Kate said.

Annie said, "Let's say that the drunk cowboys decided to have some fun and began to molest the sisters, and their father came to their rescue, unarmed. One of the cowboys, a big man who acted as their leader, shot the farmer dead and then all four of them repeatedly raped the sisters."

"How awful," Kate said.

"Yes, wasn't it," Annie said. "But worse was to come. Suppose that after the punchers left the younger sister found her father's shotgun, placed the muzzles under her chin, and managed to pull both triggers with her toes. She was a sensitive girl and couldn't bear the shame," Annie said.

"The shame was with the cowboys, not the girl," Kate said. "I would have hanged all four of them if I'd been there."

"You would, hypothetically of course?" Annie said.

"I would have strung them up without hesitation," Kate said.

"No trial."

"The testimony and physical state of the surviving sister would have been enough for me," Kate said. She remembered her own sister and a different time and place and all the hurt came back, like sharp thorns thrust into her heart. She managed a smile. "That is, had all this really happened."

"Now I ask you this, Mrs. Kerrigan," Annie said. "Would the surviving sister be justified in seeking revenge on the rapists?"

"Had it been my sister on that Kansas farm I would have hounded her rapists to the ends of the earth if need be," Kate said.

"And you would have hanged them?"

Kate smiled. "Yes, I would. After I gelded them."

Annie, in that olden time I did not geld the rapists I killed, but I did seek revenge, and I found it in a stinking New York slum.

Annie opened her mouth to speak again, but Kate said, "Let me finish this for you, Mrs. Butler. We'll suppose that the older sister could not bear to stay on at the farm, so she sold it and then somehow she learned how to use a knife—"

"And suppose her teacher was Armand Pierre de Polignac the famous Baton Rouge knife fighter, who'd taken a fatherly interest in the girl," Annie said.

"And then she got employment throwing knives in

Buffalo Bill's Wild West and discovered that three of the four rapists she sought also worked with the show," Kate said. "She killed all three and scalped them to throw suspicion on one of Bill's Indian performers." Kate smiled. "That's how it could have happened."

Annie helped herself to another piece of cake and said, "Vanilla flavor. This is a welcome change from Random Clark's bear sign." She chewed for a few moments and then said, "How would you judge such a girl, Mrs. Kerrigan?"

"I would not judge her," Kate said. "I am in no position to cast the first stone. But I would advise her to turn herself in to the Rangers and stand trial for murder. I'd tell the girl that I would do everything I can for her and that I doubt there's a jury in Texas that would convict her. More tea?"

Annie shook her head and said, "It's thin," she said. "Standing trial is always a gamble."

"Let's cut right to the chase," Kate said. "There's something I must know . . . did Ingrid Hult kill the three cowboys and Slide McKenzie?"

"I told you this was all hypothetical," Annie said. "I never mentioned Ingrid's name."

"Did she kill them?"

"No."

"Then who did?"

Annie rose to her feet. "I must go."

"Was it Jim Benson? Are he and Ingrid lovers?"

"How did—"

"I know? I don't. But Benson is closer to Ingrid than anyone else. She throws knives at him, for heaven's sake. It makes sense he'd help her, and if he loves her, that he'd kill for her."

Annie collapsed into the chair. "What I'm about to tell you isn't hypothetical, it's the truth, Mrs. Kerrigan," she said. "Ingrid was barely out of childhood herself when she tracked one of the rapists to the Cimarron River. His name was Dooly Baker, and she caught up with him at a saloon in a town called Post Oak. She killed Baker at the bar and Slide McKenzie, who was bartending, saw her do it. He threatened to tell Mr. Cody about the killing, and Ingrid was afraid Bill would hand her over to the Rangers, who would have sent her to Kansas to stand trial for murder."

"More likely the Rangers would investigate the deaths of the three cowboys," Kate said. "Miss Hult could face trial in Texas. Either way, Slide McKenzie had to die. Miss Hult did kill the cowboys, did she not?"

"Yes. And Jim Benson shot McKenzie. It was a justified killing."

"Murder is murder, justified or not," Kate said.

"That's exactly what McKenzie told Ingrid, Mrs. Kerrigan," Annie said, her eyes accusing. "Strange, that."

Kate accepted the barb without comment. What would her killing of the rapists in the Five Points be called? Justified? Of course it was.

Then Annie said, "What will you do?"

"Mrs. Butler, I'm not a officer of the law. The actions of Ingrid Hult have not harmed me or mine and therefore my answer is that I'll do nothing. Unless . . ."

"Unless what?" Annie said, suspicion clouding her face.

"Unless the Indian Cloud Passing is in danger of being blamed for crimes he did not commit," Kate said. "If he faces a mustang court and a certain lynching, then I will do everything I can to stop it. Is my meaning clear?"

"Very clear," Annie said. "Ingrid will not let the Indian hang."

"Then I'm glad to hear that," Kate said. "I strongly advise her to confess to the murders of the four rapists and take her chances in court. And Jim Benson should do the same."

Annie nodded and then stood. "I'll tell her what you said."

"Mrs. Butler, why have you taken such an interest in all this?" Kate said.

"Two reasons, Mrs. Kerrigan. The first is because I am Ingrid's friend. And the second is because I'm a woman, and rape is every woman's concern."

Kate rose and extended her hand. "You must come for tea again soon. Next time we'll have sponge cake."

After Annie Oakley left, Kate realized she could not condemn Ingrid Hult for doing something she herself had done . . . all those years ago in New York in that murderous, disease-ridden, crime-infested hell on earth they called the Five Points. It was the place where she'd spent the early years of her life and where she'd killed three men when she was just sixteen years old.

CHAPTER FORTY-SEVEN

Shannon Cotter, Kate's fourteen-year-old sister, was a willful, intelligent girl with a love of the fiddle music she often heard spilling from the saloons and the works of Sir Walter Scott, represented by a couple of volumes her father had not as yet consigned to a pawnbroker. Not as beautiful as Kate, she was pretty nonetheless with the bright blue eyes and blond hair of a Nordic ancestor somewhere back in the mists of Irish history.

But what drew the ogling attention of young men was her fully developed body, especially her bust that was large and high, and the lovely straight line of her slender back.

Shannon, eager to escape the gloomy confines of the tenements, often strolled the streets alone, trusting to daylight and the constant crowds jostling for space on the sidewalks.

But then came that fateful afternoon when a brewers' dray, drawn by two shire horses, accidentally mounted the sidewalk in front of her, and Shannon had to jump into an open doorway to avoid getting crushed.

"Watch where you're going!" the driver yelled at her. "Damned daydreamer!"

Shannon was about to yell back that it was his fault, not hers, when a large, hairy forearm clamped around her throat.

The man dragged her backward into a dark stairwell and said, "Shut your trap, girlie, and do as you're told or I'll rip your heart out."

It was an Irish accent, but born of the Five Points, not the home country.

"She's prime, Bill," another man said. "Ain't she prime?"

"A beauty, lay to that," said a second, talking through a grin.

Both were Americans, and sounded like seamen.

"Get her upstairs, Bill," the first speaker said. "And ye can have the first go."

The man called Bill dragged Shannon up stone steps that led to the upper floors of what was an abandoned warehouse.

The stairwell smelled of piss and stale vomit and was so dark the girl couldn't see her abductors.

But she knew what was in store for her, and she screamed.

Who in the Five Points ever paid heed to a woman's screams, a sound as familiar as the wails of hungry children or the chirp of a house sparrow?

The men hauled the terrified girl into a top-floor room. Its windows were boarded, and the room was as black as ink.

One man lit a match and touched fire to a candle

stub stuck onto a chipped blue plate that lay on the floor. A couple of rats scuttled from the light as Shannon was thrown onto a pile of rags in the corner.

By the feeble, guttering glow of the candle, Shannon Cotter was raped.

Later, as the three men snored, exhausted by whiskey and rape, Shannon hurriedly buttoned herself into what remained of her dress and ran into the street.

Her cries for help went unheeded.

What the passersby saw was just another whore beaten by her pimp.

It was no concern of theirs, or the law.

When Shannon got home she managed to contrive a story to explain the ruination of her dress and the bruising and abrasion of her body.

"A man tried to rob me," she said. "I fought him off, but he tore my dress and threw me to the ground."

Her father, Patrick Cotter, accepted the explanation, an everyday occurrence in the Five Points, but Kate looked into her sister's wounded eyes and saw something much more serious.

She later took Shannon aside and said, "Now tell me the truth about what happened."

It took a while before Shannon spoke again.

"Three men," she said.

She threw herself into Kate's arms.

"Two of them . . . they dragged me into a room and . . . and . . ."

Kate said nothing.

She hugged her sister close, her beautiful face like stone.

"Name them," she said.

Shannon drew back and looked at her sister in surprise.

She'd never before heard ice in Kate's voice or seen the green flame in her eyes.

"One was called Bill, I think he was Irish. Another was Tom and I didn't hear the third man's name."

"Tell nothing of this to Father." Kate said. "He's a good man, but he's not cut out for this kind of work."

"Kate, what kind of work?" Shannon said.

"The work that now falls to me," Kate said.

CHAPTER FORTY-EIGHT

Two days later, walking through the rain, Kate sought out Sam Sullivan.

The big Irish cop wore a rain cape and stood in the doorway of Nathan Goldberg's used clothing store on Swan Street.

"Have you come to fight me, then, Kate Cotter?" he said, smiling.

The girl did not smile back, but she stepped beside him.

"I need your help, Constable Sullivan," Kate said.

"Oh, it's Constable Sullivan, is it? You must need my help real bad."

"Three men who run together, probably sailors at one time."

"Now why would you be seeking out men like that, Kate?"

The girl ignored him. "One is called Bill, an Irishman, another is Tom. I don't know the third one's name," she said.

"Why are you asking me this?" Sullivan said.

"It's important it is that I find those three men," Kate said.

"Under the awning here with you," the big cop said.

For a few moments he stared at the rain making startled Vs all over the cobbled street, his face frowning in concentration.

Then he said, "The only three men I can think of are Bill Wooten, Tom Van Meter, and Chauncey Upsell. They were sailors on the same ship and now they run together, whore together, and, if the truth be known, roll drunks together."

Sullivan turned his attention to Kate and said, "Come to think of it, I saw Chauncey and Bill Wooten yesterday, and they were scratched up some."

Shannon had told Kate about her struggles as she tried to fight off her attackers and she knew she had found her men.

"Where do they drink?" she said.

"Always at the Cross Keys on Kelley Street."

Without turning, he said, "What happened, Kate?"

The girl knew that now was the time for the truth.

"Two of them—I believe, Wooten and Upsell— raped my sister. Van Meter was drunk, but he tried."

"Oh my God, that's a terrible thing to hear," the cop said. "I'll see if I can get a detective interested in the case," the cop said. "But I warn you now, a rape in the the Five Points usually goes without investigation. I'll see what I can do myself, but that will be little enough. I don't have the authority a detective has, and my orders are to walk the beat, keep the peace, and nothing else."

Kate hesitated, fearing that Sullivan might suspect something, but she had another question to ask.

"Is Ben Hollister still in town?"

"Jesus, Mary, and Joseph and all the saints in Heaven, girl, what do you want with such a man?" Sullivan said. "Is this your day to speak of ruffians?"

"He's a friend of my father's," Kate said, which was true.

Hollister was a gambler who'd worked the Mississippi steamboats, then fell on hard times. He used to visit Kate's father regularly since they both had an interest in literature, but she hadn't seen him in several months.

It was said that Hollister was a notorious dueler back in the old days and had killed eight men, but her pa said that number was probably exaggerated.

"Yes, he's still in the Five Points," Sullivan said. "He firmly believes he can outrun a losing streak that started years ago, but of course he can't. The toughs and gangs around here leave him alone, though. He has a reputation as a bad man to tangle with."

The cop stared hard at Kate. "And a bad man for you to tangle with," he said.

"My pa wants me to return one of Mr. Hollister's books," Kate said. "That's all."

"He still lives in Birmingham Lane, but bring the book to me, and I'll give it to him," Sullivan said. "The lane isn't a safe place for a young lady."

"Yes, I'll do that," Kate said. "And you'll let me know . . ."

"If I can get a detective to take the case? Yes, I will."

The girl whispered her thanks and stepped into the rain.

CHAPTER FORTY-NINE

Birmingham Lane was a narrow alley between four-story tenements, the upper apartments accessed by outside, rickety wooden stairs. It was a foul, impoverished place where pigs still roamed and its people lived lives of poverty and desperation.

As Kate Kerrigan remembered, Ben Hollister lived on the ground floor, and his door was splintered by three bullet holes, now healing over thanks to time and weather.

Kate recalled her father telling her that Hollister had killed a man attempting to steal his brass doorknocker. The three holes made a clover shape that could be covered by a silver dollar and bore eloquent testimony to the gambler's aim and temperament.

Her heart thudding in her chest, Kate used the polished knocker, and a moment later a man's voice reached her from inside.

"Go away."

"I'll do no such thing," Kate said. "This is Kate Cotter, and I demand to speak with you."

"Patrick's daughter?"

"As ever was."

"Hold on a minute."

Locks clicked and chains rattled, then the door opened and a tall, slender man, somewhere on the far side of forty, stood smiling at her.

With considerable Southern charm he bowed Kate into a small parlor, sparsely furnished but swept and clean. A hand-tinted lithograph of a Mississippi steamboat hung over the fireplace.

"I apologize that my present circumstances do not allow me to properly welcome such an honored guest," Hollister said. His clothes were much patched but had once been expensive and spoke of people and places beyond Kate's imagining. "What can I do for you, Miss Cotter? Consider me your obedient servant."

"I need to borrow a pistol, Mr. Hollister," she said. "I know you have such a thing."

"Good Lord, young lady, whatever for? What a most singular request."

Kate recalled a phrase she'd once read in a newspaper, one that Hollister would understand. "It's an affair of honor, sir," she said.

Hollister was silent for few moments, then said, "I suspect that this is an *affaire du coeur*," Hollister said. "But it is none of my concern and I will not pursue the matter."

"May I have the pistol?" Kate said, her chin determined.

"Miss Kerrigan, have you ever killed a man?"

Kate shook her head. "No, I have not."

"There's no going back from a killing," Hollister said. "After the deed is done, not all your tears, nor all your prayers, can bring the dead back again. For the rest of your life you live with it."

"I protect mine," Kate said. "And when I fail to protect them, I will exact vengeance for them."

"Since you are Patrick's daughter, I will do this for you," Hollister said. "I think you will pursue this vengeance of yours no matter what I say." He sighed and said, "Better you get the instrument of your revenge from me."

Hollister rose and stepped to a dresser. He opened the bottom drawer and brought out a rectangular walnut case. He opened the case and revealed the contents to Kate. A beautiful blue revolver with an elegant side-mounted hammer nestled in red velvet along with a powder flask, percussion caps, and both round balls and paper cartridges.

The gambler said, "This is a Model 1855 revolver designed by a Colt gunsmith named Elisha Root. It shoots a .31 caliber ball and I had the barrel cut back to three inches."

"Will it suit my purpose?" Kate said.

"I don't know what your purpose is," Hollister said.

"I think you do, sir," Kate said.

"God help me, I have an idea," Hollister said. "I have heard things, terrible, sad things."

The gambler closed the case lid, as though he had made up his mind.

"I can't dissuade you from this course?" he said.

"No," Kate said. "I am determined to see justice done."

"You have the face of an angel, Kate, an avenging angel." Hollister sighed more deeply this time and

said, "Then so be it. I'll load the Root for you before
you leave. Make sure the powder stays dry."

"I appreciate this, Mr. Hollister," Kate said.

He shook his head. "My God, you're only a slip of
a girl."

"As I told you before, I fight for what's mine," Kate
said. "And I always will."

"The Root is not a man killer like the Colt .45,"
Hollister said. "You'll need to be close and aim for the
broadest part of the body."

"How close?" Kate said.

"Within spitting distance," Hollister said. He stared
at the girl. "Changed your mind?"

Kate shook her head.

"You have the makings, Miss Cotter. I sense a
courage and a ruthlessness in you that I've found in
few men," Hollister said. "If it is His divine will, may
God help you in this endeavor."

CHAPTER FIFTY

The evening after Kate Kerrigan's meeting with Ben Hollister, her father retired to bed early with a bad cold.

Kate quickly changed into a modest green cotton dress with a high collar and threw her late mother's cloak over her shoulders. The dress had two deep pockets in front and into one of those she slipped the Root Colt. A white straw hat completed her outfit and she decided she looked like an innocent Irish girl just arrived in the Five Points.

Shannon, still recovering from her ordeal, was asleep, whimpering every now and then as her bad dreams returned and tormented her.

Kate kissed her sister on the cheek and then slipped out of the house.

According to the chipped china clock on the mantel it was nearly ten.

The Cross Keys saloon was a smoky, noisy gin mill that smelled of sweaty, unwashed bodies, cheap perfume, spilled beer, and the usual background fragrance of urine and vomit.

Kate had her bottom pinched five times before she reached the long, mahogany bar, backed by six bartenders, splendid creatures with slicked-down hair and diamond stickpins in their cravats.

When one of the bartenders, among the aristocracy of the Five Points, deigned to look in Kate's direction, she dropped a little curtsey and ordered a small sherry, "Sir, if you please."

"I'll pay that for the little lady," a rough-edged voice said behind her.

A huge, hairy forearm reached out and a massive hand grabbed the sherry glass. It looked like a tiny, amber wildflower in his great paw.

Kate turned and looked into the middle button of a man's plaid shirt.

She raised her eyes and saw a broad, red-veined face and fleshy wide nose broken to a pulp. The man had heavy-lidded eyes, pendulous, unshaven jowls, and the chest and shoulders of a village blacksmith.

He seemed as huge and indestructible as a German ironclad.

Kate thought of the revolver in her pocket and feared that its tiny ball would bounce off such a man and do him no more harm than a stinging gnat.

"So what brings you to Five Points, dearie?" the man said, his hand already tracing the curve of Kate's hip.

She played her role to the hilt.

"Oh kind sir, I've just arrived from old Ireland and I'm looking for a place to lay my poor head," she said.

"Well, am I not from the old country my ownself?"

the man said. "And is my name not Bill Wooten? We are well met, indeed."

It was only now Kate noticed that he had a fresh scratch across his low, brutish forehead. This was one of them. One of the rapists. She'd thought it might take days to find him, but here he was, big and bold as brass.

"I have the very place for you," the man said. "It's a boardinghouse run by Mrs. O'Hara, as respectable a lady as you'll ever find." He winked. "No gentleman callers, if such are to your liking."

"Oh no, sir," Kate said. "It has been in my mind of late to enter holy orders."

"Is that so?" Wooten said. "And you'll make a fine nun, I'll be bound."

He grabbed Kate's arm in his huge meaty fist.

"Come and meet my friends, two Catholic, church-going gentlemen as ever was, lay to that."

As Wooten half-dragged Kate to a table, he shouldered a slatternly woman aside. She smiled at the girl, revealing black teeth, and said, "Watch your step, dearie."

"My associates," the big man said. "The one with the white eye is Tom Van Meter and t'other with the warts all over his ugly mug is Chauncey Upsell."

Van Meter smiled at Kate. "I say we leave now," he said. "Mrs. O'Hara locks her door early."

"Good idea," Upsell said. He grinned at Kate. "You'll be safe with us, me darlin'."

The events that followed after Kate left the pub played out exactly as she feared and knew they would.

Oddly silent, but constantly exchanging grins, as the three men walked her closer to what seemed an abandoned warehouse they began to glance over their shoulders.

Satisfied that there were no prying eyes on the street, they stopped, and with considerable violence dragged Kate into a doorway.

Van Meter kicked open the door open and threw her into a dark, echoing stairwell.

"Oh sirs, what are you doing?" Kate cried out. "This is not Mrs. O'Hara's."

"You can go there later," Bill Wooten said.

"If ye can walk, that is," Upsell said.

"Please," Kate said, "I am a virgin, destined for the nunnery."

"Not for much longer," Van Meter said.

"Me first," Upsell said. "Girlie, I'm gonna bust you wide open."

Convinced they had a terrified, cowering victim in their power, the grinning Wooten thumbed a match into flame and lit a stub of candle he'd picked up from the bottom step.

For a moment, no one had a hand on Kate.

"Damn you all to hell!" she yelled.

Suddenly the Root Colt was in Kate's hand and she fired.

The bullet hit Wooten high in the chest, and he fell back, gawping at the blood pumping out of him. Deafened, her ears ringing, Kate thumbed back the hammer again, wondering at how steady was her hand. Chauncey Upsell charged toward her, cursing, his clawed hands reaching for Kate's throat.

Kate's ball, fired at a distance of a couple of feet, crashed in the thug's forehead and dropped him like a felled steer.

Tom Van Meter yelled that he was out of it.

Like the other two who sprawled on the floor, one dead, the second coughing up frothing blood, Van Meter was a skull-and-knuckle fighter and good with the club and sap against any opponent. But fighting with a gun was alien to him. Kate Cotter's revolver had turned a hundred-pound girl into more than his equal and even now, as he saw his death in her eyes, he couldn't grasp what was happening to him.

"Her name was Shannon. I am her sister," Kate said. "You raped her."

"No . . ." Van Meter said. "I didn't . . . I couldn't . . ."

"You watched these two animals rape her and did nothing."

"I'm sorry. Look, put the gun away, and I'll buy your drink."

"It's way too late for sorrow, Van Meter. Yours and mine."

She shot into the man's belly, fired again and watched him fall.

Gunsmoke fogged the stairwell as Kate stepped to Wooten.

The man was still alive.

"For God's sake get me a doctor," he said, his eyes wild. "I don't want to die like this."

Kate spat on him.

She had one ball left—the one Bill Wooten took between the eyes and rode into hell.

CHAPTER FIFTY-ONE

Kate Kerrigan rose from her chair and stepped to the parlor window. Annie Oakley was a mannish-looking girl, but she always smelled like wildflowers, and that scent lingered as Kate watched a little paint gelding throw a cussing Shorty Hawkins for the seventh time that morning.

Thrust to the forefront of her mind by the Ingrid Hult affair, the memories refused to leave her. The rape had made Shannon pregnant, and she died a few months later after giving birth to a stillborn child. Shannon had lost the will to live and had long sought death. She was buried during a roaring, flashing thunderstorm as though the gods were angry that she had met such a fate.

Kate left the parlor and asked Flossie her lady's maid to help her dress for riding. A gallop in the cool of the morning would help clear her head and rid her mind of the images of the past.

* * *

"The Indian visits Josiah Mosely's grave every night and sings death songs," Trace Kerrigan said. "Bill Cody says his people can hear him and it's scaring the womenfolk, makes then think of Judgment Day."

Frank Cobb nodded. "That means Cloud Passing believes Josiah's soul is lingering and he's trying to send it on its way. As a great warrior his spirit must travel up the long fork of the Milky Way to Seana, the camp of the dead. If his spirit lingers, it will become evil and remain on earth."

Trace and Frank sat on the top board of the corral and watched Shorty Hawkins put a young paint cutting horse through its paces. Shorty had been bucked off a dozen times, but now the paint had accepted the saddle without fuss and seemed more tolerant of the man on his back.

"Bill says he sent some men up there with one of his Sioux to chase away Cloud Passing," Trace said. "But the Sioux refused to enter the cemetery and the others said they saw no sign of the Indian anyway."

"There's no use chasing after a Cheyenne in the dark," Frank said. "If he doesn't want to be found, you won't find him." He smiled. "Lookee there. Shorty is a-settin' and a-grinnin' on that little hoss like he's the king's cousin. I reckon he don't know what he's in for. That pony has a mean eye."

"Ten dollars says Shorty stays with him this time," Trace said.

"You got it," Frank said.

"Shorty's a bronc buster from way back," Trace said.

"Is that a fact?" Frank said.

Suddenly the paint unwound like a coiled spring. All four hooves off the ground, it jumped three feet into the air, landed, and then bucked its way around the corral. Shorty held on, but he was being bounced around like a rag doll and had already lost his hat and most of his composure. "Stay with him, Shorty!" Trace yelled. "Ride him, cowboy!"

Then two unfortunate occurrences happened within a couple of seconds. First Shorty Hawkins was bucked off and hit the dirt hard in a cloud of dust. The next moment the wild-eyed paint decided he didn't much like the two humans sitting on the corral fence and sideswiped them, his heavy ranch saddle acting like a battering ram. Trace and Frank fell backward and thudded onto the ground in a tangle of chaps, spurs, and cusses.

Frank was the first to recover. He sat up, found his hat, slammed it onto his head, and extended his open palm. "Give me my ten bucks," he said. Then, groaning, he laid back and said, "Remind me to shoot Shorty Hawkins at the first available opportunity."

Before her morning ride Kate Kerrigan led her mare from the barn and chose that moment to pass the corral. She stopped and frowned at her son, her segundo, and bronc buster all lying on their backs on the ground.

"I don't pay you three to laze in the sun all day," she said. "Frank, after I come back from my ride I'd like to talk to you at the house. That is, if it's quite convenient and won't interrupt your nap."

Kate led the mare away, her back stiff.

Trace and Frank exchanged glances and then Trace

said, grinning, "Good luck, Frank. I think you're going to need it."

"And that's the whole story, Frank," Kate Kerrigan said. "I had to tell someone and I trust you to keep it to yourself."

Frank Cobb had listened in silence and now he said, "Does Bill Cody know about this?"

"No. I'm the only one Annie Oakley spoke to. Ingrid Hult is a killer, Frank, but God forgive me, I can't blame her. I think what she did was completely justified."

"It was a reckoning," Frank said. "And I can't blame her, either. But she had a hand in the killing of Slide McKenzie. Jim Benson murdered a caged, defenseless man in cold blood."

"McKenzie was a snake, Frank," Kate said. "Have you forgotten what he tried to do to me?"

"No, Kate, I haven't. But McKenzie was killed to keep him from talking. That was no reckoning, no eye for an eye." Frank shrugged. "If Benson gets a good lawyer a jury may figure it differently, but I can only tell you how I see it."

"Frank, you're saying to me that Ingrid Hult could hang for the McKenzie murder?" Kate said.

"It's possible. Not at all likely, but possible."

"That vile man still haunts us. There's just no getting rid of him," Kate said. She slapped her hand on the parlor table. "Ingrid Hult and Jim Benson work for Bill Cody. This is his problem, not mine."

"Do you really believe that?" Frank said. "Seems to

me that rape and its consequences are every woman's problem. But I'm a man, so what the hell do I know?"

"A lot, apparently," Kate said. "Well, what do we do? Wash our hands of the whole sorry business and let Mr. Cody handle it?"

"Or we can say nothing at all. Come spring Bill Cody's train will pull out and we can wave it good-bye and then get on with the business of running a ranch."

"In other words what Mr. Cody doesn't know won't hurt him. Or us."

"That's the general idea," Frank said.

Kate was lost in thought for a few moments, but then she shook her head and said, "No, I can't do it, Frank. I helped bring law and order to this part of Texas, and people depend on me as the only law west of the Pecos. Despite my sympathy for them, two murderers are right here, on my land, and I can't turn my back on my principles. I'll do what has to be done to resolve this situation, and I'll do it within the limits of Texas law."

"Kate, you once told me about your sister and—"

"I told you about Shannon," Kate said. "The difference is that there was no law in the Five Points, and where there is no law the law can't be broken."

"You were judge, jury, and executioner," Frank said.

"Yes, I was, back then in a lawless time and place. But we have laws in Texas, and I'm bound to uphold them. The Five Points was anarchy, disorder, chaos. I won't visit that same hell on West Texas."

Frank thought that through and then said, "All right, then we bring matters to a head."

"By bringing in Mr. Cody?" Kate said.

"No, Kate, by bringing in Ingrid Hult and Ducking Jim Benson."

"I don't understand," Kate said.

But then Frank Cobb explained it to her, and she understood perfectly.

CHAPTER FIFTY-TWO

"I want everybody mounted but the cook," Frank Cobb said. "This has got to look good to Bill Cody and his people."

"Thirty riders to capture one raggedy Indian?" Trace Kerrigan said. "Cloud Passing will see an army coming and light a shuck."

"He won't, because I'm going up to the cemetery to talk to him tonight," Frank said. "You know what a Cheyenne Dog Soldier with a Winchester can do? He's got to be on our side from the git-go. And Trace, make sure the hands share a few jugs of whiskey tonight. I want them likkered up good and smelling of whiskey tomorrow."

"There will be a few hangovers tomorrow," Quinn said.

"That's all to the good," Frank said. "Understand this, I don't want respectable, God-fearing KK punchers riding with me."

"That ain't likely anyhow," Quinn said. "We don't have any of them."

Frank smiled. "I know. But I need the hands to look and smell like a drunken lynch mob. You figure you can make that happen, Quinn?"

"It ain't much of a stretch," Quinn said.

"Isn't . . . isn't much of a stretch," Frank said. "I don't want your mother accusing me of not teaching you to talk proper."

"Ma wants me to go to college," Quinn said.

"And a good thing too," Frank said.

"I want to do what you do, Frank."

"My time is over, Quinn. Law and order has come to the West, and there's no room left for fellers like me. We're being crowded out."

"I want to work with cattle," Quinn said.

"No, you don't. Cowboying is something a man does when he can't do anything else. You know what I want?"

Quinn shook his head.

"I want to build me a cabin somewhere in California and grow peaches," Frank said. "I'm right partial to peaches, but I've only eaten them out of a can. I want to grow fresh peaches, eat some, sell the rest."

"If I ever drive a herd that way I'll come buy some of your peaches," Quinn said.

Frank smiled. "Sure you will, but only after you've graduated from college."

As the day faded into evening Frank Cobb made his way up the rise to the cemetery. Below, the Kerrigan mansion was lit up like Dodge City on a Saturday night and a mile or so to the west Bill Cody's tent city glowed gold and orange in the darkness, two beacons of civilization in a vast, somber landscape.

Coming up on a Cheyenne Dog Soldier in the gloom of night was an activity calculated to get a man's pulse pounding, and Frank made more noise than he had to, his eyes warily scanning the murk ahead of him.

He reached Mosely's fresh grave and looked around, but there was no sign of the Indian. Despite feeling naked without his gun—a sign of his peaceful intentions—Frank decided he would settle in for a wait.

He didn't have to wait long.

Something cold and hard pressed into the back of Frank's neck and a voice, lacking even a hint of civility, said, "Why you here?"

Frank didn't move. "Howdy, Cloud Passing," he said. "I'm here to talk to you."

"Then talk," the Indian said.

"I'd rather do it without a gun at my head," Frank said.

"Stand up."

Frank stood and Cloud Passing glanced at his waist and said, "White men are sly. Cobb, do you have a sneaky gun?"

"No, I'm unarmed," Frank said.

Cloud Passing lowered his Colt. "What you want to talk about? The spirit of Mose-ly listens."

Frank said, "I want to talk about your future, Cloud Passing."

"Indian has no future. Everybody know that, and if you don't, you are loco."

"You want to stay on with Buffalo Bill, don't you?" Frank said.

"Bill Cody good man, but big liar. His talk is mightier than his deeds."

Coyotes yipped as the moon rose and a sharp-edged breeze whispered among the cemetery headstones.

"Do you wish to stay with him?" Frank asked again.

"Why you ask these questions?" Cloud Passing said. "I think you want to hang this poor Indian."

"In a manner of speaking, you're right," Frank said. "That's what I want to talk to you about."

"White man, why you want to hang me for bad things I did not do?"

"No, no, I don't want that," Frank said. This wasn't going well. "I'm going to pretend to hang you. You know *pretend*—make believe, sham, fake—I'm not really going to hang you, Cloud Passing."

"Pretend," the Cheyenne said. "Put noose around my neck on gallows, drop trap, and then say it was pretend."

"You've seen men hung before?" Frank said.

"Seen many Cheyenne Dog Soldiers hung on white men's gallows."

"I'll put a noose around your neck, but that's just for the crowd," Frank said. "I want you to help me, Cloud Passing. Help Bill Cody. Help a lot of people."

"You will pretend hang me, Cobb?"

"That's right, old fellow. Pretend hang you."

The Indian's Colt came up fast. "This here pretend pistol. Now I pretend I blow your goddamn brains out."

"No, wait," Frank said, feeling that he was on a

sinking ship. "We need to talk about this. It doesn't need to come to shooting."

But Cloud Passing wasn't listening. The Indian's eyes stared beyond Frank to Josiah Mosely's grave. Frank turned and saw what Cloud Passing saw.

A column of gray mist hung over the grave, and as Frank watched it drifted toward the Indian and then slowly enveloped him. The mist lingered for a few moments and then moved on and slowly faded into the darkness.

Such random patches of evening fog were not rare on the prairie and Frank paid it no mind, but to Cloud Passing it was an omen and he seemed keenly affected by it. Like a man waking from sleep he blinked a few times, lowered his gun, and said, "We will talk now. Mose-ly wills it. He says to state your intentions."

The mist had arrived in the nick of time, and Frank Cobb was not one to look a gift horse in the mouth. He stepped closer to the Cheyenne and said, "All right, here's what I plan to do . . ."

"And what's in it for you, Cloud Passing, is that your name will be cleared, and you'll no longer be a hunted man," Frank said. "You can go wherever you want, do whatever you want. Bill Cody's Wild West tours Europe next year. You can go with him and see the sights."

"Cobb, if you were Indian, would you trust white man to put your head in noose and trust that he was only pretending to hang you?" Cloud Passing said.

Frank said, "No, not for a moment."

The Cheyenne stared hard at the other man and then said, "I see no lie in your eyes, Cobb. You can hang me."

"You won't regret this," Frank said. "I won't really string you up, I give you my word."

"I regret it already," Cloud Passing said.

CHAPTER FIFTY-THREE

Next morning a few lingering stars still hung in the sky as Frank Cobb led a hung-over posse of thirty punchers, including Trace and Quinn Kerrigan, in search of Cloud Passing.

Feeling wretched, martyred by last night's whiskey, the KK hands were unusually quiet, though every now and then Shorty Hawkins groaned and begged someone to shoot him and bring his suffering to an end.

Relief was at hand, though the cowboys didn't know it yet. The buckboard that brought up the rear of the column was stocked with jugs of 40-rod, well hidden under a canvas tarp.

Frank Cobb had planned it well. There was not a rowdier, wilder, and more downright dangerous creature than a hung-over waddie on the prod who'd managed to get himself likkered up again. When they rode into Bill Cody's camp his boys would be a drunken, unruly mob eager to hang a murdering savage.

"They're mighty quiet," Trace said. The only sound was the thud of hooves and the creak of saddle leather. Now and then a man coughed and a few groaned.

"I don't like doing this to them, but there's no other way," Frank said. "When we meet up with Cody's people I want a drunk, hanging posse, but I can't depend on the hands acting the part."

"So you're going to kill them all with whiskey," Quinn said.

"Like I said, there's no other way," Frank said. "I wish there was."

Trace said, keeping his voice low, "Doesn't it worry you that the boys will be so drunk they'll hang the Indian for real?"

"Out of spite, like," Quinn said.

"I'm playing with fire here, and I know it," Frank said. "But we're going to flush out a murderer and save an innocent man from hanging. The hands are young, and after a bellyful of busthead they'll sleep it off. A man can sleep off a hanging but it will take him all of eternity."

"Hell, Frank, you sure thought this thing through," Trace said.

"No I didn't. I'm taking a heap of chances here, and the odds are against me."

An example of how easily things could go wrong happened after Cloud Passing stepped out of the trees under a flaming sky bannered with scarlet and jade. The Cheyenne raised his hands in surrender and Frank Cobb thought to himself, "Well, so far, so good."

But then one of the young hands shook out his rope and kicked his horse into a dead run. Cloud Passing saw the danger and turned to face the whooping puncher. Too late. The loop settled around the

Indian's chest and he was yanked off his feet and then dragged behind the galloping pony.

The puncher let loose with a rebel yell and set spurs to his mount. The Cheyenne's body bounced and rolled across the uneven ground, a dust cloud kicking up behind him.

"Stop!" Trace yelled. "You're killing him!"

But Frank was already on the move. A two-hundred-pound man riding a twelve-hundred-pound American stud at a flat-out gallop, he angled toward the hollering cowboy and drove his horse into the man and his mount. The collision was incredibly violent and sounded like a falling boulder hitting wet sand. For a split second shock registered on the young puncher's face and then he and his horse went down and hit the ground hard. Frank drew rein as the cowboy rolled away from his kicking mount and then climbed shakily to his feet.

Frank swung out of the saddle, yelled to the puncher, "See to your damned horse," and then took a knee beside Cloud Passing. The Indian showed some scrapes and bruises on his face and hands, but otherwise seemed unhurt. Frank helped him to his feet and said, "Sorry, that wasn't supposed to happen."

"Did you tell cowboy that this only pretend?" Cloud Passing said.

"No, I didn't," Frank said. "Sorry again."

"Then tell them my hanging is pretend," the Indian said. "Your men too quick with a rope."

"Cloud Passing, you're going to hear me say some pretty hard things about stringing you up, and sich. I don't mean any of it," Frank said. "I swear, you'll be just fine."

"Tell that to your cowboys," the Indian said.

Frank turned Cloud Passing over to Trace and Quinn. "Get out the jugs from the buckboard and pass them around," he said. "And make damn sure the Indian stays safe."

"Damn sure," Cloud Passing said.

The young cowboy had his horse on its feet and was slapping dust off himself with his hat. "Are you all right? No broken bones?" Frank said. The puncher nodded and Frank stepped to the horse, ran his hand over its legs, and then patted its neck. "He seems fine," he said.

"You could've killed me, Frank," the cowboy said. "You came damn near to it."

Frank Cobb smiled. "Hell, Clem, you're young. I knew you would bounce." Then, his smile gone, "I need the Indian alive, so leave him be."

"I thought we were gonna hang him," the puncher said, his young face puzzled.

"We are, and we ain't," Frank said. "Go get yourself a drink."

"After getting damn near killed, I need one," Clem said, scowling. He threw Frank an accusing glance, turned on his heel, gathered up the reins of his horse, and walked toward the other punchers.

Frank watched the youngster go and then shook his head. It seemed that Clem Brixton was not a forgiving man. The kid got upset way too easily over little things. That was his problem.

For the next couple of hours as the sun rose higher and filtered yellow light shone through the tree canopies, the jugs were passed among the cowboys, who fell on them with delight. The best cure for a whiskey hangover was more whiskey. Everybody knew that.

Frank Cobb watched the KK riders with growing satisfaction. The boys were getting good and drunk again and would play their part well. When just an inch or two of booze sloshed in the jugs, Frank called the punchers together. Cloud Passing, his hands and feet bound, was lying on his side in the wagon.

"Boys," Frank said, "you have done something splendid today, and by that I mean the capture of the murdering Indian who goes by the name Cloud Passing, or, as I prefer to call him, the Demon Scalper."

As he knew it would, this brought cheers from the hands and a sidelong look from the horrified Cloud Passing.

"Let's string him up," someone in the crowd yelled. "A scalp for the gallant Custer."

This also drew cheers and shouts of "Hear-hear," and "Huzzah!"

Frank let the punchers see his smile. "No, not now. Boys, don't rob yourself of your glory."

Clem Brixton, still smarting over the rough handling he'd had from Frank, said, "What the hell does that mean?"

The punchers muttered to one another and there were a few calls for an immediate hanging.

Trace Kerrigan held up his hands for silence. "Listen up, men," he said. "The murders were committed in Buffalo Bill's camp. I say we take our prisoner there and let Bill Cody and his people see what kind of men we are. And what kind of men we are?" Then at a shout, "The best damn Indian fighters in Texas, that's who!"

This time the cheering was enthusiastic and prolonged, but then a dissenting voice yelled, "What about the hanging?"

Frank Cobb again took up the speechifying. "Men, we're going to invite Bill Cody's people to attend our necktie party. It's their right, and they'll appreciate our gesture of goodwill. What do you say?"

More cheering and from the hands nary a word of disagreement.

Frank smiled. So far everything was going to plan. As the jugs were passed around and drained, he stepped to the buckboard and said to Cloud Passing, "It will be all over soon and you'll be a free man."

The Indian said, "Cobb, if you hang me—"

"By mistake, you mean?"

"I'll come back as evil spirit and torment you for the rest of your life."

Frank laid a hand on Cloud Passing's shoulder. "You won't hang. Trust me," he said. "Things are going real well."

And the Cheyenne groaned.

CHAPTER FIFTY-FOUR

Amid wild whoops of triumph and festive revolvers firing into the air, the KK ranch posse rode into the Bill Cody camp like a bunch of drunk cowboys hoorawing a cow town.

Kate Kerrigan was not amused, and Bill Cody was alarmed enough to buckle on his guns. "If you will excuse me, dear lady," he said before darting out of the tent.

Kate turned to her lady's maid, and said, frowning as the shooting, cheers, and yells continued, "Flossie, go see what's happening out there. And if you happen on my sons or Frank Cobb tell them I wish to speak to them."

Flossie, a robust girl who had driven Kate's carriage in the absence of Shorty Hawkins, said, "Yes, ma'am," and stepped outside. Kate knew of Frank Cobb's plan, but she didn't think its execution would be quite so . . . boisterous.

The noise died down as Frank called for silence and he then began to speak to the crowd. Kate couldn't quite hear what he was saying, but after a couple of minutes the tent flap was drawn back. Kate expected Flossie, but it was Bill Cody who entered, his face grave.

"Everyone's been invited to a hanging, Kate," he said. "Frank Cobb has the crowd all riled up. Your KK riders captured Cloud Passing and they plan to hang him for the murders of the three cowboys and Slide McKenzie."

Playacting, but hating herself for what she had to say, Kate told Bill that justice must take its course. "The ball has opened and now there will be no stopping it." she said.

Bill Cody gave Kate a long look. "You've changed your tune, Kate. I thought you figured the Indian was innocent."

"I did, but now I'm not so sure," Kate said. "All the evidence points to Cloud Passing." She smiled. "Doesn't it?"

Before Bill could answer, Flossie stepped into the tent. Her pretty face was flushed with excitement. "They're hanging the Indian," she said. "We're all invited. Mr. Cobb says he'll string him up from the nearest tree."

Bill Cody was crestfallen and he looked at Kate in disbelief. "Your segundo plans to hang an innocent man. I . . . I can't believe you're not ordering him to stop." Then, his face stiff, "Dear lady, you've changed."

Kate could not let the man suffer any longer. She said, "Mr. Cody, are you familiar with Shakespeare's play, *Hamlet*?"

Bill looked puzzled, but he said, "I am familiar with the tormented Prince of Denmark, yes."

"Then you'll recall him saying: *The play's the thing wherein I'll catch the conscience of the king.*"

"Yes, I once heard that great thespian Henry Irving utter those immortal words," Bill said. "And from that day to this I've never forgotten them."

"Mr. Cody, today we are all actors in a play, trying to catch the conscience of . . ."

"The real guilty party!" Bill exclaimed in considerable triumph.

"Exactly," Kate said. "Now if you and Flossie will assist me, I will go outside and hopefully catch the final act of our little tragedy."

Kate guessed that several hundreds of Bill Cody's people had gathered to watch Cloud Passing hauled to his feet for their inspection. The comments from the crowd were varied and many:

"A savage-looking beast."

"Hang the murderer."

"Revenge for Custer."

"Indian animals. Hang 'em all."

And more sinister than any other, "Let's do it. Let's string him up now."

Bill Cody had provided a folding canvas chair for Kate and an upturned bucket to rest her swollen ankle. She had an excellent view of the mob and of Frank Cobb standing on the back of the buckboard, holding the rope end of the noose around the Cheyenne's neck. A Dog Soldier's pride would not allow Cloud Passing to show fear, but Kate thought he seemed resigned to his fate. She fervently hoped

Frank knew what he was doing. A hanging mob could get out of hand very quickly.

There was no sign of Ingrid Hult or Jim Benson.

Frank was doing his best to stall for time, launching into one impassioned speech after another. But the crowd and his own drunk punchers wanted a hanging . . . and they wanted it now.

Finally Frank Cobb could delay no longer. It was time to force Ingrid Hult's hand. Cloud Passing was made to lie down again and the buckboard, Quinn at the reins, rolled forward toward the tree line. The crowd, still hundreds strong, performers and roustabouts, fell in behind, including a score of solemn Sioux and Cheyenne Indians. It began to rain, a steady, dismal drizzle, and Bill Cody, his head bent, took up the rear, walking. Suddenly he looked like an old, white-haired man.

Ingrid Hult was nowhere in sight.

Frank Cobb saw Kate sitting out in the open and cantered his horse toward her. He drew rein, leaned from the saddle, and said, "Kate, it isn't working. Damn it all, Ingrid Hult isn't going to play, and it won't work."

"I can see that," Kate said. She turned to Flossie, who stood at her side, and said, "Bring the carriage. We'll go after the crowd and try to stop them."

"It's begun, Kate," Frank said. "I don't think anybody can stop it."

"We'll most certainly give it a try," Kate said.

By the time Kate Kerrigan hobbled into her carriage, the buckboard and its attendant crowd were halfway to the wild oaks. The rain had increased to a steady downpour and Kate hoped it would dampen enthusiasm for a hanging. Shorty Hawkins kept an oilskin slicker under the driver's seat and Flossie put this on as she took up the reins. After a struggle Kate pulled up the canvas top behind her and found some shelter.

"Flossie, whip up the horses and catch the buckboard if you can," Kate said.

"Yes, ma'am."

The carriage lurched forward and then it rocked violently as a cloaked woman jumped inside. Her hood slid back off her head and Kate came face-to-face with Ingrid Hult. The woman looked pale, and her eyes were reddened as though she'd cried recently. She turned and yelled to Flossie, "Catch up to them and don't even think about sparing the horses."

"Yes, ma'am," the girl said. She cracked the whip, and the team took off at a trot that quickly became a canter.

"I didn't think you'd show," Kate said.

"You know why I'm here?" Ingrid said.

"Yes. To confess to the murders of Davy Hoyle, Andy Porter, and Buck Nolan and to save an innocent man's life."

"You're well informed, Mrs. Kerrigan," Ingrid said. "And you're correct. It all ends today."

That last statement should have rung an alarm bell in Kate's mind, but surprised as she was by the woman's sudden appearance it did not register. Only a moment later, when it was too late, did she realize what it meant.

A single revolver shot racketed into the morning, and startled, Kate said, "Flossie, stop!" And then to Ingrid, "Where did that come from?"

"No, Flossie, drive on," Ingrid said. She turned to Kate. "It was nothing, Mrs. Kerrigan. Nothing at all."

CHAPTER FIFTY-FIVE

Judicial hangings in the West were pure theater since they were well attended, and the crowd had to be entertained as they watched the law at work. After a prayer, and maybe the singing of a hymn or two, the condemned man could usually be cajoled into a speech that would please the ladies in the audience. The doomed man, previously coached by the presiding lawmen, would say that whiskey and fallen women led him to this pass . . . but he had a good mother. That last would bring nods of approval from the matrons present and a few would shed a tear after the trapdoor was sprung. The ceremony seldom varied, and more often than not the condemned died with at least some of his dignity intact.

But a lynching practiced no such niceties.

The condemned man was usually abused and derided as he was dragged to the noose and then hauled aloft by willing hands to strangle to death, the jeers and catcalls of the crowd the last thing he ever heard. That was to be Cloud Passing's fate as the crowd cheered and a noose was slung over a tree branch and dangled just six feet off the ground. Unless Frank Cobb and the Kerrigan brothers stopped the hanging the Cheyenne was a dead man. Easier said than done. Frank knew he could rely on the KK punchers, but Bill Cody's people were crying for blood, especially the cowboy performers, since the murders had happened to three of their own.

As a couple of men eagerly hung the noose around Cloud Passing's neck, six or seven others grabbed onto the rope to haul him off his feet and let him swing. The Cheyenne stared at Frank through the rain, and their eyes met. There was no accusation in the Indian's gaze, just resignation and perhaps disappointment.

Frank had given Cloud Passing his word, and in the West a man's word counted for everything. To go back on it now would leave a scar on Frank Cobb's conscience that would never heal. Trace Kerrigan looked at him, horrified, and Quinn was trying, unsuccessfully, to pull men off the rope. A blue-chinned Cody cowboy grabbed Quinn by the shoulder, yanked him around, and landed a right on his chin. Quinn staggered back and then fell. Trace, his pent-up anger boiling over, went after the cowboy, blocked the man's wild punch, and delivered a right hook to his chin. Before Trace had time to recover his stance, several of the Cody men, including a huge roustabout, came at him. Trace blocked a punch, ducked under another, and then for his pains took a roundhouse to his midsection from the roustabout that doubled him over. The KK hands ran to Trace's aid and the fighting became general. Close to a hundred men whaled at each other with fists and boots while a couple of hundred more, of both sexes, cheered them on.

Frank Cobb glanced at Cloud Passing. The Indian lay on the ground where he'd been dropped when the fight started and for now at least he was safe. Frank drew his Colt, fired into the air, got little response, and fired again. This time the muddy, battered combatants dropped their fists and glared at him.

"I'll shoot the next man who throws a punch," Frank said. He looked at Trace and Quinn, who had been in the thick of the scrap and were bloodied, and added, "And I don't give a damn who you are."

All of the KK hands wore guns, as did a few of the Cody people, but most knew of Frank Cobb by reputation, a draw fighter with bark on him who was a dangerous man to cross.

Bill Cody stepped between Frank and the others and said, "That's enough, you damned fools. Stop it now before someone gets killed."

Then a voice from the crowd, "Mr. Cody is right. Let's get on with the damn hanging and stop fighting among ourselves."

This was greeted with yells of agreement and beat-up men with bloody noses and black eyes picked themselves up off the ground and after a deal of handshaking, agreed that they should call a truce and get busy with the task on hand . . . hanging a black-hearted, murdering savage.

Frank Cobb still had his Colt in his hand. He'd thought it through and made up his mind. He would keep his word to Cloud Passing even though it meant a killing . . . and even his own death.

But the chiming harnesses of Kate's carriage

horses made every head turn, and Frank holstered his revolver. Still at a distance, Ingrid Hult stood up in the carriage and called out, "Stop the hanging! The murderer is here. Right here."

Everyone stood still in the rain, and for a second time Cloud Passing's moccasins thudded to the ground as the rope was released.

Kate's carriage rattled to a halt, and Ingrid Hult pulled her red cloak around her and stepped out into the crowd. "I'm here," she said. "I killed the three cowboys. I'm the one you should hang."

Bill Cody stepped to the girl's side. "My dear young lady, what are you telling us?" he said.

"They raped me, raped my sister, and she killed herself afterward," Ingrid said. "There were four of them, and I tracked down and killed one of them in Kansas. I discovered that the other three were with the show, and I killed them one by one. I scalped them to make it look like an Indian was to blame. But I won't let an innocent man hang for my crimes."

Ingrid's speech was greeted by a stunned silence. Frank Cobb emphasized the fact that Ingrid had told the truth by stepping to Cloud Passing and removing the noose from his neck.

"Cobb," the Cheyenne said. "No more pretend."

Frank smiled. "Never again, Injun. Never again."

Bill Cody had assumed his leadership role. His voice stern, he said, "Young lady, did you also murder Slide McKenzie?"

The girl shook her head. "No, it was Jim Benson who shot him. He did it for me. McKenzie was bartending in the saloon where I killed the first"—she spat out the word—"rapist. McKenzie threatened to tell you, and we were afraid that you would turn me over to the Rangers."

Bill was shocked. "My dear, laws are made to be broken and I've broke most of them, and that is why I would never welcome the Texas Rangers here. We would have handled such an affair ourselves."

Kate Kerrigan signaled to Flossie to help her out of the carriage. By now everyone in the crowd, including Kate, was thoroughly soaked, but no one had drifted away, held in place by the drama that was unfolding.

Supported by Flossie and helped by a cane, Kate limped toward Ingrid, who turned to her and smiled, and Kate remembered why she'd liked this beautiful girl on sight.

"Ingrid," Kate said, "no matter how you wish to handle this crisis in your life I'll help you every way I can. We can hire the best lawyers in the country and go to trial, or you and Jim can leave the United States for a while and start a new life. I have relatives in Ireland, a rough-and-ready bunch to be sure, but they'll welcome you with open arms."

"Splendid suggestions, Kate, first rate," Bill Cody said. "A stay in the Emerald Isle might just be the ticket, Ingrid. Your first step in what could become, after the passage of time, the gateway to a new and joyous life."

Rain plastered Ingrid's blond hair to her forehead. Her lips trembled. "Thank you, Mrs. Kerrigan. I think we'll do that. Thank you, thank you for both me and Jim's sakes."

CHAPTER FIFTY-SIX

"Well, I've lost two of my best, but the show must go on," Bill Cody said as he sat in Kate's parlor, amber bourbon glowing in the crystal glass in his hand.

"Yes, it's a long journey to Ireland, to be sure. And a whole new life ahead of them. But at least they'll have each other," Kate said.

"I'm sure it's for the best, Kate," Bill said.

Winifred the parlor maid tapped on the door and then showed Frank Cobb inside. The segundo made a routine report about moving part of the herd to winter pasture, and after Kate nodded her approval, Bill Cody said, "Now that I have you both together I have an announcement to make that's of the greatest moment."

"I declare, that sounds exciting, Mr. Cody," Kate said.

"It is exiting, as all of Buffalo Bill Cody's proclamations are," Bill said. "I fear that recent melancholy events have robbed my people of a certain—how shall it say it?—"*joie de verve*, to wit, that gaiety, high spirits, élan, and zest for life they were wont to display. In short, they're glum."

"And you have a plan to remedy this situation?" Kate said.

"Once again, dear lady, you have gone directly to the heart of the matter," Bill said. He flicked an atom of cigar ash off a glossy, knee-high boot and said, "I plan to put on a Wild West show for the KK ranch, the very show, and I mean this most earnestly, that I will stage for the crowned heads of Europe during my tour next summer." Bill beamed and sat back on his chair. "How is that for Cody gratitude?"

Kate laughed and clapped her hands as she bounced back and forth in her chair and said, "Huzzah!"

Emboldened by Kate's enthusiastic reaction, Bill said, "And you will see, for the very first time on any continent, my new spectacular, *Buffalo Bill Saves the Denver Stage*, with a cast of hundreds, maidens in distress, bloodthirsty Indians, brave cavalrymen, stampeding bison, and, of course, my gallant self astride a noble white charger."

Once again, her eyes alight, Kate applauded, laughed, and cried, "Three cheers for Buffalo Bill!"

For his part, Bill took all this as only his due. He stood, shook his silver hair over his shoulders, and struck a gallant pose.

Frank Cobb said, "When is the show, Bill? I need to make sure all the hands are free on that day."

"One week from this very day, Mr. Cobb, rain or shine, though inclement weather stands aside when Buffalo Bill takes the stage."

* * *

Despite a thunderstorm that soaked the audience and spawned mud that more than once threatened to overturn the Denver stage, Kate Kerrigan and the rest of the KK agreed that Bill Cody's Wild West show had been a great success. Even Cloud Passing got into the act and did a very credible job as Chief Yellow Hand. He allowed Bill to slay him and then obligingly died with considerable melodramatic display. Bill would later say that the Cheyenne got so worked up it took two full days to return him to a semblance of normality. "But he's a star," he said. "They're going to love him in London."

"You will travel to Europe, Kate. Your mind is made up?" Hiram Clay said.

"This summer," Kate said. She smiled. "Yes, my mind is made up."

"Well, all I can do is to say good luck and wish you bon voyage. I'll pray for your safe return," Clay said. "You own the steamship company, so your crossing will be a pleasant one. You'll be waited on hand and foot."

Kate laughed. "I don't own White Star, Hiram, I only have shares in the company. But I'm sure the service will be first rate."

"London. You'll stay in London?"

"Yes, for a few weeks while Bill Cody's show is there, and then I'll visit the old country. Ireland is beautiful in any season, but the summer is . . . well, as close to heaven on earth as it gets. More tea?"

Clay waited until his cup was refilled and then said, "Kate, I worry about you alone in London. I've heard some very bad things about the East End. For some reason Governor Oran Roberts and the Rangers keep informed about happenings abroad, and they tell me that women are murdered regularly in what's called the Whitechapel slum district. So please, stay away from there."

Kate smiled. "I most certainly will. And besides, I always carry my trusty derringer."

"I hope you will tell us of your adventures when you return from your wanderings in foreign lands," Clay said.

"You can be assured of that," Kate said. "I plan to have many to tell."

Turn the page for an exciting preview!

THE GREATEST WESTERN WRITERS
OF THE 21ST CENTURY

*For generations, the Jensen family has staked their claim
in the heart of the American West. Now the legacy
continues as twin brothers Ace and Chance Jensen
find justice . . . swinging from a hangman's noose.*

THE BAD ALSO DIE YOUNG
In a court of law, it takes twelve jurors to convict
a killer. Two of them are Jensens. It all started
when those Jensen boys, Ace and Chance,
got roped into jury duty. It should have ended
when justice was served with the killer dancing
on the end of a rope. But no. This is just the
beginning of the death sentence for Ace,
Chance, and the ten other terrified jurors.

A JURY OF TWELVE MEN AND DEAD
He's one of the most notorious outlaws in the west.
He's also the brother of the hanged killer.
Now he's here in town—and plans to slaughter
the jurors, one by one. There's just one hitch:

*Ace and Chance aren't getting ready for Judgment Day.
They're gunning for justice—Jensen style . . .*

NATIONAL BESTSELLING AUTHORS
William W. Johnstone and J. A. Johnstone

**THOSE JENSEN BOYS!
TWELVE DEAD MEN**

On sale now, wherever Pinnacle Books are sold.

CHAPTER ONE

"Nice, peaceful-looking town," Chance Jensen commented as he and his brother approached the settlement.

"Think it'll stay that way after we ride in?" Ace Jensen asked.

"Why wouldn't it?"

"I'm just going by our history, that's all. Seems like every time we show up in a place, hell starts to pop."

Chance made a scoffing sound. "Now you're just being . . . what's the word?"

"I was thinking *crazy*," Ace said.

The brothers drew rein in front of a livery stable at the edge of town, halting Ace's big, rangy chestnut and Chance's cream-colored gelding in front of the open double doors.

Not many people would have taken them for twin brothers, despite the truth of their birth. When they swung down from their saddles, Ace stood slightly taller than Chance and his shoulders spread a little wider. Dark hair peeked out from under his thumbed-back Stetson. The battered hat matched his well-worn range clothes and the plain, walnut-butted Colt .45 Peacemaker that stuck up from a holster on his right hip.

A flat-crowned brown hat sat on Chance's lighter, sandy-colored hair. He preferred fancier clothes than his brother, in this case a brown tweed suit and a black string tie. A .38 caliber Smith & Wesson Second Model revolver rode in a shoulder holster under the suit coat, out of sight but handy if Chance needed to use it . . . which he could, with considerable speed and accuracy.

Both Jensen brothers possessed an uncanny ability to handle guns that had saved their lives—and the lives of numerous innocent people—in the past.

A tall, rawboned man in late middle age ambled out of the livery stable to meet them. He wore overalls and a hat with the brim pushed up in front. Rust-colored stubble sprouted from his lean cheeks and angular jaw, and a black patch covered his left eye. "Do you gents for somethin'?"

"Stalls and feed for our horses," Ace said.

The liveryman studied the mounts for a second and nodded in approval. "Nice-lookin' critters. Be four bits a day for the both of 'em."

Ace took two silver dollars from a pocket and handed them over. "That'll cover a few days. My brother and I don't know how long we'll be staying here in . . . ?"

"Lone Pine," the liveryman said. "That's the name o' this place. Leastways, that's what they call it now."

"Did it used to have another name?" Chance asked.

A grin stretched across the man's face. He chuckled

and said, "When it started, they called it Buzzard's Roost."

"That sounds a little sinister," Ace said.

"Just a wide place in the trail, back in them days. Couple saloons and a store. Owlhoots all over New Mexico Territory—hell, all over the Southwest—knew you could stop at Buzzard's Roost for supplies and a drink and maybe a little time with an Injun whore, and nobody 'd ask any questions about where you'd been or where you planned to go. Folks who lived here would forget you'd ever set foot in the place, happen the law come lookin' for you."

"So it was an outlaw town," Chance said.

"And now look at it," the liveryman said with a sigh that sounded somehow disapproving. "Place is plumb respectable these days."

That appeared to be true. Lone Pine had a business district that stretched for several blocks, lined with establishments of all sorts. Saloons still operated, to be sure, but so did restaurants, mercantiles, apothecaries, a blacksmith shop, a saddle maker, lawyers, doctors, a newspaper—the *Lone Pine Sentinel*, LEE EMORY, ED. & PROP., according to the sign painted in the office's front window—and even a shop full of ladies' hats and dresses.

Dozens of residences sat along the tree-lined cross streets. Lone Pine appeared to be a bustling settlement in pleasant surroundings, at the base of some foothills that rose to snowcapped peaks in the west, with green rangeland lying to the east.

Ace spotted a marshal's office and jail a short distance along the main street, too. With any luck, he and Chance wouldn't see the inside of it during their stay in Lone Pine.

He planned to hold on to that hope, anyway.

"The way you talk about Buzzard's Roost makes it sound like you were here during those days," Chance said to the liveryman.

"Oh, I was. I surely was."

"But you weren't one of the owlhoots." Chance grinned.

"Nope. Didn't have nothin' but a piece of ground with a corral on it in those days, but I rented out space in it to anybody who come along, no matter which side o' the law they found theirselves on. Had to, or risk gettin' shot. Slowly but surely, things begun to settle down, and I made enough *dinero* to start buildin' a barn." The man jerked a knobby-knuckled thumb over his shoulder at the structure behind him.

"It looks like you've done well for yourself," Ace said. "I'm Ace Jensen, by the way. This is my brother Chance."

"Crackerjack Sawyer," the liveryman introduced himself.

"Surely Crackerjack isn't your real name," Chance said.

"Castin' doubts on a fella's name ain't too polite," Sawyer said, his eyes narrowing.

"My brother didn't mean anything by it." Ace cast a warning glance at Chance. "Sometimes he talks before he thinks."

"Well, as it happens, that ain't the name my ma called me. 'Twas Jack. But I'm from Georgia, and when I come out here back in the fifties, some folks called me a cracker. That sorta got put together with my name, and it stuck."

"We're pleased to meet you, Mr. Sawyer."

"Jensen . . ." the liveryman repeated slowly, frowning. "Since you was bold enough to ask me about my name, I'll ask you boys about yours. Are you related to Smoke Jensen?"

The brothers got that question fairly often, since just about everybody west of the Mississippi—and a good number of those east of the big river—had heard of the notorious gunfighter and adventurer Smoke Jensen. Those days, Smoke was a rancher in Colorado, but he hadn't exactly settled down all that much, as Ace and Chance had good reason to know.

"Don't encourage him," Chance said to Sawyer. "My brother thinks Smoke Jensen is some long-lost relative of ours."

"As a matter of fact, we've crossed trails with him several times, and his brothers Matt and Luke, too," Ace said. "They're friends of ours, but as far as we know we're not related to them."

"A long time ago—must be goin' on ten years now—Smoke come through Buzzard's Roost. Rumor had it he was on the owlhoot then, but come to find out later the charges against him weren't true. He already had a rep as a fast gun, though. Some other hombres who were here fancied themselves hardcases and tried to prove it by bracin' Smoke." Sawyer shook his head. "Almost quicker 'n you can blink, all four of 'em wound up dead in the street. Never seen the like of it, in all my borned days."

"That sounds like Smoke, all right," Chance said.

"Well, we're not looking for any trouble like that,"

Ace added. "We're just planning on spending a little time in a nice, peaceful town before we move on."

Sawyer snorted. "Drifters, eh?"

"Let's just say we haven't found anyplace we want to settle down in yet."

"Lone Pine's peaceful enough these days . . . most of the time."

"Meaning some of the time it's not?" Chance asked.

"Bein' respectable and law-abidin' don't sit well with some people. Steer clear o' Pete McLaren and his bunch, and you'll be fine."

"Where do they usually hang out . . . so we can avoid them?" Ace said.

"Harry Muller's Melodian Saloon." Sawyer pointed. "Two blocks up, on the far corner."

"Is it the biggest and best saloon in Lone Pine?" Chance wanted to know.

"Well . . . I reckon most folks 'd say so."

"But there are other saloons in town," Ace said.

"Yeah, three or four."

"If we want to wet our whistles, we won't have any trouble finding someplace to do it. If you'll show us the stalls where you'll be keeping our horses, we'll take them in and unsaddle them, Mr. Sawyer."

"No need to do that. I got a couple hostlers who'll take care of it. Just get any gear you want off of 'em. We'll take good care of the critters for you."

Ace and Chance took their saddlebags off the horses and draped them over their shoulders, then pulled Winchesters from sheaths strapped under the saddle fenders.

Ace considered the state of their finances, then

said, "How about a hotel? Maybe not the best in town, but decent enough to stay in."

"The Territorial House," Sawyer answered without hesitation. "Next block, this side of the street."

"We're obliged to you."

Ace and Chance walked up the street to the hotel, which turned out to be a two-story, whitewashed frame building with a balcony along the front of the second floor. They stepped up onto the boardwalk and went into a lobby with a threadbare rug on the floor and a little dust gathered in the corners. An elderly man with white hair, a bristly white mustache, and hands that trembled a little checked them in.

"Mr. Sawyer down at the livery stable recommended your place," Ace commented as he slid a silver dollar across the counter while Chance signed the registration book for them. It was actually cheaper for them to stay there than it was to keep their horses at the livery stable.

"That old Reb?" the hotel man said.

Ace didn't know if he was the owner or just a clerk.

"I'm surprised he sent any trade my way. I was a Union man." He drew himself up straighter. "Colonel in the 12th Illinois infantry. Colonel Charles Howden."

"Mr. Sawyer said he came out here to New Mexico before the war."

"Yes, and then he went off and fought in the Battle of Glorietta Pass for the Confederates. Forgot to mention that, didn't he?"

"It's been quite a while since the war ended, Mr. Howden," Chance pointed out.

"Colonel Howden, if you please."

"Of course, Colonel," Ace said. "If we could, uh, get the key to our room . . ."

"Certainly." Howden took a key from the rack and handed it to Ace. "Room Twelve, on the second floor. I hope you enjoy your stay, Mister . . ." He looked at the registration book and read their names upside down, a talent most people who worked in hotels acquired. "Jensen."

The name didn't seem to mean anything to him.

The brothers went upstairs, left their saddlebags and rifles in Room Twelve—which, like the lobby, showed signs of wear and was a little dusty—and then came back down and strolled out onto the boardwalk in front of the hotel.

"Reckon it's late enough in the day we could find someplace to get supper," Ace said.

"We *could*," Chance said, "but think how much better supper would taste if we had a drink first."

"You weren't thinking about that Melodian Saloon Mr. Sawyer mentioned, were you?"

"He said it was the biggest and best in Lone Pine," Chance replied with a smile, "and it's right over there." He pointed diagonally across the street toward the building on the far corner.

"I'm going to have a hard time talking you out of this, aren't I?"

"More than likely," Chance agreed. "Anyway, that troublemaker the old-timer mentioned—what was his name? McLaren? He's probably not even there right now."

CHAPTER TWO

Pete McLaren laughed. "Shoot, Dolly, you might as well stop tryin' to get away. You know I like it when you put up a little fight."

The blonde put her hands against Pete's chest and pushed as she tried to squirm off his lap. He just tightened the arm around her waist, put his other hand behind her neck, and pulled her head down to his so he could press his mouth against hers.

Dolly Redding let out a muffled squeal and tried even harder to get away for a few seconds. Then she sighed, wrapped her arms around Pete's neck, and returned the kiss with passionate urgency.

He let that continue for a minute or so and then pulled his head away and laughed raucously. "You see, fellas, I told you this little hellcat couldn't resist me for long!"

The four other men at the table in the Melodian Saloon joined in Pete McLaren's laughter. Like Pete, they were all young, in their twenties, and dressed like cowboys, although the lack of calluses on their hands indicated they hadn't had riding jobs lately. Exactly how they got the money they spent there and in other saloons was open to debate, although nobody was going to question it too much if they knew what was good for them.

Dolly pouted. "Pete, you shouldn't make sport of me. Just 'cause I work in a saloon don't mean you shouldn't treat me like a lady!"

"Nobody's ever gonna accuse you of bein' a lady, Dolly, but hell, if I wanted a lady, I'd be chasin' after that Fontana Dupree. I like my gals, well, a little on the trashy side. Like you."

That provoked more gales of laughter from Pete's friends. Dolly just looked embarrassed as a blush spread across her face. She didn't deny what Pete had said about her, though.

To tell the truth, Dolly Redding was a good-looking young woman, and she hadn't worked in saloons long enough to acquire the hard mouth and the suspicious lines around her eyes that most doves displayed. She still had a faint flush of . . . well, innocence would be stretching it too far, but maybe remembered innocence would describe it.

Some of her thick, curly blond hair had fallen in front of her face while Pete was kissing her. She tossed her head to throw it back and told him, "I'm just sayin' you should treat me a little better, that's all. Maybe I ain't a lady now, but I might be someday if I work hard enough at it."

"Oh, you work hard at what you do. I'll give you

credit for that," Pete said with a leer on his handsome young face.

The other men at the table thought that was hilarious, too.

The commotion in the corner drew a few disapproving frowns from the saloon's other patrons. The hour was early, not even suppertime yet, so the Melodian was only about half full.

A burly, bald man in a gray suit leaned on the bar where he stood at the far end of the hardwood. He glared at the table where Pete McLaren and his friends were working on their second bottle of whiskey since they'd come in an hour or so earlier.

A young woman with light brown hair framing a face of sultry beauty came out of a door at the end of the bar and paused beside the bald man. The silk gown she wore wasn't exactly churchgoing garb, but it was more decorous than the short, low-cut, spangled getups worn by Dolly Redding and the other girls who delivered drinks in the Melodian.

"What's wrong, Hank?" the brunette murmured.

"Ah, it's just that blasted McLaren kid and his pards again," Hank Muller said as he continued to scowl. "I hate to see Dolly gettin' mauled like that."

"It sort of comes with the territory, doesn't it?"

Muller looked sharply at her. "I make no bones about what goes on here. The girls know what's expected of 'em, and they don't kick about it. Pete McLaren's too rough about it, though. Too sure of himself. Ah, hell, Fontana, maybe I just don't like the kid and the rest of that bunch."

"You're not the only one," Fontana Dupree said. "Want me to try to distract them?"

"Well . . . I don't suppose it'd hurt anything to try."

Fontana smiled and nodded. She left the bar and walked over to a piano sitting next to a small stage in the back of the barroom. At a table close by the piano, a small man with thinning fair hair sat reading a copy of the *Police Gazette*. An unlit store-bought cigarette hung from the corner of his mouth, bobbing slightly as he hummed to himself and studied the etchings of scantily clad women in the magazine.

Fontana put a hand on his shoulder. "Come on, Orrie. It's time to get to work."

Quickly, he closed the *Police Gazette* and sat up straighter. "Uh, sorry, Miss Dupree. I didn't figure we'd be starting this early—"

"It's all right," Fontana told him. "How about some Stephen Foster?"

"Sure." Orrie stood up from the table and went to a stool in front of the piano. He put his fingers on the keys and looked up at Fontana as she took her place beside the instrument. When she nodded, he began to play, and a moment after the notes began to emerge, crisp and pure, she started singing a sad, sentimental ballad in a voice even more lovely than Orrie's playing.

Chance Jensen stopped in his tracks. "I think I'm in love."

He and Ace had just pushed through the batwings and stepped through the corner entrance into the Melodian. Ace almost bumped into his brother, then moved aside so he could look past Chance. He heard the singing, and judging by Chance's intent,

love-struck expression, Ace figured he was staring at
the singer.

She was worth looking at, Ace thought, slim and
lovely in a dark blue gown. Creamy skin and features
that compelled a man to look at them twice in appre-
ciation. A small beauty mark near the corner of the
young woman's mouth gave her character and didn't
detract at all from her attractiveness.

"She sings like a . . . a nightingale," Chance said.

"Just how many nightingales have you heard
singing?" Ace asked.

"Well, then . . . a mockingbird. Only prettier."

"She *is* prettier than any mockingbird I've ever
seen," Ace admitted.

"That's not what I—Ah, just shut up and let me
look at her and listen to her."

That didn't seem like such a bad idea. They had
been in their saddles for quite a few miles and Ace
wouldn't mind sitting down. An empty table stood not
far away, so he took hold of Chance's arm and urged
him toward it. "Come on. You can see and hear her
just as well from over there."

Chance didn't argue. He went with Ace without
taking his eyes off the young woman standing beside
the piano in the back of the room.

Ace was more interested in taking in all their surroundings, however, not just one small part. As they
sat down, he let his gaze travel around the saloon.
Checking for trouble like that was just a habit he had
gotten into. The Jensen brothers might be young, but
they had run into more than their share of ruckuses.

Most of the customers in the saloon appeared to be

townies, cowboys from some of the spreads to the east, or miners from diggings up in the hills.

A group of men at one table caught Ace's eye. They wore range clothes but had a certain indefinable hard-bitten air about them that set them apart from the usual breed of puncher. For one thing, they all wore gun belts and holstered revolvers.

So did he and Chance, Ace reminded himself. That didn't mean there was anything wrong with them, just that sometimes they needed to be armed.

The bunch at that table was loud and boisterous even though the young woman at the piano was singing. One of them had a blond saloon girl on his lap and was pawing at her as he laughed. She looked a little uncomfortable, but she wasn't trying to get away from him.

The racket had started to annoy Chance and he frowned. "Don't those fellows know you're supposed to shut up and be quiet when a lady's singing? How can they not be in awe of such a beautiful voice?"

"They've probably guzzled down enough rotgut they don't care," Ace said.

"I don't care how drunk they are, they need to pipe down."

"Maybe so, but it's not our job to make 'em do it."

Chance looked like he wanted to argue, but he sighed and turned his attention back to the young woman. From time to time, he cast an irritated glance toward the noisy table across the room.

Chance wasn't the only one whose nerves those hombres were getting on, Ace realized a moment later. A bald, broad-shouldered man standing at the bar was glaring at the rowdies, too. He caught the blonde's eye, lifted a hand, and used his thumb to point at the table where Ace and Chance sat.

That had to be the boss. Crackerjack Sawyer had mentioned the saloonkeeper's name, and after a moment Ace recalled it—Hank Muller.

The blonde finally managed to wriggle free of the man who had her on his lap. She said something to him and stepped back quickly out of his reach when he tried to snag her again. Picking up a tray from an empty table nearby, she hurried across the room toward the Jensen brothers, looking relieved and worried at the same time.

As she came up to the table, she put a smile on her face. "Hello, boys," she said, trying to sound bright and cheerful but not quite managing it. "What can I get you to drink?"

Ace could tell that took an effort. "Beer for both of us." It was all they could really afford, and besides, neither of them was much of a heavy drinker, although Chance had cultivated a fondness for fine wine when they had enough dinero for it.

The blonde nodded. "I'll be right—"

A heavy footstep sounded behind her and she let out a little gasp as a man's hand grabbed her shoulder.

He hauled her around, revealing himself to be the hombre from whose lap she had escaped. "You'll get right back over to our table where you belong," he said, giving her a shove in that direction. "If these saddle tramps don't like it, that's just too damn bad!"

CHAPTER THREE

Chance sprang out of his chair instantly, and Ace was just a second behind him.

"I don't really care what you call my brother and me," Chance said in a taut, angry voice, "but you'd better apologize to the lady for treating her so rough."

"Lady?" the man repeated with a cocky, arrogant smirk on his face. "I don't see no lady here, only a saloon floozy who ain't no better than she has to be."

Ace said, "Mister, you're just making us like you even less."

The man laughed. "You reckon I give a damn about whether you like me?"

The blonde said, "Please, Pete, I told you I'd come right back after I got these boys their drinks—"

"I don't want any trouble in here, McLaren," Hank Muller interrupted her from the bar.

So the hombre gazing defiantly at them was Pete McLaren, Ace thought. The old-timer at the livery stable had mentioned him. From the sound of what

Crackerjack Sawyer had said, McLaren was the biggest troublemaker in Lone Pine.

"Stay outta this, Muller," McLaren snapped. "This is between me and these saddle tramps."

"Really," Chance said. "Do I *look* like a saddle tramp?" He gestured to indicate his suit, which was of good quality even though it wasn't particularly new.

McLaren sneered again. "No, you look more like a damn, four-flushin' tinhorn, if you ask me."

Chance clenched his fist as he took half a step toward McLaren.

At the same time, the four men who had been sitting with McLaren got to their feet. They had been content to let their leader—as McLaren seemed to be—sally forth alone, but now that combat seemed to be imminent, they clearly didn't want to miss out on any of the action.

"Take it easy, Chance," Ace said quietly.

Five to two wasn't very good odds. They would buck those odds if they had to—they were Jensens, after all. Related to the famous clan or not, they didn't run from a fight, but Ace understood why Hank Muller didn't want such a ruckus breaking out in his saloon.

"As if the way you treated this girl isn't bad enough, you ruined a beautiful song," Chance said with a nod toward the piano and the lovely brunette who stood beside it.

She had stopped singing and the piano player had stopped tickling the ivories when the confrontation began, just like the rest of the saloon's customers had halted their drinking and talking to watch the unfolding drama.

The brunette smiled at Chance's compliment, but the expression vanished a moment later when Mc-Laren chuckled coarsely and said, "Beautiful song? You mean that caterwaulin' that was going on a minute ago?"

Ace heard the hiss of Chance's sharply indrawn breath. McLaren had pushed him too far by insulting the singer.

Chance lunged forward, fist whipping up toward McLaren's face.

McLaren was fast. A few years older, he had more experience at brawling and jerked his head aside so Chance's punch went harmlessly past his ear. Stepping in, he hooked a left into Chance's midsection and then hammered a right into his chest.

Chance went backwards, his legs tangling with his brother's as Ace tried to charge into the battle. As they struggled to hang on to their balance, McLaren's friends sprang to the attack. Hank Muller bellowed for everybody to stop, but they ignored him. Customers at nearby tables scrambled to get away from the violence.

Ace and Chance got loose from each other, but only in time to be hit again. McLaren bored in on Chance, pounding him and making him retreat against one of the tables, while one of McLaren's companions punched Ace in the jaw and knocked him halfway around.

That gave one of the other men the opportunity to grab Ace from behind and pin his arms back. "Thrash him good, Lew!" the man called to his friend.

Grinning, the man who had already hit Ace once moved in, fists cocked to deal out punishment.

Ace was a little groggy from the blow to the jaw, but his instincts were still working. As Lew closed in, intent on handing him a beating, Ace jerked both knees up and lashed out with a double-footed kick that landed on the man's chest and sent him flying backwards. Lew crashed down on a table that collapsed with a splintering and rending of wood.

Ace's kick also made the man holding him stumble backwards in the opposite direction. He tripped and fell onto his back on the sawdust-littered floor, pulling Ace with him. Ace landed on top of him. Thinking clearly enough, he rammed an elbow into the man's belly and rolled to his feet.

Chance had recovered his wits and pushed off the table he was leaning against. He lowered his head and tackled McLaren as the hardcase tried to crowd him. They staggered around in a circle as Chance smashed a couple punches into McLaren's kidneys, figuring he ought to do whatever it took to win—especially when he and his brother were outnumbered more than two to one. He continued the punches, even though he knew Ace would have considered such blows to be dirty fighting.

McLaren bellowed in pain and anger, got his hands on Chance's chest, and shoved the younger man away. He threw a roundhouse punch that Chance leaned away from.

Getting his feet back under him, Chance put his own experience to work. He jabbed a right into McLaren's mouth that made blood spurt. He followed it a split second later with a left that rocked the man's head back, turning the tide of battle for a moment.

One of the other men snatched up a chair and brought it down on Chance's head. The crashing blow sent him to his knees. McLaren caught his balance, kicked Chance in the chest, and knocked him over on his back.

Ace grabbed the chair-wielder by the shoulder, jerked him around, and slammed a right to his jaw. The other man in McLaren's bunch clenched his fists together and swung them in a clubbing blow to the back of Ace's neck, knocking Ace off his feet. He landed facedown next to his brother, who was lying on his back.

"A nice, peaceful-looking town, you said," Ace groaned as he tried to push himself up.

Chance rolled onto his side. "How was I to know we'd wind up in a fight?"

Ace didn't bother answering that. He climbed onto his feet and helped Chance up. McLaren and the other four men were all standing, too, bunched together about fifteen feet away with angry glares on their bruised, bloody faces.

That pause was just a breather. The battle was about to resume.

"Everybody hold it right where you are, damn it!" The bellowed command came from the saloon's entrance, where a man stood just inside the batwings, which were still swinging back and forth a little behind him. As if his loud, harsh, gravelly voice wasn't enough to attract attention, the twin barrels of the hotgun he held looked as big around as cannons to anybody unlucky enough to be in front of them.

"Thank God you're here, Marshal," Hank Muller said. "I've already had a table and a chair busted up. There's no telling how much damage these hellions might have done if they'd kept fighting."

"Who are you calling hellions?" Chance asked resentfully. "We were just trying to help that girl who works for you."

Before Muller could reply, the newcomer stalked farther into the saloon, keeping the scattergun leveled in front of him. The customers who had tried to get away from the fight shrank back farther to make sure they were out of the line of fire.

The lawman was a medium-sized man of middle age. His clean-shaven face was tanned to the color of old saddle leather and seamed with numerous wrinkles, especially around the mouth and eyes. Thick white hair stood out in sharp contrast to the old black hat he wore. A marshal's badge was pinned to his vest. All it took was a glance to see that he still had all the bark on him, despite his years.

"I want to know who you *hellions* are," he said to Ace and Chance. "I know McLaren and his pards, but I don't reckon I've ever seen you two before."

Ace did the introductions. "I'm Ace Jensen and this is my brother Chance. We just rode into town a while ago. Mr. Sawyer down at the livery stable will confirm that, and so will Colonel Howden at the Territorial House."

"Didn't take you long to start trouble, then, did it?"

The young woman at the piano spoke up. "They

didn't start it, Marshal Dixon. McLaren and his friend did."

"That's a damn lie," McLaren said.

The brunette's face flushed angrily and she took a step forward.

The marshal told her, "You'd best just stay out of it Miss Dupree."

Chance nodded toward the blond saloon girl "McLaren was roughing up that young lady, Marshal My brother and I wouldn't have stepped in otherwise."

McLaren sneered. "There you go with that *lady* business again. You see any *ladies* in here, Marshal?"

Dixon didn't answer that.

McLaren went on. "Anyway, I didn't hear Dolly complainin' about the way I was treatin' her. Did you need somebody to protect you, Dolly?"

The blonde swallowed hard. "I . . . I guess it was all right . . . What you did, I mean, Pete. I know you wouldn't really hurt me."

"Damn right I wouldn't." McLaren cupped a hand under her chin. "You're my gal, ain't you?"

"I— Sure I am, Pete."

A disgusted look crossed Chance's face. Ace felt the same way. Even though the girl called Dolly hadn't liked the way McLaren was holding her on his lap, she was still smitten with the handsome young hardcase. Both Jensen brothers could tell that by the look in her eyes.

"Muller, who threw the first punch?" Marshal Dixon asked the saloonkeeper.

Muller didn't look happy about it, but he couldn't very well refuse to answer the lawman's question.

Besides, there were plenty of witnesses who had seen the same thing he had. "That young fella there did"—Muller pointed to Chance—"but McLaren provoked him by insulting Fontana."

"Doesn't matter," Dixon said. "Nobody appointed these two the defenders of fair womanhood." He jerked the barrels of the Greener to motion Ace and Chance toward the entrance. "You two are gonna spend your first night in Lone Pine in the calaboose."